QUARTET E

NOCTURNE AN
LOVE AN

This selection of some of
fiction makes it clear why in the minds of such men as Malraux, Valery and Joyce, he counted as one of the great creative figures of our century. 'The Sea-Going Surgeon', 'The Vigil' and 'The Virgin Orsola' all come from his earliest book of stories, *Tales of Pescara,* written in the 1880s. 'Giovanni Episcopo' (1892) was written while D'Annunzio was under the influence of Dostoevsky, whose work was just then appearing in French translation. 'Nocturne' dates from the First World War when D'Annunzio, while flying in combat, suffered an accident that blinded him in one eye and threatened the other. 'Leda Without Swan' (1916) is a fine example of D'Annunzio's ripe, most ornate, and eloquent style, and was written during his several years' stay in France.

GABRIELE D'ANNUNZIO

Gabriele D'Annunzio was born in 1863 in Pescara. His first poems were published while he was still at school; he went on to write both plays and novels – the best known is *The Triumph of Life* (1894). Flamboyant, unquestionably brave, eloquent, seductive – an inspirer and leader of men and astonishingly successful with women – D'Annunzio exerted a fascination upon his Italian contemporaries. He occupied a significant place in the social and political history of Italy, becoming closely involved with Mussolini and the rise of Fascism in the 1920s. He died in 1938.

D'Annunzio's novel *The Flame*, based on his relationship with Eleonora Duse, is also published in the Quartet Encounters series.

GABRIELE D'ANNUNZIO

Nocturne and Five Tales of Love and Death

Translated from the Italian and with an Introduction by
RAYMOND ROSENTHAL

QUARTET ENCOUNTERS

Quartet Books

Published in paperback by Quartet Books Limited 1993
A member of the Namara Group
27/29 Goodge Street, London W1P 1FD

A catalogue record for this work is available from the
British Library

ISBN 0 7943 0209 8

Printed and bound in Finland
by WSOY

Contents

INTRODUCTION

GABRIELE D'ANNUNZIO was born in 1863 in the seaport town of Pescara in the Abruzzo region of Italy, and died in 1938 in his grandiose but rather gaudy villa on Lake Garda. The dates are important because they measure not only the span of an unusually fertile and exuberant artistic life (as one critic has said, only two other writers can boast of the same long, unfailingly brilliant and evocative production: Goethe and Victor Hugo) but they also show that he came into life with the birth of the modern age in art and departed from it just after it had passed its apogee. In 1874 Nietzsche had published his great essay *The Birth of Tragedy*, and the same year Rimbaud's "Drunken Boat," *Illuminations* and *A Season in Hell* appeared together with the first large show of Impressionist painters, while Mallarmé provided the Symbolists with a manifesto with his poem "Afternoon of a Faun" in 1876. In Italy, always a little behind in the European artistic scramble, Verga published his masterpiece, *The House by the Medlar Tree*, in 1881 and Italo Svevo his second important novel, *As a Man Grows Older*, in 1898. In other words, D'Annunzio's career straddled an era of violent transition, and this innate romantic, who tried vainly over the years to become a Naturalist, a Symbolist, a Decadent, even an avant-garde modernist, never settled comfortably into any of these assumed artistic roles.

Yet he was undoubtedly a prodigy, a prodigy in the gorgeous use of words, publishing his first book of poems to critical acclaim at the age of sixteen. He had what many regarded as a dangerous facility; but, as Yeats put it, "Words alone are certain good," a good that makes up for many a failing, even for a lack of artistic maturity and of that deliberate development of a vision and a style that characterizes the greatest of writers. "I have my language," D'Annunzio declared, "as one of my most powerful instincts." The sentence is perhaps a key to his entire work because the comparison of his expressive gift to the natural, the indwelling in him—his instincts—is beautifully appropriate to the rhythms and substance of D'Annunzio's writing, whether good, bad, or indifferent. It is in fact D'Annunzio's life-long, often inspired concern with the body's sensuous life that assures him a place in serious literature. There is no writer in the late nineteenth century and the beginning of the twentieth who explored this area of experience with more subtlety, more delicacy, more power and more intensity. As the German critic Adorno rightly said, the true subterranean history of recent European consciousness is its degradation and humiliation of the body, and in this context D'Annunzio, whatever his political opinions, is unquestionably the body's least inhibited and most imaginative celebrator, the forerunner of D. H. Lawrence and Henry Miller.

Indeed, around the turn of the century nobody connected with the art of writing would have found it odd or unusual if one were to call D'Annunzio a great writer and poet. The young James Joyce thought that D'Annunzio was the only European writer after Flaubert to carry the novel into new territory, and, later on, he classed him with Kipling and Tolstoy as the three "most naturally talented writers" to appear in the nineteenth century. Henry James, whose long essay on D'Annunzio's novels is certainly the best in English, considered him a supremely gifted writer ("a rare imagination, a poetic, an artistic intelligence of extraordinary range and fineness" are some of the laudatory things he has to say about him) whose predominantly esthetic view of life seemed to James a kind of test case for this particular artistic position. In fact, in the final reckoning James felt that the esthetic stance was terribly inadequate and in some of its dealings, especially in the presentation of love affairs, even vulgar, due to the blindness it affected as regards the full complexity of human relations. And Joyce also had his critical reservations, pointing out that D'Annunzio, Tolstoy and Kipling had all been seriously compromised as writers by "their semi-fanatic ideas about religion or about patriotism." "Patriotism" was Joyce's nice way of alluding to D'Annunzio's wavering from right to left in politics throughout his life.

In any event, this praise and the strictures that accompanied it are worth recording because the worst thing that can happen to a writer has happened to D'Annunzio: if he is at all famous today—and this is certainly true of his fame outside Italy—it is not for what he wrote but for what he did. He is a gossip-star, a perennial favorite of the fashion magazines, since many of the etiolated, often perverse aristocratic or bohemian ladies he had affairs with were advance models of the prototypical "model" that graces their pages. (Fashion is a dream-world and its prime images and fantasies have changed very little since D'Annunzio's scandalous days in turn of the century Rome.) He was also an adventurer in politics and on the battlefield, a hero in combat during the First World War, a fiery orator, and the commander of a band of freebooters who seized the city of Fiume in an attempt to annex it for Italy in defiance of the agreements being made at Versailles. The expedition failed but the precedents it set in illegal activity helped Mussolini greatly in his drive to Fascist power. The fact is that Mussolini was afraid of D'Annunzio, afraid in the way a hack would naturally fear a genius, and took care to lock him away under guard in his gimcrack palace, the Vittoriale. But all this, though interesting, even entertaining, is precisely what this anthology has been fashioned to overcome, that is, to ignore the gossip-star and return to the artist, confining its selections to his best and most representative writings in prose. Of course D'Annunzio was first of all a poet, but each of the writings included in this book illustrates and underscores a stage in D'Annunzio's creative journey that will certainly enhance an eventual reading of his poetry.

The first three stories are taken from the volume titled *Tales of Pescara* [*Le novelle della Pescara*, 1884-86]. D'Annunzio was an eager conduit in Italy for all the latest European literary movements, and in these stories one can see an obvious transposition of Zola's Naturalism to Italian soil, particularly in the story "The Virgin Orsola" [*La vergine Orsola*]. The incredible description of the pathological ravages of typhus is precise and powerful, but D'Annunzio's particular talents go far beyond the Naturalistic formula. Above all he is adept at catching the movements of the spirit as they are reflected in the flesh. His marvelous account of Orsola's convalescence, the upsurge of sexual impulse that accompanies it, sharpened by the overt carnality and suggestive drama of a religious ceremony—all this is presented with a richness of nuance and implication that one hardly associates even with the most refined products of Naturalism. The sardonically romantic D'Annunzio appears again in the next two stories. "The Vigil" [*La veglia funebre*], which combines the mystery and boredom of a wake, the invasive sexuality of a languorous summer night—the very landscape seems to swell with sexual yearning—and the brutality of pure lust, is by some magic both tender and cruel; while "The Sea-Going Surgeon" [*Il cirusico di mare*] also exploits the surrounding seascape, first in a lulling calm and then a fierce storm, both depicted as the inscrutable "moods" of an indifferent nature, mirroring the impassive and indifferent cruelty of the men aboard the brig.

The long novella "Giovanni Episcopo," which was published in 1891, is another example of D'Annunzio's cultural and literary omniverousness. Dostoevsky's novels had just been issued in France and D'Annunzio, who was going through one of his periodic crises, turned in desperation to the Russian master's confessional mode in an effort to overcome his creative stasis. More sentimental than psychologically penetrating, it recreates the atmosphere of clerkly life in Rome—which had just become the nation's capital and was filling up with immigrants from all over the country—giving us an unforgettable picture of these crowds of raffish young men, living in squalid boarding houses, eating miserable meals, scrounging along on meager wages, trying pathetically to snatch some moments of pleasure. The chief characters are stock figures, the low-life "fatal woman," the inevitable bully and his inevitable butt, yet D'Annunzio's skill confers an intensity and sincerity upon what in other hands would have been absurd melodrama.

The last two selections show D'Annunzio at the height of his powers. The long story "Leda Without Swan" [*La Leda senza cigno*] was written in France in 1913 but published in Italy in 1916. Its action takes place in the Landes region of France, that sandy country of pitch pine forest along the Atlantic Coast between Médoc and Adour, bordered by great dunes which enclose the many inland ponds. "Leda Without Swan" is, among other things, a kind of summation and repudiation by D'Annunzio of the chief Decadent themes which played so great a part in both his poetry and his novels. And it is perhaps the first time that his prodigious facility has found an art form that is entirely his own and fully expresses his spirit. The "fatal woman," who gathers into herself all the world's sensuality, is shown as beautiful but miserable, more her own victim than the victimizer of others, and the usual trio of death, voluptuousness, and love as a sadistic perversity seems to have been viewed at last as squalid makeshifts that do not penetrate to the core of reality. D'Annunzio is sad about these repudiations but his sadness is more authentic and moving than many of his exultant moments and gives birth to his loveliest and most incisive prose.

"Nocturne" [*Notturno*] was written in 1916 but D'Annunzio waited until 1921 before he published it. Printed here are excerpts whose combined length amounts to about a quarter of the Italian volume. The peculiar circumstances of its creation demanded that D'Annunzio have a period of relative calm to interpret and re-order the "more than ten thousand strips of paper" on which he had inscribed his lyrical thoughts and reveries. On January 16, 1916, while on a combat flight during the First World War, D'Annunzio's plane, on which he was an observer, was forced to make an emergency landing and D'Annunzio was flung against the machine gun mounted in front of him and as a result of the blow lost the sight of his right eye. The doctors insisted that he go to bed and lie perfectly immobile, declaring that if he did not he might lose the sight of his other eye as well. So from February 23 to the end of April, in a handwriting that was nearly illegible, D'Annunzio set down this "commentary on the shadows," a succession of memories and dreams that rose spontaneously from his unconscious as he lay supine, or during the long nights of insomnia. "I had inside my wounded eye a forge of dreams which my will could neither direct nor interrupt. The optic nerve drew on all the strata of my culture and my previous life, projecting on my vision innumerable figures with a rapidity of transition far beyond the most daring lyricism." This is of course D'Annunzio with at least one foot in the camp of modernism. From then on he confined his writing to just this sort of autobiographical musing, the perfect form for an impenitent egocentric.

RAYMOND ROSENTHAL

THE VIRGIN ORSOLA

The Virgin Orsola

I

THE VIATICUM appeared under the portal of the church at noon. The season's first delicate snow lay on the streets, on the houses, everywhere snow. But on high, among the snowy clouds, large blue islands opened, dilating over Brina Palace and slowly filling with light toward the Bandiera quarter. And in the white air over the white town the miracle of the sun was suddenly revealed.

The viaticum started on its way to Orsola dell'Arca's house. The people along the streets paused to watch the priest go by, solemn and grave, striding with his bare head and purple stole under the broad scarlet umbrella, between the burning lanterns carried by the altar boys. The small handbell rang out limpidly, accompanying the psalms whispered by the priest. In the narrow lanes stray dogs scampered out of the way as the procession passed. At the corner of the piazza, Mazzanti stopped shoveling snow and bowed, uncovering his bald skull. And just then, from Flaiano's bakery, the warm, hearty smell of fresh bread spread through the air.

The people gathered at the sick woman's house heard the peals of the bell; they heard the visitors' steps mounting the stairs. Supine on her bed lay the virgin Orsola in the grip of a feverish stupor, of an inert somnolence, her rapid breathing broken by sharp, rattling gasps. On the pillow rested her head almost completely stripped of hair and her face of an almost bluish color in which the lids half-hid her viscous eyeballs and the nostrils seemed to be smeared with soot. With her fleshless hands she made small, uncertain gestures, vague attempts to seize something from the void, weird, startling signs which gave those around her a feeling almost of terror; her pale arms were shot through by muscular contractions, twitchings of the tendons; and now and then an unintelligible babble came from her lips, as if the words were caught in the soot on her tongue, the clinging mucus on her gums.

That tragic stillness which always precedes supreme events began to fill the room: a stillness in which the sick woman's breathing, her groping gestures, the raucous explosions of her cough, made the expectation of death more dreadful. Through the open windows poured the pure air, and out of them drifted the miasmas exhaled by the disease. A vivid white glare was reflected by the snow on the cornices and Corinthian capitals of the Arch of Fortanuova; at the level of the room icicles glittered like crystal flowers. Inside, on the walls, hung large, holy medallions of brass—the images of saints. Under a glass bell, her face, her breast, her arms completely black, like a barbaric idol, a Madonna of Loreto glimmered in her robe adorned with golden crescent moons. In one corner, on a small, immaculate altar, between two blue Castelli jars full of aromatic herbs, stood an old crucifix made of mother-of-pearl.

At the bedside, deathly pale, Camilla, the sister, the only relative, with a linen cloth soaked in vinegar wiped the sick woman's black lips, her encrusted teeth. The doctor, Don Vincenzo Bucci, sat staring at the silver knob of his handsome cane, at the beautiful carved cornelians set in the rings on his fingers, and waited. Teodora La Iece, a weaver who lived next door, stood erect, silent, intent on giving a sorrowful expression to her sallow, freckled face, her steely eyes, her cruel mouth.

"*Pax huic domui,*" the priest said as he entered. In the doorway, tall and emaciated on his enormous feet, with the undulating movements of a caterpillar, Don Gennaro Tierno appeared. Behind him came Rosa Catena, a woman who in her green years had made a public trade of lewdness and was now redeeming her soul by attending to the dying, bathing corpses, dressing and composing them in their coffins without taking any recompense.

Everyone in Orsola's room was kneeling, all heads were bowed. The sick woman heard nothing; a profound stupor continued to obliterate her senses. The aspersorium rose above her, flashed through the air, sprinkling the bed.

"*Asperges me, Domine, hyssopo, et mundabor . . .*"

But Orsola did not feel the purifying wave which made her whiter than the snow in the eyes of her Lord.

With frail fingers she stroked the counterpane over her chest, a tremulous movement quivered on her lips, in her throat gurgled the sound of the word she was unable to pronounce.

"*Exaudi nos, Domine sancte . . .*"

Then a loud wail echoed through the Latin words, and Camilla hid her tear-stained face against the side of the bed. The doctor had approached and encircled Orsola's wrist with his bejeweled fingers. He wanted to rouse her, prepare her to receive the sacrament from the hands of Christ's minister, get her to hold out her tongue for the Host.

Orsola mumbled, her hands again fluttered vaguely as she was being propped up against the pillows. Only a tingling sensation struck the distempered nerves in her ears—now it was a shriek, now music. As they lifted her up the bluish flush on her face immediately became a cadaverous pallor; the pouch filled with ice slipped from her head onto the sheet.

"*Misereatur . . .*"

At last she offered her trembling tongue covered by a patina of mucus mingled with dark blood, and there the virgin Host rested.

"*Ecce agnus Dei, ecce qui tollit peccata mundi . . .*"

But she was completely unconscious and so did not withdraw her tongue at that contact: the light of the Eucharist did not break through her stupor. Camilla, her reddened, swollen eyes filled with terror and grief, stared at that ashen face from which, little by little, all sign of life was fading; at the gaping mouth which looked like that of someone strangled. With the solemnity of his office, the priest slowly continued to recite the Latin prayers. All the others remained on their knees under the diffused auroral light which the noon-hour drew from the snow outside. The smell of warm bread rose with the wind and the nostrils of the altar boys quivered.

"*Oremus! . . .*"

Urged by the doctor, Orsola closed her mouth again. They laid her flat on her back as the priest intoned the first part of the sacrament of Extreme Unction. Softly, the kneeling boys recited the antiphony to the seven penitential Psalms.

"*Ne reminiscaris . . .*"

From time to time Teodora La Iece, at the foot of the bed, her face hidden in her hands, emitted a stifled sob. At her side, a yellowish secretion continually oozing from one half-closed eye, the other staring blind and white because of a cataract, Rosa Catena stood upright, fingered her rosary and muttered. And while the Psalms rose from the floor in a whisper, the sacred formula pronounced by the priest soared above the confused murmur as, making the sign of the cross, he annointed the inert woman's eyes, ears, mouth and hands.

". . . *indulgeat tibi Dominus quidquid per gressum deliquisti. Amen.*"

It was Camilla who uncovered her sister's feet: from between the sheets two feet appeared, yellow, scaly, with bluish nails, and at their touch she was filled with the disgust dead limbs inspire. And her tears fell on the dry skin, mingling with the oil of Extreme Unction.

"*Kyrie eleison, Christe eleison. Kyrie eleison. Pater noster . . .*"

The Lord's anointed now lay immobile, breathing, her eyes closed to the light, her knees drawn up and her hands squeezed between her thighs in the position typical of those stricken by typhoid fever. And after pressing the crucifix once more against her lips, and having made the sign of the cross from the center of the room with a broad gesture of his large hands, the priest went out, followed by the boys. The wan odor of incense and wax that clerical vestments give off still lingered in the room. Outside, beneath the windows, Matteo Pariello hammered away at his resoled shoes, singing to himself.

II

THE ILLNESS'S symptoms slowly lost their virulence, the fourth seven-day cycle of the disease began, and now stupefied inertness was followed by the natural quiet of sleep, a lasting calmness during which, little by little, the perturbations that had obscured her consciousness subsided, her senses' faculties grew less clouded, her respiration less rapid and agitated. But now and again a harsh fit of coughing burst from the sick woman's chest, shaking her backbone, while a painful deterioration of the skin and soft tissues at the elbows, knees, and lower back progressed day after day. When Camilla leaned over her bed calling "Orsola!" she tried to open her eyes, turn toward that voice. But her weakness weighed her down; and again lethargic apathy overwhelmed her senses.

She was hungry, hungry. A bestial longing for food tortured her empty bowels, communicating to her mouth the vague movement of jaws demanding something to chew on, sending through the pitiful bones of her hands the prehensile contractions which move the fingers of a gluttonous monkey at the sight of an apple. She was racked by the ravening hunger that accompanies the convalescence from typhus, the dreadful craving for vital nourishment clamoring from every cell of a body exhausted by long illness. Only a feeble wave of blood still circulated through the tissues; in the weakly irrigated brain all activity stagnated as in a machine deprived of the fuel's propelling energy. Only fitful vibrations stirred in her body and prompted reactions that had been habitual in her former life, nor was the convalescent woman at all aware of this muted mechanical process. Mostly she recited the litanies aloud; or painstakingly divided the senseless words into syllables; or she would threaten her pupils with severe punishments, or sing the quinary rhymes of a hymn glorifying Jesus. Almost incessantly, the index finger of her left hand ran swiftly along the cuff of the counterpane with a pointing motion, as if by that gesture she were guiding a pupil's eyes along the lines of a book. Then, at times, her voice rose, took on an almost menacing solemnity, pronouncing the admonishments of the *seven trumpets* or confusedly repeating the words of Fra Bartolomeo da Saluzzo, and perhaps before her marvelling eyes she had a vision of those old woodcuts that swarm with deformed, trumpeting angels and vanquished demons. But there was never an intelligent gaze in her eyes. The drooping eyelids half-covered her irises, those discolored irises floating contourless in the sclera which seemed covered by a film of yellow mucilage. She lay stretched out upon her bed, flat and stiff, her head supported by two pillows. She had lost almost all her hair during the illness; a dusty pallor—the kind of pallor under which it seemed impossible there should be any life left—covered her face, the hollows in her face; and beyond it was visible the skull, and through the brittle dryness of the rest of her skin transpired the skeleton, and all around that rigging jumble of bones, in the places where pressure was exerted on the bed, the connective tissue was decaying. Yet, an immense, ravenous hunger animated that ruin and tortured the intestines where the typhus ulcerations were slowly healing.

Outside, the Christmas Novena, the lovely festivity of young and old, had begun. The early evenings were luminous and freezing cold and in their light the entire town of Pescara swarmed with sailors and rang with the sound of bagpipes. The pungent odor of fish stews spread in the air from the open doors of taverns. One by one the lamps lit up at the windows, in the doorways, the streets. The sun lingered roseate on the stone balconies of Farina's house, on the chimney-pots of Menna's house, on San Giacomo's belltower. Like beacons, the shining pinnacles overlooked the town invaded by dusk. Then, all of a sudden, night began to stud the vaulting sky with stars, a sickle moon looked out from behind the bastions above the houses of Sant'Agostino, between the red lantern and the telegraph, and grew larger night after night.

All that bustle of life rose to Orsola's room with the confused buzz of an awakening bee-hive.

The bagpipers' carols approached from house to house, from door to door. Those sounds which the shepherds of Atina drew from their sheepskin bags and their bundles of perforated reeds rang with a devout and familiar festiveness. The convalescent woman heard, and rose in her bed; for that sensation aroused in her the ghosts of other, past sensations, and her eyes filled with sacred visions of radiant holy cribs and white flights of angels soaring through immaculate blues. And she began to sing praises, holding out her arms. Often, suddenly breathless, she sat there, her mouth agape as her voice faltered in her throat; she praised Jesus in a transport of sweet and ardent love, enraptured by the sound of the approaching carols, hallucinated by the holy images hanging on the walls. She ascended to heaven amid the music of cherubim, the fumes of incense and myrrh.

"*Hosanna!*"

Her voice failed her. She held out her arms. Camilla, at her side, tried to make her lie down again; Camilla felt almost subjugated by those blind outbursts of faith; her hands, her lips trembled. Orsola fell back, her head abandoned on her pillow, her throat and breast bared, her eyes showing only their whites in the dreadful pallor of her face, smiling at some invisible thing, in the attitude of a virgin martyr. The bagpipes passed; later came and passed the drunken songs of sailors brawling through the night on their way back to the boats on Pescara's river.

III

THE INSTINCTIVE craving for food became keener as her senses cleared. When the warm smell of bread rose in the air from Flaiano's oven, Orsola begged; she begged and pleaded, whimpering like a starved beggar, holding out her hand to her sister. She devoured her food rapidly, overwhelmed by a brutish pleasure of all her being, looked around suspiciously lest someone try to snatch the food from her hands.

The convalescence was long and slow but a mild feeling of well-being was already beginning to spread through her limbs and clear her mind. The healthy diet of proteins and lean meat began to produce fresh blood; her lungs, now fully dilated by air, vivified the blood laden with nourishing substances; and the tissues irrigated by the swift, warm wave, took on color and formed anew, grew back over the bedsores, which were gradually covered with epidermis; and stimulated by that even flow the brain began to function secure and steady; and the ramifications of the nerves in her sensory organs, no longer distempered and disrupted, limpidly transmitted all sensations; and under her scalp the bulbs of her hair thrived strong and dense; and from that newly re-established order of the mechanical laws of life, that surge of energies that before had been submerged by the illness, from the intense desire to live and feel alive that had seized the convalescent, from everything around her, slowly, as through a second birth, arose a more perfect being.

It was the beginning of February.

From her bed Orsola could see the top of the Arch of Portanuova, the reddish bricks among which grew tufts of greenery, the crumbling capitals where the swallows would soon build their hanging nests. The violets of St. Anna in the cracks of the frieze had yet to blossom. The sky above opened up with beatific serenity; and, at intervals, the call of bugles traveled through the air from the Arsenal.

It was during those days that, almost with a sense of astonishment, she thought about her past existence. It seemed as if that past did not belong to her, were not hers; an immeasurable distance separated her from those memories; a dreamlike distance. She no longer had a clear sense of time; in order to remember she had to look at the objects that surrounded her, to make a great mental effort, to concentrate at length. With the tips of her fingers she touched her temples where the hair was growing back soft and fine, and a vague, abstracted smile fluttered on her lips, flashed through her eyes.

"Ah!" she whispered and, gently, her fingers returned to her temples.

It had been a melancholy and monotonous life there in those three rooms, among all those small, deformed statues of saints, all those Madonnas, all those children repeating aloud and in unison, for five hours a day, day after day, always the same words chalked on the blackboard. Like the glorious martyrs of the legend, like St. Tecla of Lycaonia and St. Euphemia of Calcedonia, the two sisters had consecrated their virginity to the heavenly Spouse, to the nuptials with Jesus. They had mortified the flesh by dint of abstinences and prayers, breathing the air of the church, incense and the smell of burning tapers, living only on vegetables—beans and lentils.

They had stupefied their spirits in that long and arid spelling drill, the cold distilling of words, the mechanical to and fro of thread and needle over eternally identical white linens odorous of lavender and sanctity. Never did their hands reach out for the soft feel of their pupils' hair, the sweet warmth of those fair, angelic heads; never did their lips touch the children's brow in a sudden effusion of tenderness. They taught elementary catechism, the first religious chants. Upon those playful heads they brought down the admonitions of Lent; in grave voices they spoke of the horrors of sin, of eternal damnation, and the children's large eyes filled with wonder, their small pink mouths opened in astonishment. In the children's vivid imaginations, all around them, the sacred objects came alive: the waxen profiles of mysterious saints leaped from the background of old pictures, and the Nazarene, crowned with thorns and blood-red drops, stared from all sides with agonized, haunting eyes; and beneath the hood of the hearth each puff of smoke twisted into an atrocious shape. And this is how they instilled faith in those ingenuous souls.

Now the memory of that sterility turbidly reawakened in Orsola's mind. She thought back, back to the earliest years; compelled by an instinctive impulse of her spirit, she sought refuge at the source; and a sudden flood of jubilation bathed her as though in a single moment her entire childhood had streamed back into her heart.

"Camilla!" she called. "Camilla, where are you?"

But her sister did not answer from the next room, she was not there. She had gone out, perhaps: to church, for Vespers. Then Orsola was seized by the temptation to feel the ground with her feet, to try to take a few steps on the floor, there and then, all alone.

She laughed to herself like a shy little girl who hesitates as she is about to undertake a difficult task; she closed her eyes, lingering to enjoy the sudden delight of her thought; with her fingers she felt her knees, her frail calves, as if to gauge her strength; and she laughed and laughed because that laughter penetrated her with a sweet languor, a subtle, vibrant elation.

A dart of sunlight grazed the windowsill and lanced the water of a basin in the corner; its moving, restless reflection shimmered on the wall, like a delicate mesh of gold. A flight of doves flashed through the air and alighted on the Arch; it seemed an omen. Slowly she moved the covers aside, then she hesitated again: sitting on the edge of the bed, groping with the point of her thin, yellow foot for her woollen slipper. She found it, found its mate; but now a sudden, melting tenderness assailed her, her eyes filled with tears and everything before her wavered in a hazy, milky light, as if the objects around her were losing their substance and vanishing. Tears streaked her cheeks, gathered at her mouth, warm and salty; she drank them, savored their taste. Outside, one by one, in pairs, the doves rose again, fluttering. With a movement of her jaws Orsola forced back the surge of tears; then she leaned against the edge of the bed and pushed, and finally stood on her feet; she smiled through her tears, looking at herself. She hadn't realized how weak she was, that her legs would not support her; she felt a strange prickling sensation in her shins, a twitching in her muscles, almost the sensation of someone who, having broken a bone, gets up before it is well mended. She tried to take a step, she put one foot in front of her, timidly; she became frightened and sat down again on the edge of the bed, looking around as if to make sure no one was watching her. Then she sought a goal—the window; and she started again, carefully, her eyes fixed on the foot in front of her, balancing herself, clutching her green shawl to her chest, invaded by a slight chill. When she had gone halfway, a sudden fear froze her: she staggered, thrashed her hands, turned back toward the bed, took three or four precipitous steps, falling back onto the edge of the bed. She remained there for a short while, panting; she crawled back under the covers where she still found some warmth, bundled herself up tightly, and huddled there shivering.

"Oh Lord, how weak I am!"

And she looked curiously at the spot on the floor where she had taken those few steps, almost expecting to see her footprints.

IV

SHE DID NOT TELL her sister about that first attempt. When she heard Camilla come back home, she closed her eyes and lay motionless as if she were asleep, feeling, deep inside her, a strange pleasure at the deception, straining to hold back the laughter which tickled in her throat and tried to rise to her lips. She was delighted with her small secret; day after day she waited anxiously for the moment when Camilla would descend the stairs and leave; she would sit up and remain still, listening, until the sound of slowly descending footsteps faded; then she would get out of bed, stifling bursts of laughter, leaning against the walls for support, against the furniture, uttering startled little cries whenever her knees threatened to give way, whenever she was about to lose her balance.

Almost always, around that hour, the smell of bread rose from Flaiano's bakery to tease her. She went to the window trying to sniff the breeze; inhaling that hearty aroma, she experienced both torture and a voluptuous pleasure, her tongue swam in her watering mouth and her eyes shone with greed. Then she was seized by a frenzy to search and rummage everywhere, dragging herself fitfully through the rooms; and afterward she made vain and angry attempts to force the locks whose keys Camilla had taken with her. One time, in the hidden corner of a small table-drawer, she found an apple and sank her teeth into it with relish. For a long time, on her strict convalescent's diet, she had not tasted the flavor of fruit. This had a fresh scent of roses, the scent which gathers in certain pale and withered apples. She returned to the drawer and searched again, hoping; but she only found a kind of greenish pod which, probably, contained a cluster of seeds; she took it and examined it with curiosity, and hid it under her pillow.

Thus she spent that hour, in secrecy, with the acrid pleasure that convalescent children extract from forbidden things, small thefts, infractions of the doctor's orders. Her only witness was a cat, speckled like the skin of a snake. Sometimes he followed her around with his familiar meowing or, if the doves fluttered their wings on the Arch outside, he halted in his tracks, poised for an impossible leap. Little by little, Orsola was growing fond of that discreet companion. She welcomed him into the warmth of her bed and whispered nonsense to him, or watched him fixedly as he licked his paw with his pink tongue or offered his lizard-like throat to her endearments, a yellowish throat which throbbed with a husky and tender sound similar to the cooing of turtle-doves among the trees. Owing perhaps to a natural recrudescence of her previous mysticism, she loved the sudden fires that smoldered in the creature's eyes in the dimly lit room, the phosphorescent sparks emanating from that mysterious and silent shape crouching in the darkness.

Camilla observed her sister's strange foibles with a certain diffidence, perhaps even with rankling resentment, but she held her tongue. And slowly, almost imperceptibly, their souls drew apart, mutually repulsed.

They had lived, before, in a constant communion of habits and feelings because all the conflicting traits of their temperaments, all rebellious impulses had been equalized and placated by their shared faith, the unshakable cult of Christ's deity, the contemplative worship that had become the sole purpose of their lives. But as they were completely absorbed in this cult, the ties of their consanguinity had on the contrary gradually been covered and overwhelmed by those of their common religiosity; therefore no tender effusions, no intimate exchange of hopes or memories had ever drawn them together as sisters. They belonged to the same Church, they both were members of Christ's great family, lost on the earth and yearning for Heaven.

So that when, due to the change wrought in her first by the illness and then by her recovery, Orsola began to reveal certain unexpected tendencies, certain unusual attitudes, rejection followed immediate and inevitable, and the slumbering voice of their common blood did not rise to oppose it.

V

THE PUPILS came back—for the first time on a morning in early March. Orsola had got up; she sat on the edge of her bed with the warmth of the sun bathing the nape of her neck and shoulders. In the room hung the pungent smell of the vinegar that Camilla had poured into the dusty inkwells and, through the open windows, from time to time, the wind bore the scent of the violets that now blossomed on the Arch.

A premonition of the children's presence breathed in the room like a gust of that light March air. At first, in the doorway, a tumultuous bustle of small heads straining, one above the other, to get a glimpse inside; then hesitation, shyness, a kind of naive astonishment at the sight of their teacher, so pale and thin that they could barely recognize her.

But the virgin Orsola smiled, overwhelmed by the sudden turmoil of her blood; she called them to her, confusing their names in her excitement; she held out her hands. First singly, then in twos, threes, the children approached; they wanted to catch her hands and touch them with their lips, they recited the get-well wishes they had learned by heart at home, swallowing the words in their haste.

"No, no, no—enough!" Orsola cried, overcome as they pressed around her, but she relinquished her hands to their soft, warm mouths. She felt she was going to faint.

"Camilla, stop them, stop them!"

Each child had brought a gift: there were flowers, fruit. The violets had at once filled the air with their perfume and in that perfume, in that light, the children's faces, flushed with their healthy, plebeian blood, smiled at her.

Then, in the next room, the lesson began. The first grade chanted vowels and diphthongs, the second grade spelled out words; and above the silvery chorus, now and then, rose Camilla's admonishing voice.

"*La, le, li, lo, lu* . . ."

When there was a moment's pause, Orsola heard Matteo Pariello hammering at his shoe-leather or the clacking of La Iece's loom.

"*Va, ve, vi, vo, vu* . . ."

She grew restless. The monotony of those sounds and voices filled her head with a disagreeable heaviness, it made her drowsy. Whereas she wanted to stay awake, still sensing all around her the children's vitality, the joyous emanation of all those lives.

"*Bal, bel, bil, bol, bul* . . ."

She took the flowers and put them in a glass of water to keep them fresh. Then she smelled them, her nostrils buried for a long time in their freshness, wholly absorbed in that olfactory sin.

"*Gra, gre, gri, gro, gru* . . ."

A big white cloud veiled the sun. Orsola went to the window, leaned against the windowsill and looked down into the piazza. Across the way Donna Fermina Memma stood on her balcony wearing a pink dress, amid pots spilling out carnations; and a group of officers passed below her, laughing and striking the pavement with their ringing sabres. Farther ahead, in the park, the lilac bushes were ready to bloom, the crown of the huge pine-tree swayed in the wind. From Lucitino's tavern came Vedura, the eternal drunkard, staggering and vociferous.

Orsola withdrew. This was the first time, after so long, that she had looked out into the piazza. It was as if she were looking down from a tremendous height; she felt slightly dizzy.

"*Nar, ner, nir, nor, nur* . . ."

The chant inside still continued, on and on and on.

"*Pla, ple, pli, plo, plu* . . ."

She began to choke, her head began to reel under the torture: her poor frayed nerves were giving way. The chant continued relentlessly, following the beat of Camilla's pointer rapping on the desk.

"*Ram, rem, rim, rom, rum* . . ."

"*Sat, set, sit, soit, sut* . . ."

And a sudden fit of sobbing assailed her, flung her onto the bed. And she lay there, prone, her arms outflung, weeping, pressing her face into the pillows, racked by sobs, unable to stop.

"*Tal, tel, til, tol, tul* . . ."

VI

HER HAIR had all grown back, tightly curled and chestnut colored as before. She was anxious to look at herself in the mirror; for, with one of those mawkish exclamations that still revealed the old trollop she had been, Rosa Catena had passed a hand over her body and said: "What a beauty!"

So again she waited for Camilla to leave the house. Then she climbed out of bed and took down from the wall one of those gold-framed rococo mirrors antiqued with misty green stains; with a corner of the blanket she removed the dust and looked at herself in the glass, smiling. Her throat was bare and covered with bluish, almost protruding veins, and there was something goatlike about her small, long, oval head: the thin lips, the sharp chin, her eyes—the color of chestnuts like her hair, but lighter, almost yellow. Her translucent pallor and her smile gave her twenty-seven years a new charm, a new youthfulness.

She examined herself for a long time; and she played, holding the mirror off at a distance, drawing it closer, delighted to see her image vanish in its sea-green light as if under a veil of water and then slowly emerge again. She was conquered, dominated by vanity. She began to see many small details she had never noticed before: a beauty-mark, for instance, like a small lentil on the skin over her left temple, and a fine scar across the arch of one of her eyebrows. Then, in a transport of sudden joy, she looked around for some other pleasure.

The pod she had found hidden in the drawer had opened its valves like a sea-shell, exposing a dense bunch of blackish seeds. Each seed seemed to be attached to a strand of fine filaments with a silvery sheen, and the cluster hung together, compact. But when the virgin Orsola breathed upon it, a cloud of minute white plumes instantly rose into the air and scattered glittering in all directions: they were what people called "spies." The seeds seemed to have wings, they looked like fragile, evanescent insects which dissolved at the touch of the sun, or like swansdown, barely visible; they floated, began to descend, became entangled in Orsola's hair, grazed her face, covered her whole body. She tried to ward off the assault, to chase away that fuzz which tickled her skin and clung to her hands, but she kept laughing and could not blow it away.

At last she lay down, stretched out, and let that soft snowfall slowly drift down upon her. She kept her eyes half-closed to prolong its melting sweetness; and as a heavy drowsiness invaded her limbs she had the sensation of sinking into a deep bed of feathers. The room was filled with the pale, steady light of a March afternoon when the sun shines shyly, fading into the wide opalescent sky like a premonition of dawn.

When Camilla returned she found her sister still asleep with the mirror next to her and "spies" in her hair.

"Oh Jesus! Oh Lord Jesus!" she whispered through clenched teeth, joining her palms in a gesture of bitter compassion.

The good woman was just coming from church where she had sung the litanies for the Annunciation and listened to a sermon on the Archangel's message to the Virgin Mary. *Ecce ancilla Domini.* The preaching friar's thundering eloquence had intoxicated her; some of his admonitory words still rang in her ears.

Just then Orsola woke up with a voluptuous yawn, stretching her limbs.

"Oh, is that you, Camilla?" she asked, bewildered for a moment by that presence.

"Yes, it's me, it's me! You will lose your soul, you wretch, perdition is awaiting you!" the pious woman shouted, pointing at the mirror on the bed. "You are playing with the devil's tools."

And excited by her first outburst, she went on, raising her voice, spewing out the scorching words of the sermon, slashing the air with her hands, lashing out with threats of eternal damnation—she spoke not only to her sister, she rose to chastise a world of sinners.

"*Memento! Memento!*"

Orsola had stopped hearing, stunned by that screaming, vociferous onslaught.

Suddenly, at the corner of the piazza, the military band struck up with a crash, the clarion call of twenty trumpets.

VII

THE LAST ROOM in the rear of the house was low-ceilinged and narrow, the overhead beams blackened by smoke, reeking with odors of onions and dishwater and doused charcoal. The copper pots hung in an orderly row upon the walls, lusterless; the Castelli plates with their gay motifs of flowers and birds and laughing faces were lined up on a shelf; old-fashioned brass oil-lamps, empty bottles, scraps of withering vegetables were strewn about on the tables; and over all this, protectively, reigned St. Vincent, portrayed with the great book in one hand and a red flame bursting from his skull.

In that room, long ago, surrounded by the steam of boiling water and the fumes of vegetarian meals, Orsola had often heard, hurtling down upon her head from a tiny window high in the wall, couplets of bawdy songs followed by coarse howls of laughter. On summer evenings the singing and the laughter grew louder, amid the strumming of guitars and the stomping on the ground of dancing feet. At certain hours all the sounds of the life of the most wretched scum rose all the way to their window and made those poor brides of Christ, humbly bent over their earthenware pots filled with the ascetic innocence of beans and vegetables, tremble with horror. But now, with the coming of a new and merry spring, one day, at the sound of those voices, a strong longing to look outside stung Orsola's soul.

Camilla was not at home; it was the fifth Sunday after Lazarus. After the brief rains, the imminence of April stirred in the air with a sweeter, milder breath; and in that air the maiden sensed her re-birth more clearly and fully. And as she wandered through the rooms in idleness, she was inevitably overcome by curiosity, captivated by the morbid spell that obscene spectacles exert even upon the purest souls.

She climbed onto a chair to reach the opening, but before lifting her eyes to peer outside, she was seized by anxious tremors and, quivering, still standing on the chair, she looked to all sides, afraid lest someone surprise her in that position.

Everything around her was quiet; on and off a drop of water fell into a basin, with a pattering sound. Outside the voices rose and enticed.

Reassured, the virgin Orsola looked out. The filth in the alleyway had fermented under the rain like yeast; a black mire covered the flagstones where fruit peels, scraps of vegetables, rags, rotten slippers, hat-brims, all the decomposed rubbish that poverty flings into the streets, blended together. Facing that sewer from which the sun drew insects and putrid exhalations, a row of tiny houses seemed to pant, leaning against the barracks for support. Yet from every window, every crack, streamed carnations spilling from their pots; and the large pink and red flowers dangled in the sunshine, splendidly open, magnificent, in full bloom. And among those flowers appeared the flabby, painted faces of the whores; obscene songs, hoarse laughter trooped by; and down below, on the pavement, beneath the barracks' grilled windows, other trollops reached out to the soldiers, speaking in loud voices, taunting. And the soldiers whose blood called out those evil flowers of Aphrodite, stretched their arms between the iron bars to snatch whatever they could, like starved beasts slavering at the sight of those women long worn out by the lechery of countless drunken crews and sodden stevedores.

Orsola could not move, stunned by that spectacle of corruption which mounted all the way to her window, fermenting beneath the benign sun of Lent. She still did not turn away; but, lifting her eyes, at a dormer-window on the barracks' roof she saw a blond man looking at her and smiling. She got down from the chair in a flurry, paler than ever, for she thought she had heard Camilla's voice. She ran to her room and threw herself on her bed, dismayed, breathless, as if someone were pursuing her, threatening her.

VIII

FROM THAT DAY ON, every hour, every minute that Camilla was not at home, a diabolical temptation drew her to that spectacle. She tried at first to resist, in vain—weakly she gave in. She went to the window eager and wary like someone going to meet a lover; she lingered there for a long time, hiding behind the decrepit shutter while the miasma from the brothel aroused and corrupted her.

She observed everything, straining her eyes, trying to catch a glimpse of what went on beyond the carnations that screened the windows. The sun was hot and heavy; swarms of insects milled in the air. From time to time, when a man turned into the alleyway, the women would call out from the windows; half-naked women with bare breasts rushed into the street to offer themselves. Then the man and the one he had chosen would disappear through one of those dark doorways. The women who had been passed up would follow the couple with mocking insults and bursts of laughter, and then would go back to lying in wait behind their carnations.

And so lust began to smolder inside the virgin Orsola. The need for love, latent before, now rose from all of her being, became a torture, an incessant, ruthless torment against which she was helpless.

A warm wave of healthy energy filled her; sudden joyful feelings stirred her blood, aroused in her breast a fluttering like that of wings, filled her mouth with songs. At times a breath, one of those faint tremors in the air which spread in the sunshine, the song of a beggar, a smell, a nothing was enough to fill her with vague bewilderment, moments of abandon when it seemed to her she felt all over her limbs something like the caressing touch of the velvet of a ripe fruit. Thus she hovered weightless and lost over unknown depths of delight. The irritation of abstinence, the unaccustomed copiousness of lymph, thc continued tensing of her nerves under stimuli, all this kept her in a sort of daze akin to the first stage of intoxication. The past vanished, drowsed at the bottom of her memory, no longer sprang to life. And at every moment, everywhere, desire laid its traps for her: the saints on the walls, the Madonnas, the naked crucified Christs, the small misshapen figures of wax statuettes, all the things surrounding her, for her took on impure appearances. From all objects impurity emanated and touched her body, burningly.

"Now, now I'll go down into the street," she said to herself, unable to resist.

Then her hands trembled on the door as she opened it. The strident sound made by the bolt pulled through its iron rings dismayed her. She turned back, threw herself on the bed almost in a swoon, deathly pale, beneath the shadow of a man.

IX

ON PALM SUNDAY, after all those months, she left the house for the first time; and Camilla wanted to accompany her to give thanks to the Lord for her recovery. When the bells began to ring festively, Orsola looked out of her window. The entire town radiated the joy of Easter under the April sun. The entire community swarmed in the streets, carrying the peacful symbol of the olive branch.

She must now put on her holiday best; the people in the streets were going to see her when she went by. A frenzy of vanity seized her; she locked herself in her room, looked for the brightest dresses at the bottom of the chest. A sharp odor of camphor rose from those old clothes stored away in there for years; they were large skirts of flowery silk, green and violet and iridescent, a crinoline which, full and rich, had perhaps once swelled around the hips of a young bride; they were long bodices with full sleeves, light beige pelerines trimmed with white laces, veils meshed with silver threads, collars of fine, hand-embroidered linen; a heap of things impossible to use, uncouth, covered with mould-stains.

As if guided by a new instinct, Orsola picked up and discarded, perfuming her hands with camphor as she searched. All that useless silk and those veils irritated her. She found nothing that fit her! She slammed the chest shut angrily and shoved it back under the bed with a thrust of her foot. The church bells rang out for the third time. Then, with Camilla looking on, she hastily slipped on her usual drab, ash-gray dress, biting her lips to keep back the tears.

The bells called. Along the streets the sheaves of palm leaves emitted a mobile, silvery glitter; from every knot of country folk rose a hedge of branches; and the pure clemency of the Christian benediction filled the air from those branches, as if the Galilean were approaching, the poor, sweet king sitting on the she-ass amid the mob of his disciples, to meet the hosannas of the redeemed people. *Benedictus qui venit in nomine Domini. Hosanna in excelsis!*

Inside the church the crowd was immense beneath the grove of palms. Because of one of those currents that form irresistibly in a mass of people, Orsola was separated from Camilla; she found herself left alone in that surge, amid all those contacts, all that shoving and breathing. She tried to open a path for herself: her hands touched a man's back, there were other warm hands whose touch disturbed her. She felt her face grazed by an olive leaf, her step impeded by a knee, an elbow nudging her hip, her breasts, her shoulders offended by anonymous pressures. With that odor of incense, under the sacred palms, in the mystical dusk, in all that crush of Christian men and women jostling together little erotic sparks were set off and spread; secret loves found each other again and were carnally united. Past Orsola streamed young peasant girls with palm sprigs on their breasts, fleeting laughter in the flashing whites of eyes turned toward admirers who pursued them temptingly: and so, feeling love stream by all around her, she placed her body between those bodies straining to reach each other, became an obstacle to those hands trying to touch each other, separated those grasping hands, the tangle of those arms. But something of those interrupted caresses penetrated her blood. At a certain point she stood face to face with a blond soldier; she almost rested her head on his tunic, for a throng of people was pressing at her back. She lifted her eyes; the young man smiled at her as he had once smiled from the attic window of the barracks. Behind her the pressure continued; the fumes of the incense spread more densely, and from the depths of the church rose the voice of the deacon chanting:

"*Procedamus in pace.*"

And the choir answered:

"*In nomine Christi. Amen.*"

It was the introduction to the procession, which caused a tremendous commotion among the faithful. Instinctively, without thinking, Orsola clung to the man, as if she already belonged to him; she almost let herself be lifted by those arms which seized her hips, in her hair she felt that virile breath with its slight scent of tobacco. And that's how she walked, weakened, exhausted, crushed by the voluptuousness which had suddenly overcome her, seeing nothing but a confused dazzle before her.

Then from the main altar moved the thurifer, scattering clouds of sweet bluish smoke over the congregation; and a white procession uncoiled in the center of the church. The celebrants carried olive branches in their hands and sang.

X

THE ENTIRE HOLY WEEK protected virgin Orsola's love with its darkling complicity. The churches looked immensely vast in the crepuscular light of Christ's Passion, the crucifixes on the altars were covered with heavy purplish cloths; the sepulchres of the Nazarene were surrounded by tall white plants grown in cellars; a perfume of flowers and of benzoin hung heavy in the air.

There, upon her knees, Orsola waited, until a light step behind her made her start. She could not turn because Camilla watched her; but she felt completely embraced by the gaze of that man, as if by a subtle flame, and a turbid tenderness welled through her flesh. Then she stared at the triangle of tapers on a wooden frame near the altar. The priests chanted in front of a large book; and one by one the tapers were put out. There remained only five, there remained only two; darkness issued from the depths of the side chapels over the people absorbed in their prayers. The last small flame finally disappeared: all the benches resounded under the lashes of the reeds. Orsola in the darkness, as soon as she felt herself touched by two groping hands, rose from the marble floor with a jerk, dismayed. Then, when she left the church, the thought of having desecrated the holy place filled her with repentance; sudden and crushing, the fear of punishment reappeared. She then sank into a kind of dream where the livid figure of the dead Christ and the crash of flagellations and the thrills of her stimulated flesh and the heavy, redolent odor of the flowers and the breath of that blond man all mingled together in an ambiguous sensation of sorrow and pleasure.

XI

BUT WHEN JESUS triumphantly re-ascended to His heavenly glory, the aromatic effluvia of Easter no longer comforted the love of the virgin Orsola. For its setting her love now had the domain of alley cats and tame pigeons. The tender gestures traveled from the barracks' attic to the kitchen window; in between lay the brothel, like a slimy ditch along whose edges grew the flowers fed by putrefaction. The pigeons flew aloft, flashing the green and gray shimmer of their feathers.

Her lover had a beautiful, ancient name—hc was called Marcello and wore beautiful red and silver insignia on the sleeves of his uniform. He wrote letters brimming with eternal fire, replete with impctuous sentences which made the enamored woman nearly faint from tenderness and tremble from ill-contained voluptuousness. Orsola read those pages in secrecy, night and day kept them hidden in her bosom; because of the warmth of her flesh, the purple handwriting was imprinted upon her skin, and it was like a gentle tattoo of love, which delighted her. Her replies were endless: all the grammatical knowledge of a schoolmistress, the entire thesaurus of a devout believer's psalmistic apostrophes, all the flowing sentimentality of an over-ripe maiden poured onto the paper of the blue-lined school notebooks. She wrote and forgot herself, carried away by a wave of sonorous verbosity. It almost seemed that a newly born ability were expressing itself within her, unexpectedly taking on maniacal aspects. That great sediment of mystical lyricism accumulated through the reading of the prayer books over so many years of faithfulness to the Heavenly Spouse, now, stirred by earthly love, rose confusedly and assumed unsuspected flavors of profanity. Thus the tearful implorings addressed to Jesus became hopeful sighs of yearning for the delights of much less ethereal embraces; the offers of the flowers of the soul to the Supreme Good were transformed into tender surrenders of the flesh to the desire for the blond lover; and the aphrodisiac light of the moon was crowned with all the epithets by which the Holy Ghost is rendered radiant. Nor did the soft breezes of spring fail to waft away the heavenly scents of the festive banquets of Paradise.

XII

THEIR MESSENGER was one of those men who seem to sprout, like mushrooms, from the moistness of the tainted street and to bear upon their bodies almost a native tint of mud; one of those gray-invisible men, who burrow in everywhere, who are always there whenever a cent is to be earned, a bit of fat is to be lapped up, a rag is to be snatched—today junk-dealers and tomorrow procurers of maids or loose women, today fake mercantile middlemen and tomorrow catchers of stray mongrel dogs.

This man had an operatic name—he was called Lindoro; from the Ospedale quarter to the bastions of Sant'Agostino a great notoriety had sprung up around this name. He was born from the mating of a vagrant clarinet player with a market woman who hawked vegetables, and he had inherited his father's nomadic instincts and his mother's natural greed. He had at first dragged himself over the garbage piles of every household with broom and basket; then he had washed glasses and dishes in a tavern, where soldiers and sailors threw in his face the dregs of their cups and the bones of the badly fried fish. After the tavern he had landed in a bakery, where he pushed the loaves toward the fire on a long shovel, all night long, sweating, blinded. From the bakery he had gone on to the position of lighter of the public street lamps, wearing out his shoulder under the weight of the ladder he carried. Dismissed from that position because he stole kerosene from the large white zinc drums, he began to roam the streets, buying and re-selling old clothes, doing the most miserable kind of odd jobs throughout the workers' and artisans' neighborhoods, offering his services as a pimp and ruffian to soldiers and newcomers, striving in this way for his daily bread.

On his body and in his soul each trade had carved a mark, left behind an habitual gesture, the development of certain muscles, the debilitation of a particular organ, a callous, a cadence, an accent of the voice, a phrase of the jargon. He was small in stature, thin, with an enormous, almost bald head, patches of sparse bristles on his cheeks and boils among the bristles. His clothes were hybrid, varied, unpredictable; all manner of styles alternately covered his body, were superimposed with a jarring contrast: aristocratic, greenish morning coats over trousers once puce-colored and now patched everywhere, maroon felt hats and servants' slippers, shiny metal buttons, disks of white bone, military braids, laces—that potpourri of decayed opulence and ignoble penury which clutters the store of any Jewish junk-dealer.

XIII

NOW THIS MAN was the go-between. He delivered Marcello's epistles together with jugs of Pescara river water at Orsola's house and left with his jugs empty and her answering letters. When she heard him come up the stairs, Orsola went pale, racked her brain for pretexts to get rid of Camilla, to remain alone with this bearer of water and of joy. Then there were rapid, surreptitious, clandestine contacts; there were exchanged between her and her go-between those sidelong glances of complicity, those fleeting contractions of the facial muscles, those whispered monosyllables which are the instruments of human guile and which as time goes by form tenacious bonds between deceivers. Little by little Orsola's love was suffused by something of Lindoro's vileness; a kind of familiarity gradually established itself between the woman in love and the messenger. If he arrived during Camilla's absence, she plied him with questions, her head so close to his he could feel her breath, inadvertently placing a hand on his shoulder at times. Lindoro gave rein to his loquaciousness, interspersing bits of jargon, lewd silences, sly revelatory smiles, equivocal gestures, smackings of his tongue and lips.

He played the go-between with artistry, adroitly insinuated corruption into Orsola's spirit, cleverly lured the prey little by little into Marcello's trap. And the virgin listened to him intently and thoughtfully while a flame grew deep in her eyes and lewd excitement dried her mouth; she listened and did not interrupt him. Lindoro could tell at once that he had awakened lust in the woman; and faced by that body that was wholly tensed, completely ravaged by passion, the male in him was suddenly aroused and he was struck by the temptation to pluck the prize he was preparing for another man's pleasure. But fear rising from the depths of his cowardice restrained him and froze his ardor.

Then, finally, Orsola agreed to a meeting with Marcello. The assignation would take place in a remote house on the outskirts of town, tucked away in a deserted alleyway, where nobody would be able to see them, on a Sunday in June when Camilla stayed longer in church and Lindoro could be on the look-out.

During the days preceding the great event, Orsola was gripped by bitter excitement, a kind of fever which at times made her teeth chatter, brought a hot flush to her face and shivers to her scalp and the nape of her neck. She was unable to keep still, couldn't remain seated, because a frenzy of restlessness filled her limbs. During school, surrounded by the even, monotonous murmur of her pupils, surrounded by that unremitting drone of scanned syllables, a dazzling surge of rebellion would suddenly blind her, and she would have liked to pounce on the children, tousle their hair, overturn the blackboard, the charts, the benches, burst out screaming, smash something, stun herself. Under Camilla's cold and inquisitive eyes she came close to fainting, such was her agitation, her rage, her immense inner effort at dissimulation.

Then, when Camilla went out, she would flounce through all the rooms, move chairs from here to there, nibble at a flower, drain a large glass of water in one gulp, stare at herself in the mirror, look out the window, fling herself down across the bed, give vent in a thousand ways to her restlessness, the exuberance of her sensual vitality. Her entire body, in the belated, seething ebullience of virginhood, had become richer and fuller. Her head was not beautiful, it lacked the vigorous bold structure, the olive-tinted splendor of certain races of the Abruzzo, those pure lines of nose and chin drawn with Grecian definition upon the ample planes of the Latin face. But, though unaware of it, concealed by the clumsiness of her drab clothes, beneath their drooping, haphazard pleats and folds, she possessed a lovely, delicate body.

Those were the first days of June: the summer arose out of the spring as an aloe out of a grassy field. Between sea and river, the entire town of Pescara rejoiced in the salty breeze and in the river's cool air, as if it were reaching out its arms toward those natural boundaries of salt and sweet water. Then during those days the blandishments of the season rose to Orsola's room; lustrous insects knocked against her window panes and bounced back, like the grains of a golden hail.

The virgin, when she was alone, felt a need to stretch her limbs, to throw off her long dresses, lie down, and absorb through her skin that mysterious beguilement that hung in the atmosphere.

She began slowly to undress with lazy movements, her fingers lingering upon the laces and hooks, making faint, half-hearted efforts at pulling her arms out of sleeves, halting listlessly in the process and letting her head with its short crinkly hair fall back, that head which was so much like the head of an adolescent boy. Gradually, under her laboring, caressing hands, from out of the shapelessness of the garments, like a statue disinterred from the dross of time, the naked body appeared. A heap of coarse wool and linen cloth lay at the feet of the thus purified maiden, and from that heap as from a pedestal she rose in the light, crowning her head with her arms, while at the touch of the air a barely visible quiver rippled over her skin. In that momentary attitude all the lines of the torso softly stretched and rose towards the encircled head; the slight roundness of the abdomen, not yet disfigured by conception, flattened out; and the outline of the rounded thighs took on full relief. Then, if an insect got into the room, the hum of its wings circling around her and threatening to touch that nakedness—that hum distressed Orsola; and she tried to ward off the dreaded sting, making serpentine movements, her muscles twitching beneath her skin, her arms and legs forming frightened knots, her ankles twisting feebly, not powerful enough to accomplish anything.

Then, excited in this way by her movements and feeling warm, she was overcome by new yearnings. She opened her door, cautious and wary; and stuck out her head, peering into the adjacent room. There was a musty odor, that lifeless squalor which fills a classroom when the children are gone. On the square charts the large block letters of the alphabet and the groups of diphthongs and syllables loomed, the room's silent sovereigns. Orsola advanced, her bare feet avoiding the cracks in the irregular floor, experiencing the titubation of someone who walks barefoot for the first time over an uneven surface and the confusion of a woman who no longer feels her step impeded by the skirts she is used to wearing. She went like this all the way to the third room, where they kept the water. She plunged her hands into it, sprinkled it all over her body, bravely, shivering when a heavier drop ran down her skin. She left the room, all glittering with dew and walked to the mirror of an old chest of drawers.

On that dresser fragments of inlay still remained here and there. The mirror, which concealed a cabinet on top of the dresser, had a frame decorated with gilded and colored fretwork and at the top floated two decapitated cupids. Lured by an irresistible desire to see herself naked, Orsola strained on tiptoe before the mirror. Her entire body, still covered by fresh, cool drops of water, rose in the mist of the mirror as though in the green-blue depths of the sea. She gazed at herself, smiling. Her smile, each movement of her muscles, seemed to impart a quivering light to every contour of her nakedness, caught by the mirror as if they were those of an image seen in a reflection in the water. Then she began a kind of vain mimicry, watching all her gestures reproduce themselves in the glass, parting her lips to show her teeth, lifting her arms to show her armpits, offering her arched back and forcing her head to turn as far back as possible; until, at the sight of that view of herself, a mad burst of hilarity shook her whole body. Far, far off, in the distant background, behind the woman, the alphabet chart was reflected from the opposite wall.

XIV

NOW, DURING ONE of those moments, Lindoro, who had come up the stairs with his jars, knocked at the entrance door. Orsola cried to him: "Wait!"

And she hastily gathered her clothes up from the floor, hastily put them on, and went to open.

It was six o'clock in the evening; the white gleam from Brina Palace filled the room; all Pescara, a great asylum of swallows, was singing.

The two of them stood in the center of the room, discussing the imminent meeting. Lindoro with his loquacity was trying to dispel the girl's last hesitations; for he had already received part of his reward and was anxious to lay his hands on the rest. The game of deceitful persuasion gave a lively sparkle to his words, his eyes, his gestures. His breath smelled heavily of wine and, because of a razor's recent scraping, his face, his cheeks were studded with small pinkish and purplish spots.

As he spoke he revealed the row of his regular and healthy teeth, one of those strong sets of teeth that often grow fiercely in plebeian mouths; and this singularity stood out strikingly in the man's general look of turpitude.

Orsola resisted, expressing misgivings, fears, interrupting him; but the procurer's shameless arguments having been expressed with increasing heat thanks to his wine-induced excitement, she already became uneasy. Little by little she backed up to the wall, leaning against it for support. Glimpses of linen showed through her clothing here and there, telling of the haste in which she had dressed. Her throat was completely bare, and on her stockingless feet everything could be seen save for the toes inside her slippers.

But at a certain point, involuntarily, because of that blind instinct which warns a woman that she is faced by an aroused man, she swiftly moved her hand to fasten the hooks over her throat, her breasts. That movement by which Orsola acknowledged the man in the go-between, that unexpected gesture provoked in Lindoro's abjectness an uprush of masculine pride. Ah, he had made a woman respond to him! —And he came closer; and then, since the wine gave him courage, this time no cowardly restraint held the brute in check.

XV

ORSOLA LAY THERE inert, stretched out on the brick floor, her clothes, her entire body expressing the dishevelment of an outraged woman.

But when she heard Camilla's steps on the stairs, she rose on her elbow from the depths of her exhausted languor; rapidly ran her hands over her disordered clothing, was able to summon up speech and tell her sister that a sudden weakness had caused her to collapse in the middle of the room.

Outside night was falling. Over the town unfolded the vast,

glaucous coolness of a June evening, coming in from the Adriatic. Voices and laughter filled the piazza; all through the building rang the Sabbatical joy of its relieved tenants. From the second floor landing Teodora Lo Iece cried: "Neighbor Camilla, neighbor Camilla, are you coming?"

Orsola followed her sister—without speaking, without thinking. She had made an effort to remember: a sort of lethargy still imprisoned her memory. Teodora filled their ears with her vicious, petulant chatter.

"Have you heard, neighbor, that the daughter of Rosa Catena is getting married?"

"Oh."

"Have you heard, she's taking Giovanni Speranza, that red-headed fellow who runs a tavern at the Pesceria and has Saint Donato's sickness, God preserve us."

"Oh."

"Have you heard, neighbor, Checchina Madrigale has run off again to Francavilla. You know her, she's that fat woman who lives at Gloria's house, dark, with a beaked nose—that one."

Teodora had fallen into step with Orsola. Camilla followed a little behind, her head bowed, not paying any attention to the sin of slander the weaver's tongue was committing against her neighbor. Along the streets everyone was out enjoying the cool air; knots of women passed in cotton dresses, their arms bare to the elbow.

"Neighbor, just look at Graziella Potavigna, at the flounce she's wearing! Look at Rosa Zazzetta, with one sergeant in front and one behind . . . Oh, you didn't know?"

And here followed a tale of intrigues full of salacious indiscretions, whispered into the ear. To forget, Orsola let herself become completely absorbed by the gossip, with a kind of convulsed frenzy not giving herself the time to think, asking questions, inciting Teodora to go on wagging her tongue, fearful of pauses, filling them with bursts of laughter. She almost found a bitter pleasure in hearing other people being reviled.

"Oh, there's Don Paolo."

Walking towards them with his enviable placidity came Don Paolo Seccia, an octogenarian still as pungent and green as a juniper.

"Do come with us, Don Paolo; we can walk together."

All the butcher shops along the street, on both sides, displayed their freshly slaughtered heifers, strung up across the doorway; the odor of the raw meat spread from the gaping bellies and attacked one's nostrils. Farther on, long rows of macaroni were spread out under the light of the moon, which looked down on them from above a flagpole set on the barracks roof. Groups of shouting soldiers crowded round the fruit peddlers.

"Let's go to the Bandiera," said Teodora, stepping aside to let Don Paolo and Camilla walk ahead.

Orsola moved dazedly through all those sounds, those pungent odors. By now a vague despair was beginning to move deep inside her, twisting her lips when she laughed, paralyzing her tongue when she spoke. Certain little physical pains also molested her and called her back to reality. She could no longer run away from herself; her voice died under her teeth, anguish clenched her throat, the specter of her tremendous, irreparable sin rose before her. She now felt she would die from the effort she had to make to stay on her feet, to keep on walking—she was pounded by the ruthless bustle of life in the street which belongs to everyone.

"So, as I was saying, that one-eyed husband of hers, without knowing a thing . . ." said Teodora, picking up the thread of her momentarily interrupted back-biting.

They walked through the Bandiera quarter. To the left the bridge of barges straddled the river. On the opposite bank the stern and gloomy bulk of the bastion was outlined against the pallid sky. The old iron cannons, their muzzles solidly dug into the ground, stood in a long row with the thick hemp mooring ropes slung around them; huge iron anchors cluttered the pier. On the decks of the boats, along the embankments, sailors ate and smoked under their canvas tents; the lit-up tents with their blood-red glow clashed with the cold whiteness of the moon. Around the prows broad patches, as of putrifying matter, floated lazily.

". . . sent for Don Nereo Memma, just imagine!" Teodora continued inexorably.

"Did someone just mention Doctor Dulcamara?" broke in Don Paolo, who had heard the name, laughing, his frank mouth still spiked with shining ivory.

Orsola no longer heard anything; she was as pale as the face of the moon. At first all that profound, luminous peacefulness pouring down from the sky upon the river and all those long currents of marine odors mingling with the cool night had soothed her; for in that soft and tender scenery the phantom images of love deep within her revived, and the extreme aspirations of her feelings shone resplendent in the lunar night. Then, immediately after, there was a confused tumult in which all she heard was the throbbing of her arteries, a deafening murmur that seemed to expand and in a moment clog the whole atmosphere. The ground gave way under her feet. As dizziness seized her, the river's shore became blurred, the river invaded the street; waves—waves—waves surged all around her. Then suddenly a glitter of dazzling sparks lit up in her eyes, a glowing flicker of tiny flaming will-o'-the-wisps which exploded, intertwined, moved away, melted and vanished like writhing snakes in the darkness. In that glimmer Marcello's image rapidly appeared and disappeared, changing as in a dream. The dizziness ceased. Orsola recognized the streams of moonlight mirrored by the placid river; she continued to walk, stupefied, exhausted, almost about to faint.

"You're tired, eh? You're not used to it, of course. Lean on me, hold on," said Teodora. "Donna Mentina Ussoria's daughter, the youngest one, she's pock-marked, was standing right in front of the store, you know—on the small piazza . . ."

They reached the Coast Guard barracks. Large piles of carob pods gave off an odor as strong as tanned hides; and the road strewn with broken oyster shells crunched under their feet. Favored by the moon, two fishermen were silently pulling in eels with nets close to the shore. But the resounding sea filled the silence with its immensity. The rolling salt patches which again and again appeared shining above the veil of sweet water announced the river's mouth.

"Let's go back, my pretty ones," said Don Paolo, picking up a carob pod from the pile nearby.

Orsola let herself be led. She found it difficult to conceal her frantic gasps; for now her condition, with overwhelming dreadfulness, appeared before her and crushed all the amorous emotions, all the yearnings and excitements evoked by the voluptuous moonlit night. The inexorable fixed idea in her mind set before her the image of the living Lindoro; once again she felt herself seized and mauled by those harsh, coarse hands, suffocated by that breath inflamed with wine and lust, felt herself again being violated on the room's brick floor. But at that moment, she thought, she hadn't resisted, she hadn't screamed, she hadn't made the slightest attempt to fight him off; she had surrendered, all her strength drained, no longer able to distinguish anything, feeling only an immense joy mingled with the pain flooding through her body. Then revulsion and languor alternately seized her flesh, freezing her, inflaming her, like ice, like fire. Mindless, she stared straight ahead, pale, her eyes enlarged and darker.

"Listen to the wine singing!" said Don Paolo, pausing for a moment.

Aboard the boats the sailors lay stretched out between the coils of rope, surrounded by the smoke of their Dalmatian tobacco, and they sang about beautiful women, loudly, in chorus.

XVI

CAMILLA, on the *prie-dieu*, her bowed head against it, her hands clasped, prayed for a long time in a low voice; then for the night she lit the votive lamp before the Virgin Mary; and finally she surrendered to sleep, holding the sweeet heart of Jesus between the withered flowers of her breasts. Her devoutness was so great that even as she slept her breathing seemed to caress the sacred host lying there on its sacred paten. On the vaulted ceiling the shadows followed the flickering of the tiny flame fed by the oil in the lamp. The sounds of wood that swells and of wood-worms that gnaw, the mysterious voices of old furniture in the nocturnal quiet, broke the silence.

Orsola lay in the same bed at Camilla's side, stretched out motionless, open-eyed, for a great sleepless weariness weighed upon her limbs and the unrelenting vigilance of anguish tortured her wretched soul. She listened to the silence; she examined herself with fretful curiosity, as if to find out what change had been wrought in her being.

Of a sudden, Camilla began to mumble confused words in her sleep, fragments of incomprehensible words, barely moving her lips, and heaving deep sighs. Her head, gaunt, sharp, rigidly carved by penance and fasting, yellow in the light of the lamp, rested on the whiteness of the pillow like a poorly gilded effigy of a saint on a monstrance. Small, purplish shadows marked the inside of the nostrils, the furrows of the tense, stringy neck, the hollows of the cheeks, the deep sockets from which bulged eyeballs concealed by the lids' slack skin. Thus she seemed the corpse of a martyr, into which the spirit of God was descending.

Although this was not the first of Camilla's nocturnal soliloquies, Orsola felt her scalp turn to ice: a sudden terror gripped and oppressed her. She instinctively huddled up, tried to move away from her sister's body, retreating to the very edge of the bed; she remained still, holding her breath during the intervals of silence, her eyes fixed on the lips of the sleeping woman, feeling shaken by a dark ominous pang deep in her chest whenever those lips moved to pronounce more words. She did not understand them; but something remotely profound and solemn was contained in that uninterrupted murmur, a supernatural mystery emanated from that inert, unconscious body that spoke without hearing its own voice. The room was touched by the breath of the grave; for in the sleepless woman's distraught imagination the oscillating shadows took on the terrifying, threatening shapes of phantoms; the air seemed to be furrowed by mysterious sounds. All the objects toward which the hallucinated woman's eyes turned for refuge, all those objects changed form, became alive and advanced towards her. Then once again the thought of punishment and eternal damnation rose to haunt her conscience. She lay stricken under the incubus of her sin, crossing her arms over her breasts to protect herself from the threats of the demons, trying to pray, her tongue paralyzed by terror, with an ultimate, devout impulse clinging to the anchor of repentance, the last salvation. She felt damned, from the depths of her heart she begged for mercy from the divine Spouse she had betrayed, from kind and generous Jesus, from Him who forgives.

Camilla's voice petered out in sighs, turning into a confused and tremulous gurgle, fading away in a slow, even respiration, as the exhilaration of the mystical dream slowly abated. The shadows continued to flicker. But the Crucified did not yet descend from the wall to gather in His arms the lamb returning to the fold.

XVII

"THE LORD hath said by the mouth of his prophet Joel, son of Pethuel: 'It will come to pass that I shall pour my Spirit over all flesh, and your children will make prophecies; your elders will dream, your young people will see visions.'

"This spirit of which the Apostles gathered the first fruits and beatitudes was for them and for us a Spirit of truth, a Spirit of sanctity, a Spirit of strength . . . Oh divine love, oh holy bond uniting the Father and the Son, omnipotent Spirit, faithful consolation of the wretched, penetrate into the deep abysses of our hearts and fill them with your great light!"

So preached Don Gennaro Tierno at Pentecost, from the main altar, addressing the listening populace. Over him, high above, the third person of the Holy Trinity spread the radiant arc of its golden wings, and in the church the burning tapers diffused a reddish glow like that of a great conflagration. The huge stone columns supporting the two naves, covered with barbaric Christian sculptures, moved in heavy strides toward the altar; on the walls scintillated the remains of mosaics: here and there the head of an Apostle, the rigid arm of a Saint, the wing of an angel still emerged from the obliteration, the crumbling wrought by the centuries. Between the mosaics were hung small votive boats offered to the temple by the survivors of shipwrecks. And amid rough stones and the misty crusts of plaster gracefully lifted a group of rose-colored spiraled columns supporting the marble pulpit, which was garlanded with acanthus leaves and animated by bas-reliefs.

"Spread your sweet dew over this barren earth, so that its long aridity may cease. Send the celestial rays of your love to the sanctuary of our soul, so that in penetrating us they kindle flames to consume our weaknesses, our omissions, our despondency!" the priest continued, his eloquence and vocal power reaching their greatest heights.

Orsola, nearby, listened, absorbed in meditation. She had sought refuge in the house of the Lord, she had returned to his chamber; she wanted the Lord to purify her and welcome her once more into the benignity of his all-embracing arms. That sudden bright blaze of faith blinded her, made her forget almost every previous error. It seemed to her that the stains upon her soul were instantly erased, and that from her flesh the dregs of worldly impurity fell away. Never before had she approached the altar of God with a more profound tremor of hope; never had she listened to the word of God with greater exaltation.

From the instant in which the horror of damnation rose in her consciousness, she had gathered herself in a kind of dark, meditative concentration, standing guard over herself, over her actions, her thoughts, her slightest impulses, for fear lest that vehemence of repentance be dispersed, and with it an anxious desire to preserve intact within herself that flower of faith that had suddenly germinated. It was a kind of elevation toward Jesus, together with the repudiation of every human tie. She fed her exaltation by reading inspirational books; she plunged into the contemplation of the holy images and mysteries; she struggled against the craven frailties of the flesh, the sensuous heat of the day, the insidious snares of the night, the fragrant odors carried to her by the wind, the gusts that rose from her impure memories, the voices that seemed to caress her ears and whisper to her of secret pleasures never thought of before.

After that week of solitary torments she now laid her sacrificial offerings at the foot of the altar, drank in the soothing potion of God's word, her gaze fixed aloft on the radiant dove and feeling herself sink little by little in the sea of ecstasy.

"So descend, descend unto us, oh tender comforter of all afflicted souls, refuge in time of danger, guardian in time of despair. Oh, descend unto us, for you cleanse all souls of every stain and heal their wounds. Come, strength of the weak, support of those who have fallen. Come, star of seafarers, hope of the poor, salvation of the dying!" Don Gennaro Tierno rushed on, standing tall in his silver chasuble, his face flushed purplish red, his eyes bulging from their sockets, with gestures that seemed to reach the very heavens.

Throughout the church a dense sultriness hung over the faithful. The naves seemed to crush the columns; in a stained glass window the head of St. Luke the Evangelist sparkled, struck by the sun, and his broad mantle carved a zone of cool green dusk in the penumbra. The marble pulpit rose like a miraculous mystical flower in that vaporous cloud of light.

"Come, oh Holy Ghost, descend unto us and have mercy on us!"

Orsola kept her eyes fixed on high: on the wave of all those invocations she ascended toward the nimbus, penetrated by the ineffable bliss which draws the soul toward the scent of spiritual essences. For an instant she thought she saw the golden dove send her a lightning flash of assent, and her heart leaped jubilant in her breast, as St. John had leaped in the womb of Elizabeth at the sight of the Virgin Mary.

"For our Lord Jesus Christ. Amen."

The priest, all silver, turned toward the monstrance, reciting the Credo in a low voice. Two white-robed incense bearers flanking the altar began to swing their smoking, aromatic thurifers. A cloud of incense enveloped the violated virgin who knelt close by; and instantly an irresistible gush of nausea from the depths of her pregnancy rose to her throat and twisted her mouth.

XVIII

WAS THERE NO WAY out, then? For a good many days she had still wavered doubtfully, waiting for the final proof. Her head spun in the morning when she got up, when her feet touched the floor; confused spells of exhaustion overwhelmed her toward evening, a general listlessness in which her mind, her will, her memories seemed to blur, to fluctuate drowsily as in the early morning hours. She did everything mechanically, with the movements of a somnambulist, wearily. In the classroom, if the wind brought her a whiff of bread fresh from the oven, she felt all her strength desert her, her entrails leap suddenly into her mouth; a pungent taste of soap and ashes spread on her tongue. One day, while one of the children was sucking a cherry, a violent desire for that fruit made her squirm on her chair, turn pale and sweat. Then, after her meal, bitter with nausea, she stretched out on her bed, surrendered to a dazed inertia: the heat was heavy, the flies buzzed, the cries of a peddler selling eyeglasses passed below her window, hoarse in the silence.

Without hope, she no longer turned for help to the church; even its incense repelled her.

She stopped thinking about Marcello; she no longer saw him, of him she preserved only an uncertain memory, as of a remote dream. Her present anguish entirely possessed her.

Lindoro came to bring water, as before. He arrived upstairs, flushed and dripping sweat; he set down his jars, glancing at his victim surreptitiously out of the corner of his eye. Orsola fled to the other room or bent over her work, clenching her teeth with repressed rage. Lindoro left, like a beaten dog; but the thought of having possessed that woman stirred his blood; he would now have liked to force her to go off with him, have her for himself, own her like a piece of merchandise he could use and sell. In him sensual lust and desire for gain joined hands.

One evening he waited near the street door for Camilla to leave the house; then he rushed upstairs to catch Orsola by surprise, to find her alone at home. When he knocked at the door and Orsola recognized him, she was shaken to the core.

"What do you want from me? What?" she demanded in a muffled voice, without opening.

"Listen to me for a moment, listen! Don't be afraid; I won't hurt you . . ."

"Go away, you dog, coward, murderer . . ." the woman cried with shrill vehemence, giving vent to all her accumulated hatred of him. "Go away, go away!"

And, exhausted, she retired to her room, buried her head in the pillows, biting them and weeping.

XIX

THERE WAS NO WAY out. The daughter of Maria Camastra had drunk vitriol and had died, a three-months-old baby in her belly. The daughter of Clemenza Iorio had flung herself from the bridge and had died in the mud of the Pescarina. So she too must die.

When this thought flashed through Orsola's mind, the afternoon was ending. All the church bells were ringing out festively for the vigil of Corpus Domini; large tribes of swallows shrieked and twirled over Brina Palace and assembled in chattering groups on the Arch. A red cloud hovered over the town, similar perhaps to the cloud from which burning pitch poured down upon the godlessness of Sodom.

At the flare of this thought Orsola felt lost, frightened. Then gradually, as her feeling of shame convinced her of the necessity of that step, in her depths a dark rebellion of vitality began to seethe, her entrails quivered. She felt a sudden warmth as a rush of blood brought blotches of color to her forehead, her cheeks. She rose from her chair, twisting her arms as she struggled with herself. And at last, propelled by a nervous impulse, she left the room, went into the kitchen, looked for a glass on the tables and a box of matches. The strong odor of the charcoal turned her stomach; dizziness filled her head. She had everything she wanted: put matches in the water to dissolve, returned to her room and hid the lethal glass in a corner, underneath a chest of drawers.

"Help me, oh God, help me!"

She was now afraid to be there, alone, facing her decision. In her imagination she suddenly saw again the dead body of Christina Iorio which she had glimpsed that day as it was being carried on a stretcher to her mother's house: a body swollen like a barrel, with slime in its hair, in the eye-sockets, in the mouth, between the toes of the purple feet . . .

"God, I must die—oh God!"

And she gave a start, as if her head had been touched by a stiff, cold hand; a chill passed through her limbs, lingered for a moment on her scalp, making her feel as if a blade were cutting into it to detach the skin.

"No, no, no!" she cried in an altered voice, as though she wanted to keep something horrible from touching her. And she went to the window, leaned out, looking for some sort of refuge.

She remained there, nailed to the floor, stunned by that vision of Biblical conflagration and that horde of black birds. Turning part way around, she saw a strange gleam in the darkness of the room: the shimmer of the golden crescents on the robe of the Madonna of Loreto and the glitter of the medallions. She grew even more frightened; she flattened against the windowsill, leaned farther out; and stayed there without daring to move. Then, in that immobility, the exhaustion that came on every evening began to invade her; she clutched her heavy head between her hands, shut her eyes.

"Oh!"

Suddenly a passage opened up in her soul. —Yes, yes, how could she have forgotten! Spacone, the witch doctor, that old man with the long beard, the one who performed miracles and had a medicine for every illness . . . He'd come to town several times riding a small white mule, with two golden triangles hanging from his ear-lobes and down his front a row of buttons that looked like the bowls of silver spoons. So many women had come out on their doorsteps, had greeted and blessed him. He had cured every sort of malady with certain herbs and certain potions and certain signs he made with his thumb and certain magic words. He certainly must have a remedy for that trouble, too . . . Yes, yes, he certainly did!

And in Orsola a flicker of hope revived, while the dizziness got worse and worse. Before her eyes, objects drowned in the twilight; the crimson day, extinguished by the ashes of encroaching night, swooned away in a slow discoloration, without contrasts. A swallow, like a bat, swooped past and grazed her head. The sudden breath of summer blew into her face, strummed every vein in her body, shook the innermost roots of her life.

With an involuntary, unconscious gesture, she placed her hands on her lap and held them there for a moment. The indefinable feeling of motherhood flooded her soul. And from deep inside her, mysteriously, a memory of her distant convalescence awoke. —Oh, it was March . . . a vast laughing whiteness . . . and above her the "spies," the soft fuzzy seeds poured down on her.

XX

AND SO IT WAS that she left the house the following morning, surreptitiously; and, the town behind her, set out alone on the new road leading to Chieti.

Spacone lived in the vicinity of San Rocco. Below the majesty of a druidic oak, he performed his miracles and formulated his oracles. The entire populace for twenty miles around turned to him for help, as to an Apostle of Providence. During epidemics among the local cattle, herds of oxen and horses gathered around the oak to receive the talisman that would protect them from the disease; equine and bovine hooves traced a circle of enchantments in the plain grass that covered the ground.

When Orsola set out, the landscape surrounding Pescara was enlivened by a great play of lights and shadows. Through that Arabian sky of the month of June the wandering clouds were migrating from the seashore to the mountains, like caravans with copious provisions of water. At intervals vast tracts of land sank deep in shadow, while others emerged shining brightly; and, since the shadow was blue and flowing freely, the countryside looked like a floating archipelago luxuriant with trees and wheat. The songs of the birds praised the ripeness of the oats.

At first that sight gave Orsola a feeling of unaccustomed relief; for the freedom of the countryside, the happiness of the light on the greenery, the cordial smells in the air, by suddenly enveloping her body, revivified her blood, and with the opening up of the horizon the new hope inside her was fortified and exalted. She cast off all her anxieties and lived only for two emotions—for the hope of her physical salvation and the desire to reach her goal. Far away, at that goal, in her imagination she saw the beneficent old man rise up and become mystically illuminated. Because of her innate susperstitious propensity, she transformed that figure, endowed it with enormous powers and garbed it with Christian kindness, surrounding it with a halo. Then all the stories repeated among the populace came back to her and cast sprays of miraculous light on Spacone's brow. Then she remembered that on a distant day of her illness Rosa Catena had spoken about the Old Man with reverence, mentioning certain miracles: a blind man from Torre de' Passeri had gone to San Rocco and returned after three days with eyes that saw and a blue cabalistic sign on his temple. A woman from Spoltore, possessed by evil spirits, had returned as meek as a lamb, after she had drunk two sips of water from a small dry gourd.

Thus, gradually as she walked along the road, the coming together of so many scattered elements formed a kind of legend in Orsola's mind. And little by little, for men can do nothing without the aid of God, there also arose the conviction that the Old Man was an envoy of Heaven, a redeemer of souls from subjugation to the flesh, a dispenser of heavenly grace on earth to those who had succumbed. —Had not the extreme hope descended upon the sinner suddenly, almost by divine influence, amid signs burning in the sky? And during Pentecost, had not the dove sent down from on high, before the praying woman's eyes, a lightning flash of hopeful promise?

The promise was now being fulfilled on the holy day of Corpus Domini. So, burning with faith and exultation, Orsola went forward in the dust of the new road, indifferent to the effort that every step cost her. On both sides of the road the shrubs shone white as though covered by the droppings of birds. Clumps of rustling poplars stood along the borders; and the silvery trunks reverberated with variations of light. The peasant women of the Villa del Fuoco, dwarfs with flat, Hamitic noses and broad lips, fair-skinned Berber women, came from the opposite direction in twos and threes. The life of the clouds occupied the immense stage of the countryside.

Orsola passed the Mill, then the Villa. A nervous energy animated her step. She felt the wind blowing upon her neck and at intervals heard the poplars rustle overhead. But the wavering of shadows and the dust was beginning to affect slightly her vision; the warmth of her exertion rose to her head; her will was completely concentrated on the unaccustomed physical effort of walking. Thus she advanced in an increasing daze which was turning into a sensation of discomfort; then, overcome by fatigue and the heat, she yielded to the temptation to rest in the shade of an olive grove standing on a slope to the left of the road.

Four or five half-naked gypsies, the color of bronze, with shining amulets on their chests, went riding past, straddling reddish donkeys. One of them was whistling, striking the belly of his beast with his heels. They all held switches in their hands and leather saddle bags lay on their thighs. They looked at the woman resting among the olive trees and murmured something in a low voice, laughing.

Orsola was frightened by those eyes whose whites glistened as they looked, and she remained tense with fear until they disappeared in the distance. Discouragement was beginning to seize her; her loneliness was beginning to fill her with dread, for through the countryside ran prolonged shivers announcing rain and an almost lugubrious silence descended through the air from the gathered clouds. She was leaning against a tree trunk; intermittent cool gusts tore at her body and chilled the sweat on her skin, gusts that fell upon her with the rustling sound of a furtive animal in the grass, while all around the shimmer of sunlight seemed the glitter of remote waters. Pale flowers, yellow as sulphur, wavered at the feet of the olive trees.

A memory then descended from the good trees into the woman's soul. —That day the church was crowded with consecrated olive branches and scents; and she walked through the throng in a state of agitation, sustained by Marcello's arms . . . But as she lingered on this thought, her memory wandered; everything eluded her grasp with a dreamlike uncertainty. Yet dark throbs battered her heart; gasps of anguish quickened her breathing. She now had the blunt sensation of a torpor that seemed to crash down on her brain with the weight of a sledgehammer. A last trace of vigilant determination helped to rouse her weakly, and she stepped down onto the road.

The clouds gathered in the direction of the Maiella had taken on the diaphanous gray color of a suspended mass of water. Large waterspouts approached from the sea with heavier loads; and yet here and there a broad patch of blue fanned out high in the sky. A smell of humidity was already rising from the dust, from the entire countryside gasping heavily with expectation. Immobile, the trees seemed to absorb the light, rose black in the misty air, populated the distance with blurred, uncertain shapes.

Orsola walked on with an immense weariness, feeling that

all her strength would soon leave her. "Yes," she thought, "I'll just be able to reach that tree and then I'll fall." But she did not fall. The houses of San Rocco came into view on the right. A peasant was coming from the opposite direction at a run.

"Good man, is that San Rocco?"

"Yes, yes, you turn off at the first path."

Heavy, pattering drops were beginning to fall; then suddenly the increasing rain cut through the air with long white darts, long whips which cracked as they lashed down. A monstrous tumult now agitated the clouds: beams of light broke through here and there. All the hills, far off, beyond the sheets of rain, lit up for an instant and turned dark again. A frail, silvery brightness rose over the Maiella, seemed to sharpen like a thin sword.

Orsola tried to run toward the oak which stood about a hundred yards away. The raindrops struck the nape of her neck, coursed down her back between her shoulderblades, hit her in the face; her clothes were already wet through. Her feet slipped on the wet ground. She fell and got up again, twice. Then, half-crazed, she began to shriek in the direction of the house.

"Help me! Help me!"

A woman came through the door and ran to assist her, followed by two barking dogs.

Pale as death, her features distorted, Orsola let herself be led, no longer able to utter a word through her clenched teeth. Only after a while did she collect herself, brought round by the questions the woman addressed to her. And then, on hearing the name Spacone, she at once remembered everything.

"Where is Spacone?" she demanded.

"He went to Popoli, my saintly woman; they sent for him."

Orsola couldn't contain herself any longer; she began to sob and tear at her hair.

"What do you want, saintly woman? What is it? I am his wife, I'm here . . . " whimpered the witch, clutching her wrists, urging her to speak.

Orsola hesitated for a moment; then she told her everything, precipitously, sobbing, hiding her face.

"Hold on. There is a remedy. But it costs fifty soldi, my saintly woman," said the witch in her soft, vowel-filled idiom, chanting that beautiful interjection.

Orsola untied a knot in her handkerchief and held out five small silver coins. Then she waited, calmer.

The room was low-ceilinged but spacious. The wall, where saltpeter blossomed here and there, was flaked and greenish. Crude Christian idols made of pottery populated the back wall of that lair; strangely shaped tools and instruments cluttered the tables. It was like a rustic sanctuary guarded by a herbalist monk.

Standing in front of the hearth Spacone's wife was brewing her philter in silence. She was a tall, bony woman with an extremely pale face, a rotting nose as purple as a fig, straight red hair over her temples, an albino's tiny eyes, and with tattooes on her chin, forehead and the backs of her hands.

"Here, saintly woman! Take heart."

Orsola swallowed the liquid in one gulp; but immediately afterward she felt an atrocious bitterness claw at her palate and entrails. She remained motionless as if paralyzed, her mouth agape, pressing her belly with her hands, rapidly stamping her feet against the ground, in the spasm of the first uterine contraction.

"Be brave, saintly woman, be brave!" the witch repeated, staring at her with her milky eyes, massaging her loins. "You have just enough time to get back to Pescara . . . Go! Go!"

Orsola could not answer; only screams rose to her mouth. Cramps gripped her stomach, blocked her diaphragm, made her want to vomit. Her eyeballs turned back, as though she were showing symptoms of an epileptic attack. All through her feeble body the excessive power of the potion was now producing unexpected effects. The miscarriage took place almost immediately, with one of those terrible hemorrhages with which the forces of life quietly, imperceptibly flow away.

"Oh Jesus, Jesus, Jesus," mumbled the witch, fretfully, seized by sudden fear at the sight of that poor fallen body. "Oh Jesus, help me."

Under her proddings, Orsola regained consciousness. And since after a while the flow of blood seemed to wane, the wretched creature managed to get to her feet: went outside, pushed by the woman; reached the road, staggering, pale, as if drained of her last drop of blood, but kept alive by the hope that the greatest danger was past.

Now the fields were all fresh and luminous after the rain. A line of carts loaded with gypsum rolled past, and the big carters from Letto Manoppello, full of wine, lay sprawled on the sacks, smoking. As Orsola began to walk at the end of the line, one of them, the nearest to her, yelled: "Hey, do you want to ride up here with me, pretty girl?"

Half-unconscious, Orsola let herself be hoisted up by the man's strong arms and sat there on the sacks. She did not hear the lewd laughter and the obscene jokes that spread from one cart to the next.

With instinctive energy she held her knees tight together to stem the flow of blood. She felt a gradual dullness invade her senses, so that the frequent jolts of the wheels on the gravel caused her only a numb pain and she barely noticed the stench of the men's pipes. Then a remote murmur reached her ears, a quivering brightness became visible to her eyes. Several times she would have fallen if she hadn't been held up by the hands of the carter, who, encouraged by her docile silence, attempted a few rough caresses.

At the end of the road, silhouetted against the sun, appeared the town of Pescara, whose sounds came forth to greet them, borne upon the wind.

"The procession is out," one of the men said. All the others whipped their beasts; and the road rang with the sound of heavy hooves, the jangling of collar bells, the cracking of whips.

That violence of jolts and crashing noises recalled Orsola for a moment to a sense of the surrounding reality. But when the man put one arm around her waist and blew his wine-sodden breath on her cheek, out of blind impulse she started to scream and thrash about as if she had suddenly become delirious. And before her darkened eyes Lindoro's phantom image suddenly rose with clarity enough to awaken the revulsion of horror in her almost insensible mind. As soon as the cart halted she got down, slipping from the sacks to the ground; she began to walk, with the frenzied anxiety of someone trying to reach a safe place before collapsing.

From the opposite direction young maidens were advancing down the road, covered by their immaculate white veils, holding colored tapers in their hands, and singing. Following this angelic swarm, a great fluttering of banners and baldaquins crowded the air soothed by the recent rain. And they sang:

Tantum ergo sacramentum
Veneremur cernui . . .

Orsola, half blinded, turned into an alleyway; reached the house of Rosa Catena, entered it; overcome by vertigo, she fell on the floor. And, as the copious bleeding started once again, paralysis gripped the lower half of her body, and all capacity for voluntary movement left her.

Rosa was not at home; that day everyone in town had joined the procession. In a corner of the room, Mua', her father, a monster of human decrepitude, a blind man nailed for years to the wood of a chair by crippling arthritis, made vague attempts to probe the brick floor around him with the tip of his cane in order to discover the reason for the unexpected noise; and a slobbering mumble dribbled out of his toothless mouth.

Then, at the feet of that horrendous monster, soaked in the blood of sin, her thumbs clenched in her fists, without a cry, the violated bride of the Lord squirmed for a few moments in the throes of death.

"Out, out of here! Go! Go away!"

Thinking the butcher's mastiff had come into the house, and seeking to chase the beast away, the old man waved his cane about; and it struck the dying woman.

THE VIGIL

The Vigil

MAYOR BIAGIO MILA'S corpse, already completely dressed, a cloth drenched in vinegar and water spread over its face, was laid out on the bed, almost at the center of the room, surrounded by four lighted tapers, one at each corner. The dead man's wife and brother were keeping vigil, facing each other across the room.

Rosa Mila was about twenty-five years old. She was a woman in full bloom. Her complexion was fair, her forehead rather low, her eyebrows were traced in a long arc, her eyes gray with irises as variegated as agates. She had a luxuriant mass of hair, and, generally, unruly strands hid her eyes and the nape of her neck. Her entire person shone with the luster of health, and her fresh skin gave off the perfume of rare, delicate fruit.

Emidio Mila, the cleric, was more or less the same age. His body was thin and had the bronzelike color peculiar to people who live in the countryside exposed to the sun's full power. A soft reddish fuzz covered his cheeks; his strong white teeth lent a virile beauty to his smile, and, at moments, his yellowish eyes gleamed like new gold coins.

Both were silent; she, letting the glass beads of a rosary glide between her fingers; he, watching the rosary glide. Both were full of the indifference with which our country folk confront the mystery of death.

With a long sigh, Emidio said, "It's hot tonight."

Rosa raised her eyes, agreeing.

In the low-ceilinged room the light wavered in accordance with the restless flames of the tapers. The shadows gathered now in a corner, now on a wall, changing in shape and intensity.

The windows were open, but the shutters were closed. The white muslin curtains stirred, almost seemed to breathe. On the stark whiteness of the bed, Biagio's body seemed to be asleep.

Emidio's words sank into the silence. The woman again lowered her head, and again let the rosary glide slowly through her fingers. Beads of sweat studded her brow, and her breathing was heavy.

After a while Emidio asked, "When are they coming to take him away, tomorrow?"

"At ten, with the Congregation of the Sacrament."

Then they were silent again. From the fields came the frogs' persistent croaking and, at intervals, the scent of grass in that perfect quiet. Rosa heard a hoarse gurgle coming from the corpse and with a horrified gesture rose from her chair, as if to run away.

"Don't be afraid, Rosa. It's just liquids," her brother-in-law said, reaching out with his hand to reassure her.

She grasped the hand instinctively and held it, still on her feet. The gurgle inside the dead man's belly continued and seemed to make its way to his mouth.

"It's nothing, Rosa. Calm yourself," he added, making a gesture for her to sit down on a hope chest covered by a flowered bright cushion.

Still holding his hand, she sat down beside him. The chest was not very large, and as they sat their elbows touched.

Silence returned. The song of the peasants who were threshing rose in the distance.

"They are threshing at night, in the moonlight," she said, speaking to conquer her weariness and fear.

Emidio said nothing. And the woman withdrew her hand because the contact had begun to give her a vague feeling of uneasiness.

Both were now filled with the same thought which, all of a sudden, had risen in their minds: both were captured by an identical memory, a memory of rustic ardor at the time of their puberty.

They lived at that time in a cluster of houses called the Caldore, on a sun-drenched hill where the roads crossed. There, at the far edge of a wheat field, rose a high wall built of stones and clayey mud. On the side facing the south, which belonged to Rosa's relatives, where the sun's warmth was denser and sweeter, a family of fruit-bearing trees throve and multiplied. With the coming of spring the trees blossomed in festive communion; and the silvery or rose-colored cupolas, curving gently against the sky, crowned the wall, rocked to and fro as if to lift themselves up into the air and, all together, hummed with the drowsy sound of mellifluous bees.

Behind that wall, on the trees' side, in those days Rosa used to sing. Her voice, clear and fresh, rose and fell like a fountain beneath the flowering crowns.

Through a long season of convalescence, Emidio had listened to her voice. He was weak and famished. To escape the diet imposed on him he would often leave his house furtively, hiding a large chunk of bread inside his jacket, and follow the wall, walking along the last wheat-furrow until he reached his place of bliss.

There he sat down with his shoulders against the warm stones and began to eat. He bit into the bread and plucked a tender ear of wheat: each small grain enclosed a minute drop of juice like milk and with the fresh flavor of flour. After his long illness the sensual pleasure of tasting and hearing almost blended into a single, infinitely delectable sensation. And so, in that idlness, in that heat, among those fragrances which gave the air the hearty substance of a wine, the woman's voice also became for him a natural, strengthening nourishment, a physical food, which melted into his bloodstream.

So Rosa's voice was a cause for recovery, and even when his recovery was complete Rosa's voice continued to affect his senses.

After that period, the two families having become quite intimate, Emidio was seized by one of those silent, shy and solitary loves which devour all the strength of adolescence.

In September, just before Emidio's departure for the seminary, one afternoon the two families went together on a picnic in the woods along the river.

The day was listless, and the three carts drawn by oxen made their way along the canebrakes in bloom.

In the woods they picnicked on the grass in a circular clearing circumscribed by the trunks of giant poplars. The grass was short and crowded with tiny purple flowers which gave off a subtle perfume; here and there, through the thick leafage, large swaths of sunlight poured inside the secluded shelter.

After the picnic some of them went roaming along the river banks, while others remained there, stretched out on their backs.

Rosa and Emidio found themselves together; they linked arms and started down a path marked through the brush.

She leaned against him with abandon; she laughed and tore leaves from the branches as they passed, nibbled at the bitter stems, and flung her head back to follow the flight of the scattering jays. And with that movement, the tortoiseshell comb slipped from her hair, which suddenly slipped down over her shoulders in all its stupendous richness.

Emidio bent down with her to pick up the comb. As they straightened up, their heads bumped together lightly. Clutching her forehead with both hands, Rosa cried amid peals of laughter, "Oh God, oh God!"

The young man looked at her, feeling his body quiver through and through, feeling his face turn pale, fearing that he might give himself away. Using her fingernails, she pried a long tendril of ivy from a tree trunk, wound it round her hair with a quick twist and put an end to the rebellion by affixing the teeth of her comb at the nape of her neck. The green leaves of the ivy, some with a reddish tinge, were loosely bound and burst free at random. She asked, "Do you like me like this?"

Emidio did not say a word; he did not know what to reply.

"Oh, this is no way to behave! Are you deaf and dumb, perhaps?"

He wanted to fall down on his knees. And, since Rosa's laughter sounded disappointed, he could almost feel tears rise to his eyes from the frustration of being unable to think of some simple words to say.

They continued walking. At a certain point an uprooted sapling blocked the path. With both hands Emidio lifted the trunk, and Rosa slipped past beneath the bright green leaves which, for a second, wreathed her head like a crown.

Farther on, they found a well at both sides of which stood two rectangular stone basins that were set around and above the well. The dense trees formed a cloister of greenery. The shadow there was deep, almost damp. The verdant cupola was perfectly reflected by the water which reached halfway up the brick parapet.

Flinging out her arms, Rosa said, "How wonderful it feels here!"

Then she scooped up some water in the cup of her palm with an alluring gesture and drank. Drops of water slipped through her fingers and clung like pearls to her skirt.

When her thirst was quenched, with both palms she scooped up more water and offered it enticingly to her companion: "Drink!"

"I'm not thirsty," Emidio stammered, in a daze.

She threw the water in his face, making an almost contemptuous grimace with her lower lip. Then she lay down in one of the dry troughs as if in a cradle, letting her feet hang over the rim and shaking them impatiently. Suddenly she jumped up, giving Emidio a strange look.

"Well? Let's go."

They started back to the clearing to rejoin the others, in complete silence. The blackbirds whistled above their heads; horizontal sheaves of sun cut across their steps, and the scent of the woods grew more intense around them.

A few days later Emidio would leave.

A few months later Emidio's brother would take Rosa for his wife.

During his first years at the seminary, the cleric thought about his new sister-in-law quite often. In class, as the priests explained the *Epitome historiæ sacræ*, he daydreamed about her. In study hall, while his classmates, hiding behind their lecterns, paired off for obscene practices, he hid his face in his hands and gave himself up to impure fantasies. In chapel, as the Virgin's litanies rang out after the invocation to the Mystical Rose, he fled into distant realms.

And then, after he had learned corruption from his fellow students, the scene in the woods had appeared to him in a new light, and the suspicion of having failed to understand, the regret at having failed to pluck the fruit which was being offered to him, would then strangely torment him.

Did it mean this? Did it mean that Rosa had once loved him? Did it mean that he had unknowingly passed by a great joy?

And every day this doubt became more acute, more insistent, more goading, more anguished. And every day he fed on it with greater intensity of suffering until, in the long monotony of his seminary life, this doubt became for him a kind of incurable illness, and, confronted by the event's irremediability, he was overcome by an immense feeling of futility, an unending melancholy.

Yes, he had failed to understand.

In the room now drops of wax were falling from the tapers. Between the slats of the closed shutters entered stronger gusts of wind which made the curtains rear up.

Slowly pervaded with drowsiness, Rosa's eyelids lowered now and then; but whenever her head fell upon her chest, she would open her eyes with a start.

"Are you tired?" the cleric asked in a gentle voice.

"Not me," the woman answered, rallying her energies and straightening up on her hips.

But in the silence her senses were again overcome by drowsiness. Her head rested against the wall; now her hair covered her whole neck; through her parted lips came slow, regular breathing. She was very beautiful like that; and nothing in her was more voluptuous than the rise and fall of her breasts and the shape of her knees discernible beneath the thin cloth of her skirt. A sharp gust drew a moan from the curtains and extinguished the two tapers closest to the window.

And what if I kissed her? thought Emidio, prompted by a sudden fleshly urge as he gazed at the dozing woman.

The singing voices again cascaded through the June night with the solemnity of liturgical cadences; and from different points, always farther removed, rose the answers in varying tones, unaccompanied by instruments. The full moon must have been high in the sky because the dim light inside did not subdue the cool white light which poured copiously over the shutters and seeped through the slats.

Emidio turned to face the death bed. His eyes gliding over the rigid black outline of the corpse involuntarily halted at the hand, a swollen, yellowish hand, with nails that looked somewhat like claws, its back crossed by livid webs; and his eyes quickly shrank away from this sight. Little by little, in the unconsciousness of sleep, Rosa's head, almost tracing a semicircle on the wall, bent towards the perturbed cleric. The slow reclining of that beautiful feminine head inspired a melting tenderness; and, since the movement somewhat altered the woman's sleep, between her ever so slightly parted lids the rims of the iris appeared and immediately disappeared in the white cornea, like the petal of a violet floating in milk.

Emidio remained immobile, letting her weight rest against his shoulder. He held his breath for fear of waking the woman from her sleep, and a tremendous anguish was cast upon him by the throbbing of his heart, his wrists, his temples, which seemed to echo through the entire room. But, since Rosa went on sleeping, little by little he felt drained and drifted into an invincible listlessness, looking at that feminine throat marked with voluptuousness by Venus' necklaces, breathing in her warm breath and the smell of her hair.

A fresh breeze laden with nocturnal fragrance bent the flickering flame and blew it out.

Then, no longer thinking, no longer timorous, yielding fully to temptation, the keeper of the funeral vigil kissed the woman full on the mouth.

At that contact she awoke with a start, fixed her wide, astonished eyes on her brother-in-law's face and went very pale.

Then she slowly gathered together the hair on her neck; and then just sat there, holding herself erect, tensely guarded, staring straight in front of her at the shifting shadows.

"Who put out the tapers?"

"The wind."

Nothing else was said. They both remained on the wedding chest as before, sitting side by side, grazing each other with their elbows, in a painful uncertainty, by a mental artifice not letting their conscience judge the event and condemn it. Spontaneously, they both turned their attention to external things, injecting into this act a fictitious intensity, even helping it along by the position of their bodies. Gradually a kind of intoxication was taking possession of them.

The singing voices in the night continued, lingered in the air, and from call to call grew alluringly softer. The male and female voices wove an amorous composition. At times one single voice emerged sharp and high above all the others, striking a single note around which the harmonies swelled like waves drawn to the central current of a river. Now, at intervals, at the beginning of each stanza, rose the metallic vibration of a guitar tuned in diapente, and between one round and the next came the measured thuds of the threshing flails against the ground.

Both listened.

Perhaps because of a change in the wind, the smells were no longer the same as before. From Orlando hill, most likely, came the powerful perfume of orange and lemon groves; from the Scalia gardens, perhaps, came the perfume of roses, so thick that the air had the flavor of wedding candies; and perhaps from the swamps of Farina the damp fragrance of irises which, once inhaled, was as delightfully refreshing as a draft of cold water.

They still kept silent, sitting motionless on the chest, oppressed by the voluptuousness of the moonlit night. In front of them the last flame flickered rapidly and, bending, made tears of wax fall from the almost consumed taper. Again and again it seemed about to die. They did not move. Tense and hesitant, their eyes fixed and dilated, they watched the tremulous, moribund flame. Suddenly the inebriating wind blew it out. Then, unafraid of the darkness, with the very same avidity, at the very same instant, the man and the woman drew close, clutched, searched for the other's mouth, lost, blindly, without speaking, smothering each other with caresses.

THE SEA-GOING SURGEON

The Sea-Going Surgeon

ALONG ABOUT EVENING the brigantine *Trinità*, carrying a cargo of wheat, sailed for Dalmatia. She made her way down the calm river between Ortona's fishing boats lying at anchor in two rows, while on shore fires lit up one by one and the men just back from sea were singing. Then, gliding smoothly through the narrow mouth of the inlet, the boat rode out into the sea.

The weather was fair. In the October sky, almost skimming the water, the full moon hung like a soft, rose-colored lamp. The mountains and hills being left behind were shaped like reclining women. Up in the sky wild geese swept by without honking and vanished.

At first the six men and the cabin boy all worked in unison to set the sails to catch the wind. Then, when the sails, all red and adorned with crude images, swelled aloft, the six men sat down and began smoking quietly. The cabin boy straddled the bow and hummed a nostalgic song.

The elder Talamonte flashed a long streak of saliva into the water and, sticking his well-worn pipe back into his mouth, said, "The good weather won't hold."

At this prophecy they all looked out to the open sea and did not speak. They were tough sailors, inured to the vicissitudes of the sea. They had sailed before to the Dalmatian islands and Zara, and to Trieste and Split; they knew the way. Some of them even harbored a pleasant memory of the wine of Dignano, which has the perfume of roses, and also of the fruits of those islands.

Ferrante La Selvi commanded the brig. The two Talamonte brothers, Cirù, Massacese and Gialluca made up the crew—all of them came from Pescara. Nazareno was the cabin boy.

Since the moon was full, they lingered on the deck. The sea was strewn with fishing boats at work.

From time to time two trawlers running together passed alongside the brig and the men called out to each other with familiarity. The catch seemed to be good. When the fishing boats were left behind and the sea was once more deserted, Ferrante and the two Talamontes went below to sleep. After they had finished smoking, Massacese and Gialluca followed them. Cirù remained on watch.

Before they went below, Gialluca, pointing to his neck, said to his companion, "Look, what do I have here?"

Massacese looked and said, "It's nothing. Don't worry about it."

There was a red blotch, similar to that produced by the bite of an insect, and at the center of the blotch a small protuberance.

Gialluca added, "It hurts."

During the night the wind changed and the sea began to swell. The brig started to labor through the waves and was pulled eastward, losing headway. As they tacked and Gialluca helped trim the sails, he gave a small cry of pain now and then, for at every abrupt movement of his head he felt a dart of pain.

Ferrante La Selvi asked him, "What is it?"

In the light of dawn Gialluca showed him what hurt him. On the skin the red blotch had spread and a small pointed abscess rose at its center.

Ferrante, after examining it, also said,. "It's nothing. Don't worry about it."

Gialluca got a handkerchief and bandaged his neck. Then he began to smoke.

The brig, battered by the waves and buffeted by the head wind, still fled eastward. The clamor of the sea drowned the men's voices. At intervals a wave broke on deck with a deep, hollow sound.

Towards evening the storm abated and the moon emerged like a cupola of fire. But since the wind fell, the brig floated almost motionless in the lull; the sails fell slack. From time to time a short-lived breeze sprang up.

Gialluca complained about the pain. Being at leisure, his companions began to take an interest in his ailment. Each man suggested a different remedy. Cirù, who was the oldest, spoke up and suggested a cataplasm of flour and apples. He possessed a few vague medical notions, because back home on land his wife practiced medicine together with the arts of magic, healing illnesses with nostrums and spells. But they had neither apples nor flour. Sea biscuits would not serve the purpose.

Then Cirù went to get an onion and a handful of wheat; he pounded the wheat, chopped up the onion and prepared the cataplasm. At the touch of that poultice, Gialluca's pain got worse. After about an hour, seized by a fury of irritation, he ripped the dressing from his neck and threw the whole business over the gunwale.

To master his discomfort, he went to the stern and held the tiller for a long period. The wind had risen and the sails shivered gaily. In the bright night a small island, which had to be Pelagosa, loomed in the distance like a board resting on the water.

In the morning Cirù, who had by now taken charge of Gialluca's trouble, examined the abscess. The swelling had dilated, spreading over a great part of the neck, and had taken on a different shape and darker color, which at the apex had turned purple.

"What's happening here?" he exclaimed, perplexed, in a voice that made his patient flinch. And he summoned Ferrante, both Talamontes, and all the others.

Opinions varied. Ferrante's imagination produced the vision of a horrifying disease that could end up by strangling Gialluca. His eyes extraordinarily dilated, quite pale, Gialluca listened to the prognostications. The sky was shrouded with mist, the sea looked gloomy, flocks of gulls flashed shrieking towards land—and so a kind of terror descended upon his soul.

In the end the younger Talamonte proclaimed, "It's a malignant boil."

The others agreed: "Yes, could be."

And indeed the next day the cuticle covering the abscess was forced up by a blood-colored serum and split open. And the entire area took on the appearance of a wasp's nest from which a flow of purulent matter oozed profusely. The inflammation and the suppuration went deeper and spread very rapidly.

Gialluca, terrified, invoked Saint Rocco, the healer of sores. He promised him ten, twenty pounds of candle wax. He knelt in the center of the deck, raised his arms to the sky, made vows with solemn gestures, called out the names of his father, mother, wife and children. All around him his companions blessed themselves gravely at each invocation.

Ferrante La Selvi, feeling the approach of a powerful gust of wind, shouted a command in his hoarse voice through the roar of the sea. The brig heeled completely over on one side. Massacese, the two Talamontes, and Cirù all scrambled back to their positions on deck for the maneuver. Nazareno slid along one of the masts. The sails were dropped in a flash; only the two jibs remained in place. And the brig, listing sheerly from side to side, was broached to and began to run precipitously along the waves' crests.

"Saint Rocco! Saint Rocco!" screamed Gialluca with mounting fervor, also excited by the surrounding tumult, doubled over on his hands and knees to withstand the ship's roll.

Again and again a bigger wave than the others broke over the bow and swept the deck from end to end.

"Go below!" Ferrante yelled to Gialluca.

Gialluca, drenched, climbed down into the hold. He was plagued all over his skin by a bothersome heat and a feverish dryness, and the fear inspired by his sickness gripped his stomach. Down below in the dim light the shapes of things assumed singular aspects. He could hear the deep, resounding blows of the sea against the sides of the vessel and the creaking of the whole structure.

After half an hour Gialluca reappeared on deck completely ashen, as if rising from a grave. He preferred to be out in the open, to expose himself to the waves, see the men, breathe the wind.

Ferrante, shocked by his pallor, asked, "What's wrong now?"

The other men, remaining at their posts, began to discuss remedies, raising their voices, almost shouting so as to be heard above the roar of the storm. They became excited. Each had a treatment of his own. They argued with the assurance of full-fledged physicians. In the dispute, they forgot all danger. Two years before, Massacese had seen a real doctor operate on Giovanni Margadonna's side in a similar case. The doctor had cut, then had rubbed the wound with two pieces of wood steeped in a steaming liquid and had burnt it. With a kind of spoon he had scooped out the scorched flesh, which looked like coffee grounds. And Margadonna had been saved.

Massacese, almost in a frenzy, repeated, like a ruthless surgeon, "We've got to cut! We've got to cut!"

And with his hand he made the gesture of cutting in the direction of the sick man.

Cirù shared Massacese's opinion. Both Talamontes also agreed. Ferrante La Selvi shook his head.

Then Cirù put it to Gialluca. Gialluca refused.

With a brutal impulse that he was unable to restrain, Cirù yelled, "Then die!"

Gialluca grew even paler and stared at his companions with huge, horror-stricken eyes.

Night was falling. In the darkness the roar of the sea seemed even louder. The waves glittered, rolling beneath the gleam cast by the bow lamp. Land was far away. The men clung to a line to stand up under the waves. Ferrante was at the helm, shouting from time to time into the storm, "Go below, Gialluca!"

Because of a strange aversion to being alone, Gialluca would not go below, even though he was in great discomfort. He too hung on to the line, clenching his teeth from the pain. Whenever a wave beat down on them, the men ducked their heads and in unison gave a shout, the sort they used to accompany a common effort at work.

The moon came out from behind a cloud, reducing the feeling of horror. But the sea continued rough all through the night. In the morning, Gialluca, dazed, said to his shipmates: "Cut it." They discussed it seriously, holding a kind of final consultation; and then they examined the swelling abscess, which was now the size of a man's fist. All the craters, which before had lent it the appearance of a wasp's nest or sieve, had now become a single crater.

Massacese said, "Don't be afraid! Let's get started." He was going to be the surgeon. He tested the edge of various blades on his fingernail. Finally he chose the elder Talamonte's knife, which had been sharpened recently.

"All right. Let's go!"

Almost a shiver of expectation shook him and all the others.

The sick man now seemed to be seized by a dark stupor. He kept his eyes fixed on the knife without saying anything, his mouth half open, his hands dangling at his sides, like a halfwit.

Cirù got him to sit down, took off the bandage, while with his lips he made the instinctive sounds that express utter revulsion. For a moment they all bent down over the sore in order to look at it.

Massacese said, "This way and this way," indicating the direction of the intended cuts with the point of his knife.

Then, suddenly, Gialluca burst into a wild fit of tears. His entire body shook from the sobs.

"Don't be afraid! Don't be afraid!" the men kept repeating, grabbing his arms.

Massacese set to work. At the first touch of the blade Gialluca let out a scream; then, gritting his teeth, he breathed out a muffled moan.

Massacese cut gingerly but with determination, sticking out the tip of his tongue as he was in the habit of doing when he concentrated on anything. Since the brigantine often lurched and staggered, the cut was not the same all the way; the knife went in deeper at one place than another. The sudden blow of a wave made the blade dig down into the healthy flesh. Gialluca howled again, struggling, blood all over him, like a steer in the butcher's hands. He didn't want to submit quietly to it any longer.

"No, no, no!"

"Come here! Come here!" Massacese yelled at him, jumping up to follow him, wanting to finish the job because he was afraid that the interrupted cut could be more dangerous.

The sea, still running heavily, roared all around them, ceaselessly. Clouds shaped like upended funnels rose at the horizon and embraced the whole sky, which the birds had deserted. Now, in the midst of that tumult, beneath that light, a singular excitement seized those men. Involuntarily, while struggling with the wounded man to hold him still, they became enraged.

"Come here!"

Massacese made another four or five cuts, rapidly and at random. Blood mixed with whitish matter bubbled up from the wounds. All the men were smeared with blood, except for Nazareno, who was at the prow, trembling, overwhelmed by the atrocity of the event.

Ferrante La Selvi, who suddenly saw the boat tilt perilously to one side, shouted a command at the top of his lungs: "Take down the mainsail! Hold the tiller due north!"

The two Talamontes, Massacese and Cirù sprang to carry out the order, trimming the sails. The brig continued to scud ahead, pitching up and down. They could see Lissa in the distance. Long zones of sunlight flooded the water, the light pouring down from among the clouds; and the zones varied in accordance with the clouds in the sky.

Ferrante remained at the tiller. The other members of the crew returned to Gialluca. They had to even out the cuts, cauterize it with fire, and cover the wound with a dressing of frayed hemp.

Now the wounded man was in a state of profound prostration. It seemed that he could no longer understand anything. He stared at his comrades with deadened, bleary eyes, already murky like the eyes of animals when they are about to die. He kept repeating at intervals, as if to himself, "I'm dead! I'm dead!"

Cirù tried to clean him up with some raw hemp; but he had a rough touch and irritated the wound. Massacese, wanting to follow the example set by Margadonna's surgeon to the bitter end, was carefully sharpening some strips of fir. The two Talamontes were busy with the tar, since boiling tar had been chosen to cauterize the wound. But it was impossible to light the fire on the deck, which at every moment was being flooded by waves. The two Talamontes went below.

Massacese yelled to Cirù, "Wash him with sea water!"

Cirù followed the advice. His teeth chattering, Gialluca submitted to everything, whimpering all the time. His neck had swollen enormously, was completely red and in some places almost purple. Around the cuts a few dark brown patches began to appear. The sick man was finding it hard to breathe or swallow, and he was tormented by thirst.

"Put your soul in Saint Rocco's hands," Massacese told him. He had just finished sharpening the pegs of wood and was waiting for the tar.

Propelled by the wind, the brigantine was now off course, going up toward Sebenico, losing sight of the island. But, although the waves were still high, the storm gave signs of abating. The sun stood in the center of the sky surrounded by rust-colored clouds.

The two Talamontes came up with a terra-cotta jar full of boiling tar.

Gialluca knelt to pray again to the saint. They all made the sign of the cross.

"Oh, Saint Rocco, save me! I promise you a silver lamp and enough oil for years and thirty pounds of candles! Oh, Saint Rocco, save me! I have a wife and children . . . Have pity on me! Have mercy, my dear Saint Rocco!"

Gialluca kept his hands clasped; he spoke in a voice that no longer seemed his. Then he sat down again, saying simply, "Go ahead!"

Massacese twisted some hemp around the pieces of wood, and as he proceeded he dipped the prepared swab into the boiling tar and with this rubbed the wound. To make the cauterization deeper and more effective, he also poured some water into the cuts. Gialluca did not cry out at all. The men watching shivered in dismay at seeing that terrible pain.

Ferrrante La Selvi, from his place at the tiller, shook his head and said, "You've murdered him!"

The other men carried Gialluca below and laid him on a pallet. Nazareno stayed with him to watch over the sick man. He could hear Ferrante's guttural cries as he ordered the crew to trim the sails, and then the sailors' rapid steps on deck. The

Trinità swerved sharply, creaking in every joint. Suddenly Nazareno noticed a hole which was letting in water; he yelled. The sailors came down in a tumult, excited, all shouting at the same time, trying hastily to stop the leak. It looked as though the boat was going to sink.

Although completely drained of strength and spirit, Gialluca sat up on the pallet, thinking that the boat was about to go down; and he clutched one of the Talamontes with desperate hands. He was begging like a woman, "Don't leave me! Don't leave me!"

They reassured him and stretched him out again. He was frightened. He blurted out meaningless sentences. He cried. He didn't want to die. Since the growing inflammation filled his whole neck and cervix and had also spread little by little down his chest, the swelling had become even more monstrous. He felt that he was being strangled. Every so often he would open his mouth wide to gulp some air.

"Take me on deck! I can't breathe down here. I'm dying down here . . ."

Ferrante called the crew on deck. The brigantine was now tacking, trying to gain headway. The maneuver called for a lot of work with the sails. Ferrante would watch the wind and then give the appropriate command from his place at the tiller. As evening approached, the waves grew calmer.

After some time Nazareno rushed up on deck, completely distraught, crying, "Gialluca's dying! Gialluca's dying!"

The sailors ran to him; they found their shipmate already dead on the pallet, his body lying in a twisted position, his eyes wide open and his face swollen like a man who has been strangled.

The older Talamonte said, "And now?"

The other men stood there silently, bewildered at the sight of the corpse.

They went back on deck, silently. Talamonte repeated, "And now?"

The light slowly retreated from the surface of the water. Calm filled the air. Once again the sails hung slackly and the ship did not move. They caught sight of the island of Solta.

The sailors, all assembled at the stern, discussed what had happened. All of them were gripped by a sharp feeling of anxiety. Massacese was pale and pensive. He said, "What if they say we killed him? What if we get into trouble?"

This fear already tormented the minds of these superstitious, distrustful men. They replied, "That's the truth."

Massacese went on, "Well? What should we do?"

The older Talamonte said simply, "Is he dead? Let's throw him in the sea. We'll pretend that we lost him overboard during the storm . . . It's sure to work."

The other men agreed. They called Nazareno.

"Listen, you . . . mum as a fish, you hear." And they sealed the secret in his soul with a menacing gesture.

Then they went below to bring up the corpse. Already the flesh on the neck gave off a noxious smell; at every jostle the pus in the suppuration dripped out.

Massacese said, "Let's put him in a sack."

They got a sack; but only half of the corpse could fit in it. They then tied the sack at the height of the knees, and the legs stuck out. As they were working on the corpse they looked around them, instinctively. They couldn't see any sails; after the storm, long, slow, ample, rolling waves covered the sea; the island of Solta looked all blue over there on the horizon.

Massacese said, "Let's put in a rock, too."

They got a rock from the ballast and tied it to Gialluca's feet.

Massacese cried, "Let's go!"

They lifted the corpse over the side and let it slide into the sea. Gurgling, the water closed over it; at first the body descended with a slow oscillating motion; then it quickly disappeared.

The crew went back to the stern and waited for the wind.

They smoked and didn't talk. Now and then Massacese made an involuntary gesture, as men who are brooding will sometimes make.

The wind rose. After fluttering for an instant, the sails filled out. The *Trinità* began sailing in the direction of Solta. After two hours of good sailing, they passed through the inlet.

The moon lit up the shore. The sea had the tranquil look of a lake. From the port of Spalato came two ships which sailed out to meet the *Trinità*. Their crews were singing.

Hearing the song, Cirù cried, "Say! They're from Pescara."

Seeing the marks and numbers on the sails, Ferrante said, "Those are Raimondo Callare's brigs." And he shouted to them.

The sailors from their home port answered with loud shouts. One of the boats was carrying a cargo of dried figs, the other young donkeys.

When the second boat passed about ten meters from the *Trinità*, they exchanged greetings. One voice shouted, "Hey, Gialluca! Where's Gialluca?"

Massacese answered, "We lost him at sea during the storm. Tell his mother."

Then some loud cries and exclamations rose from the brig carrying the donkeys; and then cries of farewell.

"So long! So long! See you at Pescara."

And as they sailed off, the crews began singing again under the light of the moon.

GIOVANNI EPISCOPO

Giovanni Episcopo

Ego autem sum vermis, et non homo;
opprobrium hominum, et abjecto plebis.
Omnes videntes me, diriserunt me . . .
Psalm XXI, 7,8.

Judica me secundum justitiam tuam.
Psalm XXXIV, 24.

SO, YOU want to know . . . What do you want to know, my dear sir? What should I tell you? —Oh, *everything*! —So you want me to tell it all, from the very beginning.

All, from the beginning! How can I? I no longer know anything; I no longer remember anything, truly. How can I do it, sir? How?

Ah, my God! Well, here it is . . . —But wait, please, wait. Be patient. The truth is I don't know how to talk. Even if I could remember anything, I wouldn't be able to tell it. When I lived among men, I kept silent. I was silent, even after I'd been drinking: always silent.

Well, not always. I used to talk with *him*; only with him. On certain summer evenings, outside the city's gates, or in the piazzas, or the public parks . . . He would link his arm in mine, that poor, emaciated arm, so frail that you could barely feel it. And we would walk together, discussing this and that.

Eleven years old—think of that, sir—he was eleven; and he conversed like a grown man, he was sad like a grown man. It seemed that he already knew everything about life, that he had borne all of its sufferings. His mouth already knew the bitter words, the words that hurt so much and can't be forgotten!

But who ever forgets anything? Who?

I told you that I no longer know anything, I no longer remember anything . . . But it wasn't true.

I remember everything, everything, everything. Do you understand? I remember his words, his gestures, the way he looked at you, his tears, his sighs, his cries, every act of his existence from the time he was born until the time he died.

He's dead. It's already sixteen days since he died. And I'm still alive! But I must die; I must die as soon as possible. My little son wants me to leave. Every night he comes, sits, watches me. He's barefoot, poor little Ciro! I have to strain my ears to hear his footsteps. All the time, continually, from the moment it gets dark, I sit there listening; continually. When he sets his foot on the threshold, it's as though he put it on my heart; but gently, gently, without hurting me—oh, so lightly . . . Poor soul!

He's barefoot now, every night. But, take my word for it, never, never in his life did he go without a pair of shoes. I swear it: never.

I will tell you something. Now listen carefully. If someone dear to you should die, be sure that he doesn't lack for anything in his coffin. Dress him yourself; if you possibly can, do it with your own hands. Dress him completely, minutely, as though he were to live again, get up, walk out onto the street. Nothing must be missing for someone who leaves this world, nothing. Remember what I tell you.

Here, look at these shoes. —Do you have children? —No. Well, you can't know, you can't realize what these two worn-out shoes which contained *his* feet, which have preserved the form of *his* feet, mean to me. I could never tell you, no father could ever tell you; no one.

At that moment, when they entered the room and came to take me away, weren't all of *his* clothes there, on the chair next to the bed? Why didn't I look for anything but the shoes, anxiously, under the bed, feeling my heart burst at the thought of not finding them, and didn't I hide them, as if in them a little of *his* life were left? Ah, you can't understand.

On certain cold winter mornings, when the time came to go to school . . . He suffered from chillblains, poor child! During the winter, his feet were covered with sores, bleeding. I used to help him put on his stockings, his shoes. *I knew how to do it* very well. Then, when I laced them up, stooping over I could feel his hands resting on my shoulders tremble already from the cold. And I would try to procrastinate . . . No, you can't understand.

Then, when he died, this was the only pair; this pair I'm showing you. And I took them off him. And so of course that's how he was buried, like a poor little waif. Who loved him, except for his father?

Now, every evening, I take these two little shoes and put them one next to the other on the threshold for him. Do you think he sees them as he walks by? Perhaps he sees them, but he doesn't touch them. He knows perhaps that I would go crazy if I couldn't find them there in the morning, in their place, one next to the other . . .

Do you think I am crazy? Oh, no? I think I can read in your eyes . . . No, sir; I'm not crazy yet. What I'm telling you is true. *Everything is true.* The dead come back.

That *other one* also comes back, sometimes. Horrible! Oh, it's horrible!

You see: I have trembled like this for whole nights, my teeth have chattered and I couldn't stop them; I thought that the terror would shake my bones loose at the joints; I felt the hairs over my forehead stiffen like needles until morning—hard, rigid. Isn't my hair all white? Tell me: isn't it white?

Oh, thank you, sir. You see: I'm not shaking anymore. I'm sick, very sick. How many days of life would you still give me, judging from the way I look? You know: I must die, as soon as possible.

But yes, yes, there, I'm calm, perfectly calm. I'll tell you the whole story from the beginning, as you wish. Everything, in the proper order. I still haven't lost my wits. Believe me.

So, here it is. It was in the house in the new section of Rome; a kind of private *pensione*, about twelve or thirteen years ago. There were about twenty clerks living there, both old and young. We would go there to dine in the evening, all together, at the same hour and at the same table. We all knew each other, more or less, although we didn't all work in the same office. That's where I met Giulio Wanzer, twelve or thirteen years ago.

Did you see . . . his corpse? Don't you think there was something extraordinary about that face, those eyes? Ah, but the eyes were closed . . . Not both eyes, though; not both of them, I know. I must die, at least to remove from my fingers the feel of those eyelids that resisted me . . . I feel it, I feel it here, always; as though a little of that skin had stuck to them—here. Look. Isn't this a hand that has already begun to die? Look at it.

Yes; it's true. One shouldn't think of it. Forgive me. Now I'll go straight on to the end. Where were we? I'd begun so well and immediately went astray! It must be due to not eating; nothing else, surely, nothing else. For almost two days now I haven't eaten a thing.

At first, I remember, when my stomach was empty, I experienced a slight delirium, very strange. I felt my mind was wandering; I saw things . . .

Oh, of course, that's right. I remember now. You're right. I was saying that that's where I met Wanzer.

He lorded it over everyone there; he bullied them; he couldn't bear to be contradicted. He always raised his voice; sometimes, his hands. Not an evening passed that he didn't get into a quarrel. He was hated and feared there, like a tyrant. Everyone spoke badly of him, they murmured against him, plotted; but as soon as he appeared, even the angriest of them fell silent. The timid ones would smile at him, flatter him. What did that man have?

I don't know. At table he sat almost directly opposite me. I tried not to, but somehow I kept looking at him, continually. I had a strange feeling, which I can't quite express: a mixture of revulsion and attraction, indefinable. It was like an evil fascination, very evil, which that robust, sanguine, violent man exerted over me, so weak then, sickly and irresolute; and, to tell the truth, something of a coward.

One evening, as we were finishing the meal, a dispute started between Wanzer and a certain Ingletti who sat next to me. As usual, Wanzer began to shout and got furious. Ingletti, emboldened by the wine, refused to back down. I sat there stiffly, my eyes fixed on my plate, not daring to raise them; and my stomach all knotted up, horribly. Some insulting words were exchanged. Suddenly Wanzer picked up a wine-glass and threw it at his adversary. He missed him; and the glass smashed on my forehead, here, where you can see a scar.

As I felt the blood running down my face, I fainted. When I came to, my head was already bandaged. Wanzer was there, looking sorry; he muttered some excuse. Together with a doctor he took me home; he watched as I received the second medication; he wanted to stay in my room late into the night. He returned the next morning. He visited me often. And that started my slavery.

The only attitude I could have toward him was that of a frightened dog. When he walked into my room, he was the master. He would pull open my drawers, comb himself with my comb, wash his hands in my basin, smoke my pipe, rifle through my papers, read my letters, carry away with him any object he happened to fancy. Day by day his domination became more relentless, and day by day my spirit became more groveling, more feeble. I had lost my will. I no longer had a will. I submitted to him completely, without the least protest. He robbed me of all sense of human dignity, just like that, suddenly, with the same facility with which he would have tweaked out a hair.

And I wasn't in a daze. I was aware of everything I did, I was conscious of everything: of my weakness, my abjection and, especially, *of the absolute impossibility* of escaping from that man's power.

I can't explain to you, for example, the profound, obscure emotion that that scar inspired in me. And I can't explain the enormous perturbation that swept over me one day when my executioner took my head between his hands to look at this scar which was still tender and completely red. He passed his finger over it a number of times and then said:

"It's healed perfectly. In a month you'll no longer see a thing. You can thank the Lord."

Instead it seemed to me from that moment on I bore on my forehead not a scar but a mark of servitude, a shameful, very visible sign that would remain there for my entire life.

I followed him wherever he wanted to go; I waited for him for hours in the street, in front of a door; I stayed up late into the night recopying papers from his office for him; I would carry his letters from one end of Rome to the other; a hundred times I climbed the stairs of the public pawnshop, rushing panting from money-lender to money-lender to procure him a certain sum of money that was supposed to save him; a hundred times I stood behind his chair in a gambling den until dawn, dying of weariness and nausea, kept awake by his fusillades of profanity, the acrid smoke clawing at my throat; and he would be annoyed by my coughing, would blame his bad luck on me; and then if he had lost, when we left, walking down the deserted alleyways, surrounded by the mist, he dragged me along like a rag, gesticulating and cursing, until a shadow would loom up at a corner and offer to sell us some brandy.

Oh sir, who will be able to unravel this mystery for me before I die? So there are indeed men on earth who, when they meet other men, can do what they wish with them, can make them their slaves? So the will can be taken away from a man just as one takes a blade of straw from between a man's fingers? Can one do this, sir? But why?

Confronted by my executioner, *I no longer had any will.* And yet I was intelligent; and I too had a head full of thoughts; and I'd read many books, knew a great deal, understood a great deal. One thing, one thing above all I understood: that I was *lost*, irremediably lost. I felt continually in my depths a fright, a tremor; and ever since that evening I was cut, I had a fear of blood, a vision of blood. The crime stories in the newspapers upset me, kept me from sleeping. On certain nights when, coming back with Wanzer, we passed through a dark passageway, down a dark stairway, and the matches were hard to light, I felt a shiver down my back and my hair became prickly, sensitive. I had the idea fixed in my head that some night he would murder me.

That didn't happen. Instead what happened was *that which could not happen*. I used to think: to die by those hands one night, atrociously, this surely is my destiny. Instead . . .

But listen to me. If that evening Wanzer had not come to look in Ciro's room; if I had not seen the knife on the table; if *someone* had not entered into me, suddenly, to give me that terrible push; if . . .

Ah, it's true. You're right. We're still at the beginning and here I'm speaking of the end! But you wouldn't be able to understand if first I didn't tell you everything. And yet, I'm tired already; I'm confused already. I have nothing more to say, sir. My head is light, light, like a bladder full of air. I have nothing more to say. Amen, amen.

There, it's passed. That's enough. Thank you. You are very kind; you have pity for me. Nobody has ever pitied me, nobody on this earth.

I feel better; I can continue. I'll tell you about *her*, about Ginevra.

After that business with the wineglass some of our companions left the *pensione*, others declared that they would stay only if Giulio Wanzer was excluded. So Wanzer received a sort of dismissal from the landlady. After cursing and yelling as usual at all of them, he left. And when I was able to go out, he wanted to take me with him; he expected me to follow him.

For a long time we wandered listlessly from trattoria to trattoria. Nothing was sadder for me than what for other working people is a relief and, sometimes, a form of escape. I barely ate, forcing myself, disgust growing in me at the noise my fellow diner's jaws would make: a mastiff's jaws, formidable, that could have crushed steel. And little by little I began to develop that *thirst* which, once it starts, lasts until death.

But one evening Wanzer left me free. And the next day he told me that he had found a very pleasant place, to which he wanted to take me immediately.

"I found it. You'll see. You'll like it."

In fact the new *pensione* was perhaps better than the old one. The terms were to my liking. Some clerks from my office lived there. Also, several others were not completely unknown to me. I stayed. Nor would I have been able—as you know—not to stay.

That first evening, when the soup was brought to the table, two or three men asked with unusual intensity, in unison: "What about Ginevra? Where's Ginevra?"

The answer came that Ginevra was sick. Then they all inquired about her illness, they all showed great concern. They were told that it wasn't serious. In the conversation the absent woman's name was on everybody's lips, spoken amid ambiguous phrases betraying a sensual desire which perturbed all those men, old and young. I tried to catch what they were saying up and down the table. A dissolute young fellow sitting across from me spoke at length about Ginevra's mouth, becoming quite excited; and he looked at me as he talked, because I was listening so attentively. In my imagination, I remember, there then took form a figure of the absent woman that was not very different from the woman I later actually met. I shall always remember Wanzer's expressive gesture and the curl, I would say, almost of voracity his lips took in pronouncing an obscene sentence in dialect. And I remember that when we left I was already infected with the contagion of desire for that woman I had not seen—and also a slight disquietude, and a certain very strange, almost prophetic sense of exaltation.

We left together—I, Wanzer, and a friend of Wanzer's, a certain Doberti, the same man who had talked about her mouth. As we walked the two of them continued to talk coarsely about sex; and they would stop now and then to laugh long and loudly. I stayed a bit behind them. An almost oppressive melancholy, a quantity of obscure, confused thoughts swelled my already humiliated, quaking heart.

Even now, after about twelve years, I can remember that evening. I haven't forgotten a thing; not even the most insignificant detail. I know now, as I sensed then, that on that evening my fate was decided. From whom then did I get the warning?

Is it possible? Is it possible? The mere name of a woman, three ringing syllables, can open before you an inevitable abyss, which you can see, which you know to be inevitable. Is this possible?

Premonition, clairvoyance, inner vision. . . Words! Words! I've read them in books. It's not that way, it's not that way. Have you ever looked inside yourself? Have you ever examined your soul?

You suffer. Does your suffering seem new to you, *never experienced before*? An error, an illusion. Everything has been experienced, everything has taken place. Your soul is composed of thousands, hundreds of thousands of fragments of souls which have lived a whole life, which have produced all phenomena, have seen all phenomena. Do you know where I'm heading? Well, listen to me carefully, because what I am telling you is the truth; the truth discovered by someone who has spent year after year continually looking inside himself, alone among men, alone. Listen to me carefully because this is a truth much more important than the events you want to know about. When . . .

Another time? Tomorrow? Why tomorrow? So you don't want me to explain my idea to you.

Oh, the facts, the facts, always the facts. —The facts are nothing, they don't mean anything. There is something in this world, my dear sir, which matters much more.

Ah well: another mystery. Why did the real Ginevra resemble most faithfully the image which had flashed into my mind? Well, let's leave that aside. —After two or three days' absence, she reappeared in the dining room, carrying a large soup tureen that veiled her face in steam.

Yes, my dear sir, she was a waitress, serving meals at a clerks' *pensione*.

Did you ever see her? Did you know her? Did you ever talk to her? And did she ever talk to you? Well, you too, I'm sure, experienced that sudden, inexplicable perturbation, if she touched you with her hand.

All the men desired her, every one of them wanted her; they still want her. Wanzer is dead; yet she will still have a lover, a hundred lovers, until she grows old, until her teeth fall out of her mouth. When she walked down the street, the prince in his coach turned round, the beggar stopped to look at her. I've caught the same gleam in all eyes, I've read the same thought.

She's changed, changed a lot. At that time she was twenty. I have always tried in vain to *see her again* within myself, just as I saw her that first time. There's the secret. Have you ever noticed this? A man, an animal, a tree, anything whatsoever, presents its true aspect only once, that is, in the fleeting moment of that first perception. It is as though it gave us its virginity. Immediately after, it's no longer the same; it's something else. Your soul, your nerves transform it, falsify it, obscure it. Farewell.

Ah well, I've always envied the man who saw that creature *for the first time*. Do you understand me? Maybe you don't. You think that I'm raving, that I'm getting confused and contradicting myself. It's hopeless. Let it go. Let's get back to the facts.

. . . A room lit by gas lights, overheated, with an arid heat that dries up the skin; and the smell, the steam rising from the food; and a confused noise of voices, and over all those voices Wanzer's harsh voice, which made every word crude and rough. Then, all of a sudden, an interruption, a silence that seemed frightening to me. And a hand brushes past me, picks up my plate, sets down another; it makes me shiver as though it had given me a caress. All of them around the table, one after the other, experienced the same thrill: it was visible. And the heat became suffocating; ears began to turn red, eyes began to glisten. A base, almost bestial expression appears on the faces of those men who have eaten and drunk, who have attained the only goal of their daily lives. The emanation of their impurity wounds me so deeply that I think I'm going to faint. I gather myself together on my chair, draw in my elbows to increase the distance between myself and my neighbors. A voice cries through the hubbub: "Episcopo's got a belly-ache."

Another voice shouts: "No, Episcopo is feeling *sentimental*. Didn't you see the look on his face when Ginevra changed his plate?"

I try to laugh. I raise my eyes and meet Ginevra's fixed on me with an ambiguous expression.

She leaves the room. Then Filippo Doberti makes a clownish proposal.

"My dear friends, there's only one way out. One of us must marry her . . . on behalf of the others."

That isn't exactly what he said; he used the coarse word; he indicated the act, the role of the others.

"Let's vote. Let's vote. We've got to elect a husband."

Wanzer yells: "Episcopo!"

"Episcopo and Associates Incorporated."

The brawl increases. Ginevra returns, perhaps she's heard. She smiles a calm, assured smile, which makes her seem intangible.

Wanzer yells: "Episcopo, ask for her hand."

Two other men, with studied gravity, get up and ask in my name for Ginevra's hand.

With the same smile, she replies: "I'll think it over."

And again I meet her eyes. And I really don't know if it is I they are talking about, if I am the one this is addressed to, if I am that Episcopo they're laughing at. And I can't possibly imagine the expression on my face. . . .

A dream, a dream. That whole period of my life is like a dream. It's impossible for you to understand or imagine the sense I had of my own being and the consciousness I had of the things I was doing. In a dream I re-lived a part of life already lived; I watched the inevitable repetition of a series of events that had taken place already. When? Who knows? You can add that I was not sure of being I, myself. Often it seemed to me that I had mislaid my personality, at times I felt I had an artificial one. What a mystery a man's nerves are!

I'll cut it short. One evening Ginevra quit her job; she said she was leaving that sort of work; she said that she didn't feel well, that she would go to Tivoli, would stay there for a few months at her sister's house. All of them, when they said goodbye to her, clasped her hand. Smiling, she kept saying to them: "We'll see each other."

And then, laughing, to me: "Remember, Signor Episcopo. We are *betrothed*."

That was the first time I touched her; and it was the first

time I looked into her eyes with the intention of trying to penetrate her thoughts. But she remained a secret for me.

The following evening the meal was almost gloomy. They all seemed disappointed. And Wanzer said: "You know, Doberti's idea wasn't bad."

Then some of them turned to me and stupidly prolonged the mockery.

The company of those idiots had become unbearable to me; but I made no attempt to get away. I continued to go to that house where, amid the jesting and laughter, I could feed my dark sweet fantasies. For many weeks, undergoing the worst material difficulties, humiliations, anxieties and terrors of my slavish life, I experienced all the anguish of the most delicate and violent love. At twenty-eight a kind of belated adolescence had suddenly manifested itself in my spirit, with all the languors, all the tender feelings, all the tears of adolescence . . .

Ah, my dear sir, you can imagine this miracle in a creature like myself, already old, withered, parched to the marrow. Picture an unexpected flower that suddenly sprouts on a dry stalk.

Another extraordinary, unexpected event astonished and overwhelmed me. For several days now Wanzer seemed harder, more irascible than usual. He had spent five or six nights in a gambling den. One morning he had come up to my room looking pale as a corpse, had flung himself in a chair; two or three times he had tried to speak; then, suddenly, giving it up, he had left without saying a single word, without answering me, without looking at me.

I didn't see him again all that day. I didn't see him at dinner. I didn't see him the following day.

We were at table when a certain Questori, a colleague of Wanzer's, came in and said: "You haven't heard? Wanzer's run away."

At first I didn't understand it or I didn't believe it; but my heart leapt to my throat.

Some of the men said: "What are you saying? Who's run away?"

"Wanzer, Giulio Wanzer."

I really don't know what I felt; but certainly my first feeling of agitation was in great part composed of joy. I made an effort to contain myself. And then I heard all the resentments, all the rancors, all the repressed hatreds explode against the man who had been my master.

"And what about you?" the most ferocious of the men shouted at me. "Don't you have anything to say? Weren't you Wanzer's servant? Didn't you carry his suitcases to the station?"

Another man said to me: "You've been marked on the brow by a thief. You'll get ahead."

Another man: "Whose lackey will you become now? Will you move on to the police?"

That's how they insulted me, for the sheer pleasure of hurting me, because they knew I was a coward.

I got up and left. I walked down the streets, wandering at random: free, free, free at last!

It was a night in March, serene, almost warm. I climbed the slope of Via Quattro Fontane, turned up toward the Quirinale Palace. I was looking for broad open spaces; I wanted to drink in a single breath an immensity of air, look at the stars, listen to the sound of water, do something poetic, dream of the future. Continually I kept repeating within myself: Free, free; I am a free man. I still couldn't reflect, gather my thoughts, examine my state. I was assailed by childish whims. I would have liked to perform a thousand deeds all at once to prove my freedom to myself, to savor my freedom. Passing by a café, I was washed by a wave of music and it stirred me to the depths. I walked in, my head held high. I felt that I had a proud air. I ordered a cognac; and I made the waiter leave the bottle on the table. I drank two or three glasses.

It was suffocating in that café. The act of taking off my hat reminded me of my scar, reawakened in my memory the cruel sentence: "You've been marked on the brow by a thief." —Since I felt that everyone was looking at my forehead and had noticed the mark, I thought: "What can they think? They most likely think it's a wound received in a duel." —And I, who would never have fought, was pleased by this thought. If someone had come to sit next to me and struck up a conversation, I certainly would have found a way to describe that duel. But nobody came. After some time a gentleman came to take the chair opposite me, on the other side of the table. He didn't look at me, didn't ask my permission; he didn't notice, when he took the chair, whether or not I was resting my feet on it. It was rude of him; don't you agree?

I left, started walking about the streets again, aimlessly. I felt deeply unhappy, without quite knowing why. Gradually a vague disquiet arose from that bewilderment; and as my disquiet grew it suggested a thought to me: "Maybe *he* is still in Rome, hidden? Maybe he's going about the streets in disguise? Maybe he's waiting for me in the dark, on the stairs?" —I was afraid; I turned round two or three times to make sure I wasn't being followed; I went into another café, as one goes into a place of refuge.

When it was late, very late, I finally made up my mind to set out for home. Every appearance, every noise frightened me. A man stretched out on the sidewalk in the dark looked to me like a cadaver. —"Ah, why didn't he kill himself?" I thought. "Why didn't he have the courage to kill himself?" And indeed it was the one thing he should have done—I realized then that rather than news of his flight, only that of his death would have calmed me.

I slept little and it was an anxious sleep. But in the morning, as soon as I opened the shutters, a sense of relief began again to spread through my whole being: a peculiar feeling, which you can't understand because you have never been a slave.

At my office I got a detailed report on Wanzer's flight. It

was due to grave irregularities and a theft of bonds from the Central Treasury, where he had been a clerk for a number of years. An order for his arrest had been issued, but with no result. Some people thought he had already reached some safe place, far from the police.

Then, securely free, I lived only for my love, my secret. I felt that I was convalescing; I had a lighter sense of my body, less troubling; I cried very easily, like a child. The last days of March and the first days of April had for me a sweetness and sadness whose memory alone, now that I am dying, consoles me for having been born.

For that one memory I forgive Ciro's mother, the woman who did us so much harm. You cannot understand, sir, what the revelation of his own hidden goodness, the discovery of a vein of tenderness in the core of his own being is for a man hardened and warped by sufferings and injustice. You can't understand, and perhaps can't even believe what I'm saying. Well, I tell you. At certain moments, may God forgive me, I felt in me something of Jesus. I have been the most miserable and the best of men.

Here, let me cry a little. Do you see how I am able to cry? In all those years of martyrdom I learned to cry like this, without sobs or outward signs, so as not to be heard, so as not to trouble the person who loved me, the person who made me suffer. There are few people in the world who know how to cry as I do. Well, sir, this at least will be marked down in my favor, when you remember me. You'll say, when I'm dead, that poor Giovanni Episcopo at least knew how to cry silently, all his life.

How was it that on that Sunday morning—Palm Sunday—I found myself going to Tivoli on the tram? Actually, I have an uncertain memory of it. Was it a fit of folly? Was it the act of a somnambulist? Truly, I do not know.

I went toward the unknown, I let myself be dragged along

by the unknown. Once again the sense of reality eluded me. It even seemed to me I was surrounded by a peculiar atmosphere that isolated me from the outer world. I don't know how to express it. The Roman countryside, for example, the countryside I was going through, seemed to me indefinitely far away, separated from me by an incalculable space . . .

How can you form a picture of so extraordinary a mental state? What I'm describing must seem to you necessarily absurd, inadmissible, unnatural. Well, just think that I have lived amidst these disorders, these perturbations, these alterations almost continually until today. Paraesthesis, dysaesthesia . . . They've even told me the names of my illnesses. But nobody has been able to cure me. I have lived all my life on the brink of insanity, aware of it, like a man bending over and looking down into an abyss, waiting from one minute to the next for the final spell of dizzyness, the great moment of darkness.

What do you think? Will I lose my reason before I close my eyes? Is there some hint on my face, or in what I say? Do you notice anything? Answer me frankly, dear sir; answer me.

And what if I do not die! If I must survive for a long time in an insane asylum, a lunatic!

No; I must confess that this is not my real fear. You know . . . that *they* might come at night, both of them. Some night, I'm sure of it, Ciro will meet that *other one*: I know it, I foresee it. And . . . then? —The explosion of rage, of furious madness, in the dark . . . Oh, my God, my God! Will this be my way of dying?

Hallucinations, yes; nothing else. You've put it perfectly. Oh, yes, yes, you've put it well: all I need is a lamp to be tranquil, because I sleep deeply; yes, yes, a lamp, simply a lamp. Thank you, my dear sir.

Where were we? —Ah, yes, at Tivoli.

. . . A sharp stench of sulphurous water; and then, everywhere, all around, olive trees, olive trees, groves of olive trees; and in me the strange primitive sensation that one is being dispersed in the wind as our tram speeds ahead. I get off. There are people in the streets; strips of palm leaf glisten in the sun; the church bells toll. I know that *I will meet her*.

"Oh, Signor Episcopo? How did you come? Why are you here?"

It's Ginevra's voice; it's Ginevra, with her hands outstretched, standing right in front of me, who am overwhelmed.

"Why so pale? Have you been sick?"

She looks at me and smiles, waiting for me to manage to speak. Is this the woman who walked around the table in the smoke-filled room, under the gaslight? Is it possible that this is the woman?

Finally I stammer out a few words.

She insists: "But why are you here? What a surprise!"

"I'm here to see you."

"So you remembered that we're *betrothed*?"

She laughs and adds: "Here's my sister. Come with us to church. You'll stay with us today, won't you? We'll act as if we're engaged. Say you will."

She's gay, talkative, full of unexpected ideas, of new seductiveness. She's dressed simply, unpretentiously, but with grace, almost with elegance. She asks news of our friends.

"And that Wanzer!"

She learned it all from a newspaper, by chance.

"You two were great friends. Weren't you?"

I do not reply. A short silence; and she seems pensive. We go into the church bedecked with sacred palms. She kneels alongside her sister and opens a prayer book. I am standing behind them and I stare at her neck; and the discovery of a small brown mark gives me an ineffable thrill. At that very moment she turns around a little and flashes a glance at me out of the corner of her eye.

The memory of the past is abolished, the anxiety for the future is calmed. There is only the present; there is nothing on this earth for me but this woman. Without her the only possibility is to die.

Leaving the church, without speaking she offers me a palm. I look at her, without speaking; and it seems to me that from that look she has understood everything. We walk towards her sister's house. I am invited in. Ginevra says to me, going towards a balcony: "Come, come here for a while, to enjoy the sun."

We are on the balcony, side by side. The sun strikes us with its full force; the roar of the church bells passes over our heads. She says softly, as though talking to herself: "Who ever would have thought it!"

My heart swells with a boundless tenderness. I can barely stand it. I ask her, in a voice become unrecognizable: "So we're betrothed?"

She remains silent for a moment. Then she replies slowly, blushing just a trifle, lowering her eyes: "Do you want it? Well, yes, we are."

They call to us from inside. There's her brother-in-law; some other relatives; the children are there, too. I am really the fiancé! At the table Ginevra and I are placed next to each other. At a certain point we hold hands, under the tablecloth; and I think that I am going to faint, the feeling of voluptuousness is so keen. The brother-in-law, sister, relatives suddenly look at me with mixed curiosity and astonishment.

"But how is it that nobody knew about this?"

"But how is it that you, Ginevra, never told us anything about it?"

We smile, embarrassed, confused, also astonished at what is happening with the ease and absurdity of a dream . . .

Yes, absurd, incredible, ridiculous; above all, ridiculous. But it happened in this world between a man and a woman of this world, between me, Giovanni Episcopo, and the living Ginevra Canale, just like that, just as I have told it to you.

Ah, sir, you may laugh, if you wish to. I won't be offended.

A *tragic farce* . . . Where did I read this phrase? —Truly, nothing more ridiculous, nothing more ignoble and nothing more atrocious.

I went to her mother's home in an old house on Via Montanara, up some narrow, damp and slippery stairs, like the steps leading down to a cistern, a dubious, greenish, almost sepulchral light filtering down from a slit overhead: unforgettable. I remember it all! As I went up I paused upon almost every step; because I felt I was losing my balance at every moment, as if I were treading on moving ice. The higher I climbed, the more that staircase, in that light, seemed fantastic to me, full of mystery, of a grim silence, where certain very distant, incomprehensible sounds seemed to come to die. Suddenly I heard a door open violently on the landing above; and an outburst of profanity shrieked by a female voice resounded through the whole stairwell; and then the door closed again with a loud crash that made the house shake from top to bottom. And I shook too, intimidated; and I stayed there, hesitating. A man was gradually coming down, indeed he seemed to slither along the wall like some soft thing. He was grumbling and whimpering beneath the turned-down brim of a whitish hat; but when he bumped into me, he raised his head. And I saw a pair of dark glasses, the kind that are enclosed in a protective mesh, enormous, jutting out from a face red as a piece of raw meat.

The man, thinking he recognized me, called: "Pietro!"

And he grabbed me by the arm, breathing his wine-laden breath into my face. But he realized his mistake and resumed his way down. Then I continued my climb, automatically; and I was sure, I don't know why, that I had met a member *of the family*. I found myself before a door on which I read: "Emilia

Canale, pawnbroker attached to the Public Pawnshop, authorized by the Commissioner of Police, Rome." To end the anguish of hesitation, I made an effort and pulled the bell-rope; but I pulled it much harder than I intended and the bell began ringing furiously. An irate voice answered from within, the same voice that had shrieked the curses; the door opened; and I, seized by a kind of panic, without seeing, without even waiting, gaspingly said, swallowing my words: "I am Episcopo, Giovanni Episcopo, clerk . . . I have come, as you must know . . . for your daughter . . . as you already know . . . Excuse me, excuse me. I pulled it too hard."

I was standing before Ginevra's mother, a still good-looking, florid woman, dressed *à la* pawnbroker, wearing a gold necklace, two huge gold ear-rings, and gold rings on all of her fingers. And I was timidly asking for Ginevra's hand in marriage—you remember?—the famous proposal made by Filippo Doberti!

Ah, my dear sir, you may laugh if you wish. You won't offend me.

I must tell you everything, in detail, day by day, hour by hour—isn't that so? You want all the little scenes, all the little events, all my life of those days, so bizarre, so senseless, so comic and miserable, right down to the *great event*? Do you want to laugh? Do you want to cry? I can tell you everything. I read my past as in an open book. This great clarity comes to someone who is near death.

But I am tired, I'm weak. And you, too, you must be a little weary. It's best to cut it short.

I'll do that. I know you'll readily agree.

The pawnbroker seemed already informed as to my job, my pay, my situation. She had a ringing voice, a determined way of gesturing, a malign rapacious look, which at certain moments became caressing, almost lewd, somewhat resembling Ginevra's. When she spoke to me, standing up, she came too close to me, touched me continually; now she gave me a little push, now she pulled at one of my jacket buttons, now she flicked a speck of dust from my shoulder, now she picked off a hair, a thread. I felt deeply upset, all my nerves tense. It was torture, that continual touching on the part of that woman who more than once I saw lift her fists in her husband's face.

And her husband was in fact the man on the stairs, the man with the green eyeglasses, a poor idiot.

He had worked as a typographer, this man. An eye disease now prevented him from working. And he lived on his wife, his children and son-in-law, badly treated by all of them, martyred, like an intruder. He had the vice of drinking wine, the habit of getting drunk on it, the *thirst*, the terrible thirst for it. Nobody at his house gave him a penny for drink; but, in order to earn a little money, he must certainly have earned it on the sly, God knows on what street, God knows in what shop, from what people—plying some ignoble little trade, base, facile, hiring out by the day. When he got the chance he would snatch up some stuff from the house and run off to sell it, so he could drink, so he could abandon himself to his unrestrainable passion; and even the fear of curses and blows didn't stop him. At least once a week his wife threw him out, pitilessly. For two or three days he would not have the courage to return, to knock at the door. Where did he go? Where did he sleep? How did he live?

From that first day, the day I met him, I liked him. While I sat there and bore the chatter of my future mother-in-law, he sat facing me with a smile on his face, a continuous smile that made his lower, somewhat pendant lip tremble, but it did not come from the sort of cage in which his poor sick eyes were enclosed. When I rose to leave, he said in a low voice, with obvious fear: "I'll come too."

We left together. His legs were pretty weak. Going down the stairs and seeing him hesitate and lurch, I said to him: "Do you want to lean on me?"

With me as his support we went down, and out on the street he continued to hold his arm under mine, although I made a movement to free myself. He kept silent for a while; but now and again he turned to me and brought his face so close that he touched me with the brim of his hat. He still smiled, accompanying his smile with a peculiar sound in his throat, to break the silence.

I remember it was almost dusk; a pleasant evening. People were sauntering along the street. Two musicians, a flute and guitar, were playing an aria from *Norma* in front of a café. I remember: a wagon went by, transporting a wounded man sitting between two policemen.

Finally he said, squeezing my arm: "I'm happy; you know? Really happy. What a good fellow you must be! I already like you a lot, you know."

He said all this with a kind of anxious haste, having one fixed idea, one desire, and being shy about expressing it. Then he began to laugh, stupidly. Another pause. Again he said: "I'm happy."

He laughed again, but convulsively. I realized that he was gripped by nervous agitation, and that it made him suffer. When we were in front of a glass window with red curtains which glowed brightly, being lit up from inside, he said suddenly, rapidly: "Shall we have a glass together?"

And he halted and detained me at that door, in the reddish reflection staining the pavement. I could feel he was shaking; and the light helped me to see his poor inflamed eyes behind those lenses.

I replied: "Let's go in."

We entered a tavern. There were a few customers; they were playing cards in a group. We sat down in a corner. Canale ordered: "A liter, of red."

He was seized by a sudden hoarseness. He poured the wine in the glasses, shaking like a paralytic; then drank his down in one gulp; sucking his lips, he poured himself another glass. Then he laughed, setting the bottle on the table; and naively he confessed: "For three days I haven't had a drink.

"Three days?"

"Yes—three whole days. I haven't any money. At home nobody gives me a cent. You understand? You understand? And I can't work anymore, with these eyes . . . Look, my boy."

He lifted his glasses; and so much had the expression of his face changed, it almost seemed to me that he had lifted a mask. His lids were ulcerated, swollen, without lashes, filled with decay, horrible; and in the midst of that redness and that swollenness barely opened two tear-filled pupils, infinitely sad, with that profound and incomprehensible sadness one can see in the eyes of a suffering animal. Faced by that revelation, a mixture of disgust and pity stirred in me. I asked: "Does it hurt you? Does it pain much?"

"Oh, you can imagine, my boy! Needles, needles, jagged edges of wood, splinters of glass, poisonous thorns . . . If they stuck all this in me, it would be nothing in comparison, my boy."

Perhaps he exaggerated his sufferings, because he saw himself being pitied by me, pitied as a human being and who knows after how many years! Who knows how many years had passed since he had heard a pitying voice! He exaggerated perhaps to increase my feeling of compassion, to feel himself consoled once again by a fellow human being.

"Do they hurt you very much?"

"Very much."

Very slowly he passed over his lids a kind of rag which had neither color nor shape. Then he lowered his glasses again; and drained his second glass in one gulp. I drank too. He touched the bottle and said: "There's nothing else in the world, my boy."

I looked at him. Nothing in him, truly nothing reminded one of Ginevra: not a feature, not an intonation, not a gesture, nothing. I thought: "He isn't the father."

He drank again; ordered another liter of wine; then went on talking in a tone of voice which rasped like a falsetto: "I'm happy that you're going to marry Ginevra. And you can be happy too . . . The Canales are an honest family! If we hadn't been honest . . . by now . . ."

Lifting his glass, he wore an equivocal smile that disturbed me. Then he went on: "Eh, Ginevra . . . Ginevra could have been a treasure for us, if we had wanted. You understand? We can say these things to you. Not one, not two, but ten, twenty offers . . . And what offers, my boy!"

I felt I was turning green.

"Prince Altini, for instance . . . All the time he was on my neck! He even wanted me to come to his palace one evening, a few months ago, before Ginevra left for Tivoli. You understand? He wanted to give her three thousand lire right away; and then he would rent a house for her, and so on, and so on. Ah, no, no. Emilia has always said: It doesn't pay, it doesn't pay. We married off the first girl, we'll marry the second. A clerk with a good career, a halfway decent salary . . . We'll find him. You see? You see? You came. You're named Episcopo, isn't that so? What a name! So it's Signora Episcopo; Signora Episcopo . . ."

He had become loquacious. He began to laugh.

"How did you see her? How did you meet her? In Rome, right? At the *pensione*. Tell me, tell me. I'm listening."

At that point a man came in, a man with an ambiguous look, repugnant, something between a waiter and a hairdresser, with a pale face covered with reddish pimples. He greeted Canale.

"To your health, Battista!"

Battista called him over, offered him a glass of wine.

"Teodoro, drink to our health. Here is my future son-in-law, Ginevra's fiancé."

The stranger, surprised, muttered something, looking at me with whitish eyes that made me shiver, as if I had felt a cold, slimy touch on my skin. He murmured: "Oh, so, the gentleman . . ."

"Yes, yes," Battista broke in quickly. "Signor Episcopo."

"Ah, Signor Episcopo. It gives me great pleasure . . . Congratulations . . ."

I didn't say a word. But Battista laughed, his chin on his chest, assuming a sly, nasty look. After a while, the other man stood up to leave.

"Goodbye, Battista. We'll see each other again, Signor Episcopo."

He offered me his hand, and I gave him mine.

When he had left, Battista said to me in a low voice: "You know who he is? Teodoro, the . . . *confidant* of Marchese Aguti, the old one, who has a palace nearby. A year he's been pestering me about Ginevra. You understand? The old man wants her, wants her, wants her; he cries, shrieks, stamps his feet like a child, because he wants her. Marchese Aguti, the man who has them tie him to the iron bars of a bed, has his women whip him until the blood runs . . . We've heard the howls, from our house . . . Then the police intervene . . . Ha, ha, ha, poor Teodoro, how disappointed he looked! Did you see how he looked? He didn't expect that, he didn't expect that, poor Teodoro!"

He went on laughing stupidly, right in front of me, who was dying of anguish. Suddenly he stopped and spat out an imprecation. Beneath the rim of the glasses his cheeks were streaked by two trickles of impure, yellowish tears.

"Oh, these eyes! When I drink, it pains me even more!"

And again he lifted those frightening green eyeglasses; and again I saw that whole deformed face, which seemed almost flensed, red like the behinds of certain monkeys—you know? You can see them in the zoo. And I saw those painful pupils in the middle of those suppurating wounds. I saw him pressing that rag against his lids.

"I must go. It's already late for me," I said.

"Good, let's go. But wait."

And he started to rummage comically through his pockets,

as if to take out some money. I paid; and we got up and walked out. Again he put his arm under mine. It seemed that he didn't want to leave me that evening. Every so often he laughed like an idiot. And I felt that the excitement of just before was returning, the agitation, the inner laughing, as of someone who wants to say something but doesn't dare and is ashamed.

"What a lovely evening!" he said; and he gave the same convulsed laugh as before.

Suddenly, with the same effort a stammerer makes when he gets stuck, his head low, hiding beneath the brim of his hat, he added: "Give me five lire. I'll return them to you."

We stopped. I put five lire in his hand which was shaking a great deal. Immediately he turned and walked away, vanishing in the dusk.

Ah, sir, what a sad business! The man who is devoured by vice, the man who struggles in the grip of vice and feels himself being eaten up and lost and doesn't want to be but who can't save himself . . . What a piteous thing, sir, what a piteous thing! Can you think of anything more profound, more enticing, more obscure? Tell me, tell me: what, among all human matters, is sadder than the tremor that seizes you faced by the object of your desperate passion? What is sadder than hands that shake, knees that buckle, lips that twist, a human being racked in every part by the implacable need of a single sensation? Tell me, tell me: what upon this earth is sadder? What?

And to see this enemy all around you, to see it with prodigious lucidity, to discern all its traces, divine all its corrosions, its *hidden* devastations. To see—you know what I mean?—to see the suffering in each man, to comprehend, always to comprehend, and to have fraternal pity for every strayed soul, for every wretched person, and to feel within oneself in the depths of one's own flesh the voice of this great human fraternity, and not to regard any man on the street as a stranger

. . . You understand? Could you understand this in me, in me whom you regard as pusillanimous, abject, almost idiotic?

No, you cannot understand. And yet, that's how it is. There are men who walk among the people as though among a forest of completely identical, indifferent trees; and there are some men, continually anxious, who search in every face for the silent reply to a silent question. For such men there are no strangers upon this earth.

Alas, his heart is for everyone, no heart is for him.

I know, I know. Who cares about him? Who is concerned about his goodness and his love? Every man harbors a secret dream which is not goodness or love but rather a reckless desire for pleasure and self-aggrandizement. I know. No human creature loves another human creature—man has never been loved by another human creature. I have never dared confess the horrible truth to myself, for fear of dying of it.

Well, sir, from that evening on I felt tied to that wretch, I became his friend. Why? Through what mysterious affinity? Because of what instinctive foresight? Perhaps because his vice was beginning irresistibly to overpower me too? Or because I was attracted by his unhappiness without hope and without possibility of escape which was so much like mine?

After that I saw him almost every evening. He would come looking for me everywhere; he waited for me outside my office; he waited for me at night on the stairs of my house. He would not ask me for anything; nor could he speak with his eyes, since they were covered up. But it was enough for me to look at him to understand. He would smile his usual silly or convulsed smile; and he never asked for anything, just waited. I was unable to resist him, I would not send him away, humiliate him, greet him with a frown, speak to him harshly. —But did that mean I was being subjected to another tyranny? That Giulio Wanzer had a successor? —Often his presence troubled me acutely; and yet I did nothing to free myself from him. Sometimes he was given to ridiculous or saddening effusions of love for me, which wrenched my heart. Once he said to me, wrinkling up his mouth as children do when they are about to cry: "Why don't you call me papa?"

I knew that he was not the father; I knew that his wife's children were not his. Perhaps he also knew this. And yet I called him papa, when nobody could hear, when we were alone, when he needed to be consoled. Often, to gain my pity, he would show me a bruise, the mark of a beating, with the same gesture with which beggars display their deformities or misfortunes to elicit alms.

I discovered, by chance, that on certain evenings he stationed himself in the shadows, away from the street lamps, and would beg in a low voice, adroitly, without attracting attention, walking for a way alongside the passer-by. One evening, at the corner by the Forum of Trajan, I was approached by a man who was muttering: "I am an unemployed worker. I am nearly blind. I have five children who haven't eaten for twenty-four hours. Give me something to buy a piece of bread for those poor creatures of God . . ."

I recognized his voice immediately. But there in the darkness, barely able to see, he didn't recognize me. Fearful that he might I quickly walked away, I fled.

Even the basest action did not revolt him, provided he could satisfy his atrocious thirst. One time he came to my room; he seemed upset. I had just got back from the office and I was washing up. I had laid my jacket and vest on the bed, and in the pocket of my vest I had left my watch, a small silver watch, a memento of my dead father. I was washing behind a screen. I heard Battista move about the room in an unusual way, as if he were nervous. I asked him: "What are you doing?"

He answered a bit too promptly and in a voice that seemed a trifle different: "Nothing. Why?"

And he immediately came behind the screen, with a bit too much concern.

I dressed. We went out. At the foot of the stairs, I reached into my pocket for my watch to see what time it was. I failed to find it. It wasn't there.

"My goodness! I left my watch up in the room. I must go back up again. Wait for me here. I'll only be a moment."

I went up, lit a candle, looked everywhere for the watch. After a few minutes of futile search, I heard Battista's voice asking: "Well, did you find it?"

He had come up; he stood in the doorway, swaying a little.

"No. It's strange. And yet I think I left it in my vest pocket. Have you seen it?"

"I haven't seen it."

A suspicion had already flashed through my mind. Battista remained in the doorway, standing there, his hands in his pockets. I started searching again, impatiently, almost angrily.

"It's impossible that I mislaid it. I had it before, before I undressed; I know I had it. It must be here; I must find it."

Battista had finally moved. I turned suddenly; and I read the guilt on his face. My heart sank.

He stammered, confused: "It must be here; we'll find it."

And he picked up the candle and bent over to search around the bed; he got down on his knees, lurching a bit; raised the covers, looked underneath the bed. He was upset, troubled, panting; and the candle was dripping on his unsteady hand.

That bit of play-acting irritated me. I shouted at him harshly: "Enough! Get up; and don't make such a fuss. I know where we ought to search . . ."

He put the candle on the floor; and stayed there for a while on his knees, hunched over, trembling like someone about to confess a misdeed. But he didn't confess. He got up with an effort, without speaking. Once again I read the guilt on his face; and I felt a sharp pang. I thought: "Of course, he has the watch in his pocket. I should force him to admit it, to give me back the stolen object, to repent. I should stand here and watch him weep with repentance." But I didn't have the strength. I said: "Let's go."

We left. On the stairs the guilty man followed me slowly, clinging to the railing. How sad it was!

When we reached the street, he asked me in a feeble voice: "So you think I took it?"

"No, no," I replied. "Let's not talk about it any more."

After a while, I added: "I'm sorry, because it was a memento of my dead father."

I noticed that he made a slight, quickly repressed movement, as if he had the intention of taking something from his pocket. But it was nothing. We continued to walk.

After another interval he said to me, almost brusquely: "Do you want to search me?"

"No, no. Let's stop talking about it. Goodbye. I'm leaving now because I have some business to attend to this evening."

And I left him, without looking at him. It was so sad!

During the following days I did not see him. On the evening of the fifth day he showed up at my house. I said, gravely: "Oh, it's you?"

And without pausing for a moment, I went back to working on certain office documents. After an interval of silence, he dared to ask me: "Did you find it?"

I pretended to laugh, and went on writing. After another long interval, he added: "I didn't take it."

"Yes, yes, all right; I know. It's still on your mind?"

Seeing that I remained seated at my table, he said, after another pause: "Good night!"

"Good night, good night!"

I let him leave just like that; I didn't stop him. But I was sorry; I wanted to call him back. Too late; he had already left.

He did not come around for another three or four days. As I was entering my house late one evening, just before midnight, he was standing there before me, under a street lamp. It was drizzling.

"Oh, it's you. So late!"

He could barely stand upright; he looked drunk. But, when

I looked more closely, I realized that he was in a miserable state: covered with mud as if he had rolled in a ditch, haggard, distraught, with a face that looked almost purple.

"What's happened to you? Tell me."

He began crying wildly and came close to me as though about to collapse in my arms; and he stood like that, close to me, sobbing and trying to tell his story between sobs that were choking him, through tears that dripped down into his mouth.

Ah, sir, under that street lamp, in that rain, what a terrible thing! What a terrible thing, the sobs of a man who hasn't eaten for three days!

Do you know what it means to go hungry? Have you ever looked at a man half dead from hunger, who sits down at a table and lifts to his mouth a piece of bread, a piece of meat, and chews the first mouthful with poor, weak teeth that wobble loosely in his gums? Have you ever seen that? And wasn't your heart pierced by sadness, by sympathy?

I really didn't want to talk so much about that wretched man. I let myself be carried away; I forgot all the rest—why, I don't know. But the truth is that in my life that wretch has been my only friend and I have been his. I have seen him cry and he has seen me cry, more than once. And I have seen my vice reflected in his, as in a mirror. And we also had in common the same trouble, we have suffered the same injury, we have borne the same shame.

No, he wasn't Ginevra's father; he had not given his blood to the veins of the creature who has done me so much harm.

I've always thought with restless, unsatisfied curiosity about the *real* father, the unknown man, the nameless one. Who indeed was he? Surely not a plebeian. A certain physical fineness, certain naturally elegant features, a certain cruelty and certain complicated perfidies, and, besides, the instinct for sexual pleasure, the facile disgust, that very special way of wounding, crushing a person with a laugh—all these things and others revealed the presence of aristocratic blood. Who was the father then? Perhaps an obscene old man like Marchese Aguti? Or perhaps a priest, one of those gallant cardinals who strewed offspring through all the households of Rome?

I've always thought about it. And sometimes there appeared in my imagination the figure of a man, not vague or shifting but rather well defined, with a particular physiognomy, a special expression, who seemed to live an extraordinarily intense life.

Of course, Ginevra must know or at least *sense* that she had nothing in common with her mother's husband. In fact, I was never able to detect in her eyes, when they were looking at the unfortunate man, any gleam of affection or, at the very least, of pity.

Instead, indifference, often disgust, contempt, aversion, even hatred appeared in her eyes when she looked at the poor man.

Ah, those eyes! They said everything; they said too many things in an instant, too many different things; and they made me forget and bewildered me. When by chance they met mine, they seemed made of steel, gleaming, impenetrable steel. Then, suddenly, they were covered as if by a pallid veil and lost all sharpness. Think, my dear sir, of a blade misted over by a breath . . .

But no, I cannot talk to you about my love; I can't, I can't talk about my love. Nobody will ever know how much I have loved; nobody. She has never known; she does not know now. I know that she has never loved me even for a day, even for an hour, an instant.

I knew it from the start; I knew it even when she gazed at me with those misted-over eyes. I didn't deceive myself. My lips never dared to proffer the tender question, the question all lovers repeat: "Do you love me?" And I remember how, being close to her, feeling myself swept by desire, I would think more than once: "Oh, if I could kiss her on the face and *she did not notice my kisses!*"

No, no, I cannot talk about my love. I will tell you the facts, the petty, ridiculous facts, the small miseries, the little moments of shame.

The marriage was set. Ginevra stayed on in Tivoli for another few weeks, and I would often travel out there on the tram. I would stay for half a day, a couple of hours. I was glad that she was living outside Rome. My constant worry was that some of my office colleagues might discover my secret. I employed no end of precautions, subterfuges, excuses, lies, to hide what I had done, what I was doing, what I was about to do. I didn't go to the usual places; I met all questions with evasive replies; I ducked into a shop, a doorway, a side street when I recognized from far away some of my old acquaintances from the *pensione*.

But one day I could not avoid Filippo Doberti. He overtook me, in fact, to put it more accurately, he sank his claws into me.

"Oh, Episcopo, so long since we've seen each other! What have you been doing? Have you been sick?"

I couldn't control my unreasonable agitation. I answered thoughtlessly, "Yes, I've been sick."

"It's obvious, obvious. It does look like that, you look green. But now what sort of life are you leading? Where do you dine? Where do you spend your evenings?"

I told some morc lies and tried to keep from looking at his face.

"We were talking about you the other night," he went on. "Efrati said he saw you on Via Alessandrina, arm in arm with a drunkard."

"With a drunkard?" I cried. "Efrati's been dreaming."

Doberti burst out laughing.

"And you blush, eh? You're always looking for fine company, aren't you . . . A propos, have you heard the news about Wanzer?"

"No, I don't know anything."

"What! Don't you know he's in Buenos Aires?"

"I don't know a thing."

"Ah, poor Episcopo! Goodbye; I leave you. Take care of yourself, take care of yourself, you hear? You look pretty bad to me, pretty bad. Goodbye."

He turned up another street, leaving me in a state of agitation that I couldn't repress. All his words on that far-off evening when he had talked about Ginevra's mouth came back to my memory—precise, vivid. And I remembered other, crueler, more vulgar words. And again I saw that room lit by gas, I saw the long table at which all those men, their bellies now full, excited by the wine, a trifle hazy, were united by the same obscene interest. And again I heard the laughter, the hubbub, my name yelled by Wanzer, acclaimed by the others; and then the atrocious motto: "Episcopo and Associates Incorporated." And I thought that the horrible thing could actually come true . . .

It could come true! It could. —But is such an ignominy possible? Is it possible that a man, apparently not crazy, not moronic, not a half-wit, could let himself be trapped by such ignominy?

Ginevra returned to Rome. The marriage day was set.

Together with the pawnbroker, in a hansom cab, we drove around to find a small apartment, to buy the nuptial linen and other necessary furnishings—in short, to make all the usual preparations. I had withdrawn from the bank a deposit of fifteen thousand lire, my whole fortune as an orphan.

So we went around the city in an open carriage, all over Rome, triumphantly: I crouching on the small front seat, and the two women facing me, our knees touching. Whom did we meet? Who recognized us? Although I kept my head lowered, out of the corner of my eye I more than once saw someone waving at us from the sidewalk. A very elated Ginevra leaned out, turned, saying each time: "Look, it's Questori! Look, it's Micheli! And there's Palumbo, together with Doberti!"

And so the word spread. For my colleagues at the office, for my old *pensione* companions, for all my acquaintanceship, it was an occasion for endless merriment. In all their looks I could read irony, derision, malign hilarity, sometimes even a kind of insulting pity. Nobody spared me his little jab; and I, just to do something, would smile at each joke, producing the same grimace, like an impeccable automaton. What else could I have done? Act insulted? Fly into a rage? Give way to violence? Hand out a few slaps? Fling an inkwell at some of them? Brandish a chair? Fight a duel? —But all these things, wouldn't they too have been ridiculous, my dear sir?

One day at the office two "young wits" staged an interrogation. The dialogue was between a judge and Giovanni Episcopo. To the judge's question: "What profession?" Giovanni Episcopo replied: "A man who has no self-respect."

Another day I overheard these words: "He has no blood in his veins; not a single drop of blood. The little he did have Giulio Wanzer took out of his forehead. That's right, you can see that he hasn't got one drop of blood left . . ."

It was true, it was true.

But how did it happen that I suddenly decided to write a letter to Ginevra to ask her to release me from my promise? Yes, I wrote a letter to Ginevra to call off the marriage—I, I wrote her, with this very hand! And I took it to the post office myself.

It was evening, I recall. I walked past the post office a number of times, excited, like a man who is about to decide to commit suicide. Finally I stopped and slipped the letter into the slot; but it seemed I couldn't detach my fingers from it. Did I remain for a long time like that? I don't know. A guard tapped me on the shoulder, asked me: "What are you doing?"

I opened my fingers; let the letter drop in. And I nearly fainted, right there in the arms of the guard!

"Tell me," I stammered, almost whispering, "what can I do to get that letter back?"

And at night, the anguish I was prey to at night! The next morning, visiting the new apartment, the conjugal apartment already prepared to receive the married couple and suddenly rendered useless . . . turned into a mortuary.

Oh that sun, those beams of almost cutting sunlight on all those new, polished, untouched furnishings, giving off a warehouse smell, an unbearable smell . . .

That afternoon at five, leaving the office, I met Battista on the street and he said to me: "They want you at my house, right away."

We set out for it together. I was trembling, like a captured criminal. At a certain point I asked, in order to prepare myself: "What do they want?"

Battista knew nothing. He shrugged his shoulders. When we got to the street door, he left me. I climbed the stairs slowly, sorry now that I had obeyed the summons, thinking with insane fright of the pawnbroker's hands, those terrible hands. And upon reaching their landing, and raising my eyes and seeing the door open and on the threshold the pawnbroker all ready to pounce on me, I cried immediately: "It was a joke, a joke."

And so a week later the marriage took place. My witnesses were Enrico Efrati and Filippo Doberti. Ginevra and her mother had insisted that as many of my colleagues as possible be invited to the wedding feast, so as to dazzle the poor folk on Via Montanara and in the surrounding neighborhood. All my fellow diners from the *pensione* were present, I think.

I have a confused, vague, fragmented memory of the ceremony, the banquet, the crowd, those voices, that hubbub. I believe that at a certain point there passed over that table something akin to the ardent, impure breath which in the past had passed over that *other table.* Ginevra's face was ablaze and her eyes were amazingly bright. Many other eyes around her glistened; many smiles gleamed.

I remember how a heavy sadness swooped down on me, filled me, blurred my consciousness. And I can still see, down there at the end of the table, all the way down, at an incredible distance, poor Battista, who drank, drank, drank. . . .

At least one week! I don't say a year, a month, but just a week: at least the first week! —No, not at all; without the slightest pity. Not even a single day did she wait; she began immediately on the very night of our marriage to treat me cruelly.

If I were to live one hundred years I could never forget that burst of unexpected laughter that froze me to the core in the darkness of our bedroom and mocked my timidity and my awkwardness. I couldn't see her face in the dark; but for the first time I felt all her nastiness in that bitter, mocking, shameless laughter, which I had never heard before, unrecognizable. I felt that a viper lived at my side. Ah, my dear sir, she had laughter in her teeth, as snakes have poison.

Nothing, nothing served to make her less cruel: not my silent submission, my silent adoration, my pain, my weeping, nothing. I tried everything to touch her heart—to no avail. Sometimes she listened to me with a serious face and grave eyes, as if on the point of comprehending; and then, suddenly, she would begin to laugh, with that frightening laughter, that inhuman laughter which flashed more from her teeth than her eyes. And I stood there, annihilated . . .

No, no, it is impossible. My dear sir, permit me not to talk about it; let me pass over it. I can't speak about her. It's as if you had forced me to chew something bitter, something mortally, unbearably bitter. Can you not see that telling it twists my mouth?

One night—it was about two months after the wedding—

in my presence she had an indisposition, a sort of fainting fit . . . You know; the usual scene . . . And I who, all aquiver, was secretly waiting for that revelation, that indication, that fulfillment of my highest wish, that immense joy in my misfortune, I fell on my knees, as though before a miracle. —Was it true? Was it true? —Yes, it was; she told me, confirmed it. She had *another life* growing inside her.

You can't understand. Even if you were a father, you couldn't understand the extraordinary emotion that then overwhelmed my soul. Just imagine, sir, imagine a man who has suffered everything a man can suffer under the sun, a man on whom all the ferocity of other men has been relentlessly, ceaselessly vented, a man who has never been loved by anyone and yet in his depths preserves a great wealth of tenderness and goodness, a wealth to be lavished, inexhaustibly; think, sir, of the hopes of this man who looks forward to a creature of his own blood, a son, a delicate, sweet being—oh infinitely sweet—whose love he could win . . . you understand?—finally to be loved!

It was September, I remember. Those were calm, golden days, a trifle sad—you know very well—when the summer dies. Always, always I was dreaming about him, about Ciro.

One Sunday, at the Pincio gardens, we ran into Doberti and Questori. Both were very glad to see Ginevra; they joined us, to continue their stroll. Ginevra and Doberti walked ahead, I and the other man stayed behind. But those two ahead seemed to trample on my heart at each step. They were talking a lot, laughing together; and people turned to stare at them. Their words came to me indistinctly through the waves of music from the band, even though I strained my ears to catch something of what they were saying. My anguish was so apparent that Questori called out to them: "Go slow! Don't get so far away from us. Episcopo's here and he's dying of jealousy."

They joked, made fun of me. Doberti and Ginevra continued to walk ahead, laughing and talking, amid the crashing music which most likely exalted and intoxicated them, while I felt so unhappy that, walking along the parapet, I had the crazy idea of taking a sudden leap over the wall to end all that suffering once and for all. Also Questori, at a certain point, fell silent. I noticed that he was looking attentively at Ginevra's figure, and that his desire for her upset him. Other men, walking towards us, turned two or three times to look at her; and they had the very same glitter in their eyes. It was always that way, always, when she was out and there were others around: walking among them, it was as though she produced a furrow of impurity. It seemed to me that all around us the air was contaminated by that impurity; it seemed to me that none of them could get their minds off this woman they desired and thought easy to get, all, it seemed to me, had a single obscene image fixed in their brains. The waves of music spread out through the dense light; all the leaves on the trees glistened; to my ears the wheels of the carriages made a deafening racket. And in that light, that noise, that crowd, surrounded by that confused spectacle, seeing before me that woman who was gradually letting herself be captivated by that man, feeling the impurity all around—I thought with terrible anguish, with a wrench of all of my most delicate fibres, of the tiny creature that was starting to live, the little, unformed being who was perhaps at that very moment suffering the contractions of that womb from which he would start life . . .

Oh my God, my God, how that thought made me suffer! How many times that idea lacerated me before *he* was born! Do you understand? The thought of contamination . . . Do you understand? It was not so much the infidelity, the guilt that afflicted me, but the son who was not yet born. It seemed to me that something of that shame, that ugliness would cling to him, would certainly dirty him. Do you understand my horror?

And one day I had a surge of unusual courage. One day, when my suspicion was most tormenting, I found the courage to speak out.

Ginevra was at the window. I remember: it was All Saints' Day; the church bells were ringing; the sun was pouring down on the windowsill. Truly, the sun is the saddest thing in the universe. Don't you agree? The sun has always made my heart suffer. In all my most painful memories there is a little sunlight, a few yellow sunbeams as though around mortuary drapes. When I was a child they once left me for a few minutes in a room where my sister's corpse was laid out for viewing on a bed, surrounded by wreaths of flowers. I still feel I can see it, that poor white face all carved with purplish shadows, which, during his last moments, Ciro's face so much resembled . . .

Ah, what was I saying? My sister, yes, my sister lying on the bed, amid the flowers. Good; that's what I was saying. But why? Let me think a bit . . . Ah, here it is: I approached the window, dismayed; a small window looking out on the courtyard. The house opposite seemed to be uninhabited; one never heard human voices from it; nothing stirred. But on the roof a huge throng of sparrows kept up a heartbreaking chatter, continuous, endless; and beneath the gutter, on the gray wall, in the gray shadows, a streak of sunlight, a yellow line, straight, very sharp, was gleaming wickedly, with incredible intensity. I no longer dared turn around, and stared fixedly at the yellow line, as if under a spell; but I *felt* behind me—you understand?—while my ears were filled with the din of that immense chattering, I felt within me the frightening silence of the room, that cold silence which congeals around a corpse . . .

Oh, sir, how many times in my life have I seen that tragic streak of sunlight again! How many times!

Very well, what was I saying? So, Ginevra was standing at the window; the church bells were ringing; the sun washed into the room. There was also, on a chair, a wreath of evergreen with a black ribbon which Ginevra and her mother were going to take to the Verano cemetery to put on some relative's grave . . . —What a memory! you must be thinking. Yes, indeed, I now have a terrible memory!

Listen to me. She was eating a piece of fruit with that provocative sensuality she brought to everything she did. She didn't notice me, she wasn't aware that I was looking at her. And never had that profound indifference toward me pained me as it did on that particular day; never had I realized with such clarity that she did not belong to me, that she could belong to everyone, that in fact she would inevitably belong to everyone, and that I would never be able to lay claim to any right of love, even any right based upon force. And I kept looking at her, looking at her.

Has it ever happened to you, when looking for a long time at a woman, to suddenly lose all notion of her humanity, her social condition, the emotional ties which bind you to her, and *to see*, with an obviousness that terrifies you, the bestiality, the sheer femaleness, the blatant brutality of sex?

This is what I *saw* as I looked at her; and I realized that she existed only for the carnal, for an ignoble function. And another terrible truth rose in my mind: human life, all human preoccupations are based on ugliness—a horrible, horrible truth!

Well, what could I do? Nothing. But that woman bore in her womb *another life*, fed with her blood the mysterious creature who was my constant dream and highest hope, my adoration . . .

Yes, yes, even before *he* was born I adored him, I wept tenderly for him, I said unimaginable things to him in my heart. Think, think, my dear sir, of this martyrdom: not to be able to separate an innocent image from an ignominious one; to know that the object of your ideal worship is tied to a being from whom you expect the worst infamies. What would a zealot feel if he were forced to see the Sacrament on his altar covered by a filthy rag? What would he feel if he could not kiss the divine object save through a veil smeared with filth? What would he feel?

I don't know how to put it. Our words, our acts are always

vulgar, stupid, insignificant, whatever may be the grandeur of the emotion from which they spring. I had within me that day an immense confusion of painful, stifled feelings; and it was resolved in a cynical little dialogue, in buffoonery and humiliation. Do you want the facts? Do you want the conversation? Well, here it is.

So she was standing at the window, and I went over to her. I remained there for a bit, in silence. Then, with an enormous effort, I took her by the hand and asked her: "Ginevra, have you already deceived me?"

She looked at me, amazed, and said: "Deceived you? How?"

I asked her: "Do you already have a lover? Doberti . . . perhaps?"

She kept staring at me, for my whole body was trembling horribly.

"But what sort of scene is this? What's eating you now? Are you going off your rocker?"

"Answer me, Ginevra."

"Are you crazy?"

And while I was trying to seize her hand again, she shouted, pulling away from me: "Don't bother me! Enough!"

But I, like a madman, threw myself on my knees, holding her by the hem of her skirt.

"Please, I beg you, Ginevra, I beg you! Have pity on me, a little pity! Wait at least until the poor creature . . . my son . . . is born . . . Mine—isn't that true? Wait until he's born. Afterward, you can do whatever you want; and I'll keep quiet and bear everything. When your lovers come, I'll leave. If you order me to do it, I'll clean their shoes, in the next room . . . I'll be your servant, I'll be their servant; I'll endure it all. But wait, wait! First give me my son! Have pity on me . . ."

Nothing, nothing. In her look there was only a kind of mocking curiosity. She stepped back, repeating: "Are you going crazy?"

Then, since I continued to beg her, she turned her back on me, left and shut the door behind her. She left me there, kneeling on the floor.

There was the sun on the tiles; and that funeral wreath on the chair; and my sobs did not change a thing . . .

What can we change? Do our tears have any effect? —Each man is *just anyone*, to whom just anything can happen. This is the whole story; there is nothing else. Amen.

We are tired, my dear sir; I from telling my story, you from listening. After all, I have wandered a bit, perhaps too much; for—you know very well—this is not the question. The *real point* lies elsewhere. It will take another ten years to get to the *point*; ten years, ten centuries of pain, misery, and shame.

And yet, everything could still have been remedied. Yes, that night when I heard the howls of the woman giving birth, inhuman howls, unrecognizable, the howls of an animal in the slaughterhouse, I thought, with a convulsion of my entire being: "If only she died, oh, if only she would die and leave me the baby alive!" —She was howling so dreadfully that I thought: "Anyone who howls like that cannot die." —I had this thought; well, yes, I had this hope. But she didn't die; she survived in order to be the agent of my and my son's damnation.

He was my son, truly mine, the son of my flesh and blood. On his left shoulder he had the same peculiar mark I have had since birth. May God be blessed for that mark which helped me recognize my son!

Now, should I tell you about our ten years of affliction? Should I tell you everything once again? No, it can't be done. I would never reach the end. And then, perhaps, you wouldn't believe me; because what we suffered is incredible.

Here, in a few words, are *the facts*. My house was turned into a brothel. Sometimes I even met strange men, when I entered my house. I never got so far as to do what I had said—

I never cleaned their shoes in the next room; but in my own house I was nothing but a menial. Battista was less unhappy than I; Battista was less humiliated. No human humiliation could ever be compared to mine. Jesus would have wept all His tears for me; because I, among all men, have touched the bottom, the very depths of humiliation. Battista, believe me, could have pitied my state.

And it was comparatively easy, during the first years, when Ciro did not yet understand. But when I realized that his intelligence was awakening, when I saw that in that weak, frail creature intelligence was developing with prodigious speed, when I heard from his lips the first cruel question—oh, then I saw myself damned forever.

What could I do? How could I hide the truth from him? How could I save myself? I saw that I was truly lost.

His mother did not take care of him; she forgot about him for days on end; sometimes she would even make him go without necessary things; she even beat him now and then. And for long hours I was obliged to be away, far from him; I could not always give him the protection of my sympathy and tenderness; I couldl not make his life sweet, as I had dreamed, as I would have wished. The poor thing spent nearly all his time in the company of a maid in the kitchen.

I put him in school. In the morning I myself would take him there; in the afternoon, at five, I would go and pick him up; and then I didn't leave his side until he went to sleep. In short, he learned how to read, to write, he was well ahead of all his classmates; he made extraordinary progress. You could see the intelligence in his eyes. And when he looked at me with those large dark eyes, which already illuminated his entire face, and were so deep and sad, sometimes I felt within me a kind of dread; and I couldn't bear his look for long. Oh, sometimes in the evening at table, when his mother was there and silence descended upon us three . . . Then all my silent anguish would be reflected in those pure eyes of his.

But the really terrible days were still to come. My shame was too widely known, the scandal was too serious, *Signora Episcopo* was too famous. Besides, I neglected my duties at the office; my paperwork was filled with mistakes; on certain days my hand shook so violently that I wasn't able to write. My colleagues and superiors considered me a dishonored, degraded, brutalized, benumbed, cowardly man. I received two or three warnings; then I was suspended from the job; and finally I was dismissed in the name of outraged morality.

Until that day I had at least represented the value of my salary. From that day on I was not worth as much as a rag, a peel one finds on the street. Nothing can give you an idea of the ferocity, the rage my wife and her mother showed in torturing me. And yet they had taken from me the few thousand lire I had left; and the pawnbroker had opened up a dry goods store at my expense. It was on the basis of that small business that the family still managed to live.

They considered me a hateful parasite; I was put on a par with Battista. On certain nights I too found the door of my house locked; I too went hungry. And I adapted myself to all sorts of trades, all kinds of work, all the lowest, most menial tasks. To get my hands on a few cents, I worked as a messenger boy. I was a prompter in an operetta company. I was doorman at a newspaper, I worked as a clerk in an employment bureau. I did everything I got a chance to do, I crawled before all sorts of people, accepted all sorts of filth, bent my neck to every yoke.

Now, tell me: after all this travail, all these interminable days, did I not deserve some small respite, some little escape? In the evening, when I could, as soon as Ciro had closed his eyes, I would go out. Battista was waiting for me on the street, and we would go together to a wine shop, to drink.

Respite? Escape? Who has ever really known the significance of these words: *to drown one's sorrows in wine*? Ah, sir, I have always drunk because I felt that I was parched by an unquenchable thirst; but wine has never given me an instant of joy. We sat opposite each other, and we did not feel like talking. In fact in there nobody talked. Have you ever gone into one of those very quiet wine shops? The drinkers are all by themselves, their faces are tired, they prop their temple on the palm of a hand; and before them stands the glass. Their eyes stare at the glass but perhaps do not even see it. Is it wine? Is it blood? Yes, my dear sir, it is both.

Battista had become almost blind. One night, as we were walking together, he stopped under a street lamp and, palping his stomach, said to me: "You see how swollen it is?" Then, taking my hand to have me feel the hardness of the swelling, he said to me in a voice altered by fear: "What could it be?"

He had been in that condition for many weeks without revealing that he was sick. Some days later I took him to the hospital to be examined by the doctors. It was a tumor, indeed a group of tumors that were growing rapidly. One could attempt an operation. But Battista didn't want it, though he wasn't resigned to dying.

He dragged his illness about for a few more months; then he was forced to go to bed, and he never got up again.

What a long and atrocious death! The pawnbroker had shut the wretched man up in a kind of closet, a dark, stifling little hole, far away so they wouldn't have to hear his complaints. And every day I would go in there and Ciro wanted to come with me, wanted to help me . . . Oh, if you could have seen him, my poor child! How courageous he was in that work of charity, next to his father.

I would light a bit of candle to see a little more clearly, and Ciro would hold it. And then we saw that great deformed body which moaned, which did not want to die. No, it was not a man invaded by a disease; rather—how should I put it?—it was rather an image of disease, a thing outside nature, a monstrous being, living on its own, to which were attached two miserable, thin human arms, two miserable human legs, and a small, fleshless, reddish, revolting head. Horrible! horrible!—and Ciro would hold the light; and then into that taut flesh which shone like yellowish marble I injected some morphine with a rusty hypodermic syringe.

But that's enough, enough. Peace be with that poor soul. Now I must come to *the point.* I cannot digress any more.

Destiny! —Ten years had passed, ten years of a desperate life, ten years of hell. And one evening, at the table, in Ciro's presence, Ginevra said to me right out of the blue: "Did you know? Wanzer's come back."

Certainly I didn't turn pale: because, you see, my face had long been this color, unchanging, which not even death will change and I will take it with me just like this under the ground. But I remember that I couldn't manage to move my tongue.

She stared at me with her sharp, cutting look, which already filled me with the same apprehension an extremely sharp knife inspires in the pusillanimous. I realized that she was staring at my forehead, at the scar. She wore an irritating, intolerable smile. And she said to me, alluding to the scar, knowing she would hurt me: "You haven't forgotten Wanzer, have you? After all he did leave a fine souvenir on your forehead . . ."

Then Ciro also stared at my scar. And I could read on his face all the questions he wanted to ask me. He wanted to ask me: "How is that? Didn't you once tell me that you fell and cut yourself? Why did you lie? And who is this man that gave you the scar?" But he lowered his eyes again and didn't say a word.

Ginevra went on: "I ran into him this morning. He recognized me immediately. At first I didn't recognize him, because he has let his beard grow. He knew nothing about us. But he told me he'd been looking for you for three or four days. Our friend wants to see you again. He must have made his fortune in America, judging at least from how he looked . . ."

As she talked she continued staring at me and continued smiling inexplicably. From time to time Ciro cast a quick glance at me; and *I felt that he felt I was suffering.*

After a pause, Ginevra added: "He's coming tonight, quite soon."

It was raining heavily outside. And it seemed to me that that steady, monotonous noise did not come from outside but rather from within me, as if I had swallowed a large dose of quinine. And suddenly I lost my sense of reality; and I was surrounded by that *offensive atmosphere* which I've already mentioned once before, and again I had profoundly *the feeling of the repetitiveness of what was happening and was about to happen.* Do you understand me? I thought again that I was again witnessing the inevitable repetition of a series of events which had already taken place. Were Ginevra's words *new*? Was the anxiety of my waiting *new*? Was it *new*, that malaise produced by my son's gaze turned too often, perhaps involuntarily, to my forehead, to this cursed scar? No, *nothing was new.*

All three of us around that table were silent. Ciro's face expressed an unusual anxiety. There was something extraordinary in that silence: a profound, very obscure significance which my mind could not succeed in penetrating.

Suddenly, the doorbell rang.

We looked at each other, I and my son. Ginevra said to me: "It's Wanzer. Go and let him in."

I went. The act was in my person, so to speak, but the will was outside my person.

Wanzer entered.

Must I describe the scene? Must I tell you his words again? There was nothing extraordinary in what he did and said, in what we did and said. Two old friends met again, embraced, exchanged the usual questions and the usual answers: that was the appearance.

He wore a large rainproof cape with a hood, thoroughly

drenched by the rain, glistening. He seemed taller, broader, prouder. He wore three or four rings on his fingers, a pin in his tie, a gold bracelet. He spoke without embarrassment, as a man completely sure of himself. Was this perhaps the thief who had returned to his country after the expiration of the statute of limitations?

Among other things he said to me, looking me over carefully: "You look much older. But Signora Ginevra is even younger looking than before . . ."

He stared at Ginevra from beneath half-closed lids, a sensual smile on his face. He already desired her and was thinking that he would possess her.

"But to tell the truth," he added, "wasn't I the person who arranged this marriage? Of course it was me. Don't you remember? Ha, ha, ha! Remember?"

He began laughing and Ginevra laughed too; and I also tried to laugh. I was really playing Battista's role very well, I believe. That poor Battista—peace to his soul—had bequeathed to me his convulsed, stupid way of laughing. Peace to his soul!

But Ciro kept looking incessantly at me, at his mother, and at the stranger. And his gaze when it rested on Wanzer took on a hard expression I had never seen before.

"He looks a lot like you, this boy," Wanzer continued. "He looks more like you than his mother."

He stretched out a hand to caress his hair. But Ciro jumped, avoided that hand with so proud, so violent a movement of his head that Wanzer was dumbfounded.

"Take this," his mother cried, "you little boor!"

The slap resounded loudly.

"Take him away, take him away immediately," she ordered me, pale with anger.

I got up; I obeyed. Ciro hung his head, but he didn't cry. His teeth were clenched and I could just hear the gritting sound they made.

When we were in our room, I lifted his head as gently as I could; and I saw on his poor emaciated cheek the imprint of her fingers, the red mark left by the slap. My eyes filled with tears.

"Does it hurt? Tell me: does it hurt very much? Ciro, Ciro, answer me. Does it hurt you very much?" I asked him, bending with desperate tenderness over that poor offended cheek which I wanted to cleanse not with my tears but with some miraculous balsam.

"Ciro, Ciro, my son, answer me!"

He didn't answer. He jerked away from me, walked to his bed and began undressing without a word. I started to help him with almost timid, humble gestures, feeling myself die at the thought that he might have a grievance against me. I knelt before him to untie his shoelaces; and I lingered there on the tile floor, bent over his feet, holding my very heart at his feet, a heart that weighed like a ton of lead, that I felt I could never lift up again.

"Papa, Papa," he burst out suddenly, grasping me at the temples.

And he had the dreadful question on the tip of his tongue.

"Speak, go ahead! Speak to me!" I implored him, still at his feet.

He stopped, didn't say another word. He got into bed, drew up the covers, sank his head into the pillow. And, after a bit, his teeth began to chatter, as would happen on certain bitterly cold winter mornings. My caresses didn't calm him, my words did not seem to do him any good.

Ah, sir, anyone who has gone through what I did then deserves to go to heaven.

Did only an hour go by? —At last it seemed that Ciro had become quieter. He closed his eyes as though to fall asleep; gradually his face became more composed; the trembling ceased. I remained next to the bed, immobile.

Outside it continued to rain. From time to time a flail of

rain would shake the windowpanes; and Ciro would open his eyes wide, and then shut them again.

"Sleep, sleep! I am here," I repeated each time. "Sleep, my dear son!"

But I was afraid; I couldn't stifle my fear. Above me, all around me, I felt a terrible menace. And each time I repeated: "Sleep, sleep!"

A sharp, lacerating shriek burst over our heads. And Ciro sat up in bed, grabbed my arm, gasping, dismayed.

"Papa, Papa, did you hear that?"

And both of us, hugging each other tightly, overwhelmed by the same feeling of terror, listened, waited.

Another, longer shriek, like that of a person being murdered, reached us through the ceiling; and then another and even longer, even more heart-rending, which I now recognized, which I had heard before on a night long ago . . .

"Calm yourself, calm yourself. Don't be afraid. It's a woman giving birth upstairs. You know her? Signora Bedetti . . . Calm yourself, Ciro. It's all right."

But the howls continued, piercing the walls, piercing our ears, becoming more and more bestial. It was like the death-throes of a clumsily slaughtered animal. I had a vision of blood.

Then, instinctively, both of us stopped our ears with our hands, waiting for the agony to end.

The howls ceased; the pelting crash of the rain began again. Ciro lay down under the bedclothes again, shut his eyes. I repeated: "Sleep, sleep. I won't go away."

An indefinite amount of time went by. I was in the grip of my destiny, like a defeated man at the mercy of an inexorable conqueror. I was lost now, lost, inexorably lost.

"Giovanni, come. Wanzer's leaving."

Ginevra's voice? I was startled; I realized that Ciro had also been startled, but his eyelids had not moved. So then he wasn't asleep yet? —I hesitated before obeying. Ginevra opened the door to the room and repeated: "Come. Wanzer's leaving."

Then I got up, tiptoed out of the room, hoping that Ciro would not notice.

When I reappeared before that man I could read clearly the impression I made upon him. A dying man, still kept alive by some unnatural force—that is how I must have seemed to him. But he had no pity for me.

He looked at me, spoke to me in the same way as in the past. He was the master who had found his servant again. I thought: "During all the time I was in there, what did they say, what did they do, what have they *plotted* together?" I noticed a change in both of them. When she spoke to him, Ginevra's voice had a different accent than before. When it rested on him, Ginevra's gaze was covered *with that veil* . . .

"It's raining too hard," she said. "You must go down and find a carriage . . ."

You understand? It was an order given to me. Wanzer didn't object. It seemed quite natural to him that I should go and search for a carriage. Hadn't he already called me back into his service? —And I was barely able to stand! And certainly both of them could see that I was barely able to stand.

Inconceivable cruelty. But what could I do? Refuse? Begin a rebellion just at that moment? I could have said: "I don't feel well." Instead I didn't utter a word, I took my hat and umbrella and left.

On the stairs the lamps were already doused. But in the darkness I could see a multitude of flashes and gleams, and in my brain there appeared one after the other, with the rapidity of lightning bolts, strange, absurd, disconnected thoughts. I remained for a moment on the landing, thinking that I could hear madness coming through the shadows. But nothing happened. Distinctly, I heard Ginevra laugh; I heard noises from the tenants above. I struck a match; I went down the stairs.

As I was just about to go out on the street, I heard Ciro's

voice calling for me. I actually had a *real* sensation then, like the laughter, like the noises. I turned, climbed back up the stairs in an instant with inexplicable ease.

"So soon?" Ginevra cried, when she saw me reappear.

I couldn't speak because of my great agitation. Finally I blurted out desperately: "I can't . . . I must go in the other room . . . I feel sick."

And I rushed to my son.

"Did you call me?" I immediately asked as I came in. I found him sitting up in bed, as if he were listening. He replied: "No, I didn't call you."

But I felt he wasn't telling me the truth.

"Perhaps you called me while you were dreaming. Weren't you asleep before?"

"No, I wasn't asleep."

He looked at me, uneasy, suspicious.

"What's the matter with you?" he asked me. "Why are you panting? What did you do?"

"Come, be calm, Ciro," I begged, not replying to his questions, stroking him. "I'm staying here with you; I won't leave again. Now sleep, sleep!"

He let himself fall back on the pillow with a sigh. Then he closed his eyes in order to please me, pretending to go to sleep. But a few minutes later he opened them again, opened them wide. And he said, in an indefinable tone: "*Hasn't he left yet?*"

From that night on, the tragic presentiment was always there. It was a kind of vague, mysterious horror, which condensed in the depths of my being, where the light of consciousness can never reach. Among all the many abysses I have found within myself, that abyss remained inscrutable and seemed the most frightening of all. Continually I watched it, I would almost say that I craned over it with tremendous anxiety, hoping that a sudden flash might illuminate it for me, might reveal it to me completely. Sometimes I felt that I could hear this *unknowable* thing rise little by little and approach the zone of consciousness, almost touch it, graze it, then suddenly return to the depths, plunge back into the darkness, leaving me with an extraordinary perturbation. Do you understand? Imagine, my dear sir, so as to understand me, imagine that you are standing at the brink of an incalculably deep well. Down to a certain point the well is illuminated by natural light; but you know that in the lower darkness is hidden some unknown, terrible thing. You can't see it, but you hear it move around confusedly. And little by little this thing rises up, reaches even to the borders of the darkness where you can almost make it out. Just a bit more, just a bit more—and you will see it. But the thing halts, draws back, vanishes; it leaves you shaken, disappointed, terrified . . .

No, no . . . Childishness, childishness . . . You can't understand.

Well, *the facts*—here they are. A few days later Wanzer had taken possession of my house, he had established himself in it as a boarder! And as a result, I continued to be the trembling servant. Do I at this late date have to tell you how these things went? Do I have to explain them to you? Do they seem strange to you, perhaps? And must I enumerate all of Ciro's sufferings?—his silent, livid angers, his bitter words to which almost any poison would have been preferable; and his sudden cries and sobs in the night, which made my hair stand on end; and the cadaverous immobility of his body in bed, frightful; and his tears, his tears, those tears that sometimes began suddenly trickling down from his eyes which remained open and pure, which did not become inflamed or red . . . Ah, my dear sir, one had to see that child weep to know *how the soul weeps.*

We deserved heaven. Oh Jesus, Jesus, haven't we deserved Your Heaven?

* * *

Thank you, thank you. I can continue. Let me go on at once, otherwise I'll never get to the end.

We're getting closer—you understand—we're getting closer; we're already there. What is the date today? The twenty-seventh of July. Well, it was the ninth of July, this month! It seems a century ago; it seems yesterday.

I was in the back room of a grocer's, sitting at a desk working on the accounts, worn out from weariness and the heat, eaten up by flies, nauseated by the smell of the spices. It was most likely about three in the afternoon. I would often interrupt my work to think of Ciro, who at that time was feeling more unwell than usual. I was brooding in my heart over his constitution consumed by suffering, thin and pale as a candle.

Take note, sir, of one thing. From a tiny window—set in the wall to which my back was turned, and therefore above my head—slanted down *a beam of sunlight.*

And notice, my dear sir, these other things. A delivery boy, young and fat, was sleeping stretched out on the sacks, inert; and the flies were buzzing above him, countless flies as though around a carcass. The boss, the grocer, entered and went towards a corner where there was a basin. His nose was bleeding and, as he walked stooped over in order not stain his shirt, blood dripped on the floor.

Then followed a number of minutes of a silence so deep that it seemed a suspension of life. Not a customer entered; not a carriage passed by; the delivery boy wasn't snoring any more.

Suddenly I heard Ciro's voice: "Is Papa here?"

I saw him appear before me—in that squalid place, among those sacks, kegs, piles of soap, while he was so delicate, almost diaphanous, looking like a pure spirit!—I saw him appear before me like an hallucination. His forehead was drenched with sweat, his lips were trembling; but he seemed animated by an almost savage energy.

"What are you doing here?" I asked. "At this hour? What is the matter?"

"Come, Papa, come."

"But what's happened?"

"Come, come with me."

His voice was hoarse but determined.

I put aside the work I had been doing, saying: "I'll be back soon."

And I went out with him, terribly upset, my legs unsteady.

We were on Via del Tritone. We turned up the street in the direction of Piazza Barberini which was a lake of white fire and looked deserted. I don't know if it was really deserted, for all I could see was the fire. Ciro clutched my hand.

"Well, won't you tell me? What's happened?" I asked for the third time, still fearful of what he was going to say.

"Come, come with me. Wanzer has beaten her . . . beaten her."

His fury made his voice choke in his throat.

He seemed unable to say anything more. He quickened his pace, dragging me along.

"I saw it," he went on. "From my room I heard them shouting; I heard what they were saying . . . Wanzer cursed her, called her every name you can think of . . . Yes, all the names . . . Do you hear? And I saw him when he jumped on her, his hands flying, yelling . . . 'Take this! And take this!' And he called her all the names . . . you know them . . ."

That voicc was unrecognizable: raucous, shrill, sibilant, broken by the suffocation of so furious a hatred that I thought with terror: "Here, now he's going to fall; he's going to fall right here and lie stricken on the sidewalk."

But he didn't fall; he continued walking quickly, dragging me along beneath that ferocious sun.

"Do you think I hid? Do you think I just stood there and was afraid? No, no, I wasn't afraid. I went up to him; I began yelling at him; I grabbed him by the legs, I bit his hand . . .

that's all I could do . . . He knocked me down on the floor; then he jumped on Mama again, grabbed hold of her hair . . . Oh, what a coward, what a coward!"

He broke off, choked.

"What a coward! He pulled her by the hair; pulled her to the window . . . He wanted to throw her out . . . But then he let her go . . . "I'm leaving, if I don't, I'll kill you.' That's what he said. And he left; ran out of the house . . . Oh, if I only had a knife!"

He broke off again, gasping. We were on street past San Basilio, deserted. Afraid that I would fall, that I would see him fall, I begged him to stop: "Stop for a while, Ciro! Let's rest here in the shade for a little. You can't go on like this."

"No, we've got to get there quick, we've got to get there in time . . . Suppose Wanzer comes back to the house to kill her? . . . Mama was afraid, she was afraid he'd come back and kill her. I heard her tell Maria to get the suitcase, and put her clothes in it, so she could leave Rome right away . . . go to Tivoli, I think . . . to stay with Aunt Amalia . . . We've got to get there in time. Would you let her go? Would you?"

He stopped, only to look straight in my face and to hear my answer. I stammered: "No . . . no . . ."

"And will you let *him* come back in the house? Won't you say anything to him? Won't you do anything to him?"

I didn't answer. And he didn't realize I was dying of pain, of shame. He didn't see it; for, after an interval of silence, he suddenly yelled in a different tone from before, his voice shaking with deep emotion: "Papa, Papa, you aren't afraid, are you? You aren't afraid of *him*, are you?"

I stammered: "No . . . no . . ."

And we continued walking toward the house in the hot sun, over the plots of wasteland around Villa Ludovisio, through chopped down trees, piles of bricks, deep lime pits, which dazzled and attracted me. —Better, better to die burnt alive in one of those lime pits, I thought, than to confront the unknown event. —But Ciro had grabbed me by the hand again and was pulling me along blindly toward my destiny.

We got there; we went up the stairs.

"Have you got the key?" Ciro asked me.

I had it. I opened the door. Ciro went in first; he called: "Mama, Mama."

No answer. The house was empty, full of light and a suspicious silence.

"She's left already?" Ciro said. "*What will you do?*"

He went into a room. He said: "Here's where it happened."

An overturned chair still lay there. On the floor I saw a broken hairpin and a red bow. Ciro, who was looking at the same spot, stooped down and picked up some very long hairs and showed them to me.

"You see?"

His fingers and his lips trembled; but his energy was exhausted. His strength was gone. I saw him sway, then he fainted in my arms. I called to him: "Ciro, Ciro, my boy!"

He did not stir. I don't know how I managed to surmount the faintness that I felt too. One thought flashed in my head: "What if Wanzer comes in now?" I don't know how I succeeded in lifting the poor creature, to carry him all the way to his bed.

He came to. I said to him: "You have got to rest. Do you want me to undress you? You have a fever. I'll get the doctor. Now I'll undress you slowly. All right?"

I said these words, I performed these acts, as if nothing else was to happen, as if the ordinary things in life, the care of my son, were to occupy me for the rest of that day. But I felt, I knew, I was sure that it wouldn't be that way, that it couldn't be that way. But a single thought was actually digging into my brain, the anxiety of a single expectation was twisting my guts. The horror, already accumulated in my very depths, was now spreading throughout my being, was making my hair bristle.

I repeated: "Let me undress you and put you to bed."

Ciro said: "No; I want to keep my clothes on."

His new voice, his new words, also grave, did not interrupt within me the incessant repetition of that simple and terrible question of his: "*What will you do?*"

"What will you do? What will you do?"

I could conceive of nothing at all. It was impossible for me to settle on a course of action, imagine a resolution of the situation, reflect on an attack, a defense. Time passed, and nothing happened. —I should have gone to get the doctor for Ciro. But would Ciro let me go out? If he agreed, he would be left all alone. I might meet Wanzer on the stairway. *And then?* Or Wanzer might return during my absence. *And then?*

In accordance with Ciro's demands, I must not let him come back into the house, I must tell him something, do something. Well, I could have locked the door from the inside with the bolt. Not being able to open the door with his key, Wanzer would have pulled on the bell-rope, would have knocked, made a racket, furiously. *And then?*

We waited.

Ciro was lying in bed on his back; I was sitting alongside him and holding one of his hands, pressing my forefinger on his pulse. The beats were getting faster, much, much faster.

We didn't talk; we thought we were listening to all the noises and we weren't listening to anything but the sound of our blood. In the window's opening the blue sky foundered; the swallows swooped past, as if about to enter; the curtains swelled as though a gust of wind had filled them, on the tile floor the sun traced the window's rectangle exactly, and the shadows of the swallows played across it. For me all these things had ceased to be real, they were only an appearance; they were no longer life, but rather simulated life. Even my anguish was imaginary. —How much time went by?

Ciro said to me: "I'm very thirsty. Get me some water."

I got up to get him a drink. But the bottle on the table was empty. I took it and said: "I'm going into the kitchen to fill it."

I left the room, went to the kitchen, placed the bottle under the faucet.

The kitchen was next to the entrance hall. Quite distinctly I heard the sound of a key being turned in the lock. I was petrified *by the absolute impossibility of moving.* But I heard the door open, I recognized Wanzer's step.

He called out: "Ginevra!"

Silence. He took a few more steps. Again he called: "Ginevra!"

Silence. More steps. Obviously he was now looking through the rooms for her. *The absolute impossibility of moving.*

Suddenly I heard my son cry out, a savage scream, which instantly dissolved my rigidity. My eyes ran to a long knife gleaming on the bread-box; and, at the same moment, my right hand darted out to grasp it and a prodigious strength filled my arm; and I felt myself swept to my son's doorway, like a whirlwind; and I saw my son clinging with feline fury to Wanzer's huge body, and I saw that man's hands on my son . . .

Two, three, four times I drove the knife into his back, right up to the handle.

Ah sir, please, please, don't leave me, don't leave me alone! Before evening, I shall die; I promise you that I shall die. Then you can go, close my eyes and go. No, I'm not asking even for this; I, I myself, before I breathe my last, will close them.

Do you see my hand. It touched those lids; and it turned yellow . . . But I wanted to lower them, because every now and then Ciro would stiffen in his bed and cry: "Papa, Papa, he's looking at me."

But how could he look at him if he was covered up? Can the dead look through sheets, perhaps?

And the left eyelid wouldn't close, it was cold, cold . . .

* * *

All the blood! Can a man contain a sea of blood? One can barely see the veins, they are so fine one can barely see them. And yet . . . I didn't know where to put my feet; my shoes were soaked through like two sponges—it's strange, eh?—like two sponges.

One person, and so much blood; and the other, not even a drop: a lily . . . like a lily . . .

Oh, my God, a lily! So there are still white things in this world?

All the lilies, so many, so many!

But you see, you see, sir, what I feel? What good things I am still able to feel?

Yes, before evening, before evening.

A swallow flew in . . .

Let it come in . . . that swallow . . .

Rome, January 1892

LEDA WITHOUT SWAN

Leda Without Swan

I HEARD all this yesterday just before nightfall on the flat pontoon which the low receding tide was little by little leaving behind it, while all around we heard the rustle of the hidden life of the sands and from time to time the horned owl complaining to the brush along the shore, luxuriant with weeds and marine rushes. I heard it from Desiderio Moriar, most exquisite artist, innocent of works and fame, who knows as do I that in living even more than in reading nothing is as precious as attentiveness.

But his voice resembles one of those turbid days in March, all silver flashes, sudden gusts of wind, crashes of rain and hail, and pauses pregnant with melodiousness, when things not yet born seem even more powerful than those which have already come into life. And this voice flows from a mouth avid and dissatisfied like that of a greedy child who, clutching a crimped counterfeit coin, lingers before the window of a pastry shop. And at certain words his dark glance darts between the flickering lashes with a disquietude that seems to set fire to a drop of blood in the corner of the lid close to the nose, like that living touch of cinnabar one sees in certain Mannerist portraits. Sometimes, though, his eyes seem to retract their gaze deep inside themselves and to float on some remote dream-waters like two smooth hazelnut shells.

Nor is he, when seen fullface, the same man he reveals in profile. To an adventurous sensuality, intolerant of constraint but bent on discriminating despite desire's suddenness, he seems to oppose when turning to face you the abnegated will of one who unfailingly discovers the same dreadful emptiness behind both the most facile and the most difficult of life's caprices. His beautiful hands, now fluttering like those of a great violinist between bow and fingerboard, now boneless and soft like those of a famous couturier preparing to fit a *grande dame* for a dress, with a brisk gesture drew again and again a crepitating sound from their fingers as if to test the pitch of the concealed skeleton. Then certain rapid, sensitive quivers passed over his cheek bones, while his temples and chin reminded me of the extremely tender skin of a thoroughbred horse and, at times, even of a rabbit's comical, endearing nose.

What an admirable living instrument with which to assess by a gesture, an inflection, a pause, a look, the values of visible and invisible things!

Yesterday evening, prompted by the boyishness and magical that are mingled in him, he said: "Isn't the night omnipresent and perpetual? If I clench my fist under the full sun of noon, why, look, I create night in the hollow of my palm." And so, as he told the story, he constantly made me feel that miraculous darkness on which shapes and events are traced, those divine shadows that fill the fold of a skirt or the fissure in a heart.

I despair of reproducing even approximately his lively art, and so in recounting some of his stories I try to imagine that the incidents happened to me personally, that I am the protagonist.

I was going through one of those days of tedium which, they say, were invented by Nero's tutor for ambiguous temperaments, days when life's active goodness withdraws from the circles of the soul like water from the pond of a fulling press or mill, leaving behind the drained ditches cluttered with debris and with filth clinging to the inert mechanism.

One seems to scent an odor of fermenting slime in one's every thought. One's body is itself unsheathed, as it were, a broken stump: it tries to hold itself upright, to lean against something, to find respite in some enduring attitude, but it resembles those battered old crucified Christs stripped of the cross that in antique shops seem nailed to new torments, no matter where they stand and no matter what contraption they are put up against.

The season also contributed to all that misery, for on the barrens it rained and didn't rain. A sieve-like cloud sprinkled a stretch of sand with fat, sparse drops that were almost lukewarm and seemed to dribble from a ladle. But beyond the moist band you could make out bone-dry sand and farther on another sprinkled patch and farther yet another strip of dryness, so that the earth too seemed to be unwell, like those pregnant women whose skin feels hot and cold in spots while within at an indefinable depth something shapeless is startled.

I was standing at the gate of the garden, just about to part from one of those sweet tiresome creatures who, after encountering Dante's youthful vision, insist on carrying about on their sleeves, endlessly, their disappointed love—"wrapped lightly in a blood-red cloth"—for they cannot resolve to bury it and would have us feast on their dear heart as if it were pure spirit, and yet it is not consumed. *Vide cor meum.*

The sound of that well-known lamentation reached me like the drone left by quinine in the ear of a malaria patient after an attack, and I stood there neither in nor out, because the stone slab of the threshold lay between us strewn with yellow pollen. And I saw that wild dust cling to the fresh paint of the new gate, fill the interstices, envelop on a cross-bar of that not wholly dead pinewood a bubble of resin which swelled like a blister rising on the palm of a hand before turning into a callus.

A small terracotta crock hanging from a stripped tree had suddenl received so much resin at the first upsurge of the sap that it had overflowed with long filaments of an almost sugar-like aspect; and seeing it I had the urge to offer her a mouthful of it, so as to besmear her vexatious tongue and glue the inopportune words to her palate. Here and there, beneath the limpness of a milky, irresolute cloud, the birds sang off-key like listless choirboys. And all of life had for me the quality of one of those allegories that long ago my rhetoric teacher used to propose to us at the long examination bench. And I had done such a shabby job of writing it that, by way of punishment, I was condemned to carry the sheet attached to my back by two pins.

Then, as I was heading towards the Ville d'Hiver along the paths through the woods, I thought with envy of the few shepherds left on the barrens—the last descendants of those extraordinary old men who, on their tall stilts, used to cross the ponds and marshes of that sandy wasteland and could, with their long strides, go as fast as a galloping horse in the Pyrenees.

I had met one of them in the brush a few days before. The legendary poles reduced in length to two modest stumps, his faded green umbrella and brownish satchel slung over his shoulder, his mushroom-shaped beret pulled well down over his ears, he spent the entire day absolutely immobile, leaning on his cane, busy with his knitting needles, as untouched by worries as his dog, as indifferent to the flight of time as an hour-glass, his tongue stored in the silence of his saliva like a sardine preserved in the oil of its tin.

Far from loved or no longer loved eyes, the light seems to be different. To enter our room, the sky waits for all the lights to be extinguished.

In between the freshly scarred pine trees (from a distance their trunks looked as though they had nailed to them those reddish goat-hides that usually hang in front of butcher shops) I made out the varicolored town of Phthisis smoldering beneath a clammy, oven-like warmth, just as repulsive as the air one inhales in certain Turkish baths transported to the West, where fat men sweat with zest and anguish, reading the newspaper of their persuasion spread out over their dripping bellies.

The villas seemed gracefully built of papier-mâché and perforated tinfoil by a mediocre, moderately republican architect with a goatee on his chin and a flourish in his tie, who has tried to blend together in his hospitable art the spirit of the Italian Riviera and that of the Lake of Lucerne, both equally soothing.

Inscribed in Art Nouveau letters each façade dutifully bore its name gleaned from mythology, botany, civic glories, or sentimental idiocy. Each interior undoubtedly contained its vase with artificial flowers covered by a glass bell, its large, warty conch, its statuette of Joan of Arc in black plumbago armor, and its cuckoo clock to summon happiness or death.

Mounds of shawls and blankets, stirred from time to time by a fit of coughing, rested on long wicker chairs behind crystal-clear windowpanes which, like the tanks of an aquarium, seemed to enclose a far-off world. Along the white roadway an interminable file of caterpillars descending from God knows where moved toward eternity with a slight and eerie contraction of its myriads of rings. Their fuzzy nests at the tips of numerous branches presented the image of a hurt hand swathed in shredded cloth. A piano up there which had inherited from a distant relation the soul of a barrel organ, played one of those pieces that carry a number printed above each note to guide each finger to the proper key; and an unknown romantic ancestor awakening somewhere inside me seemed anxious to know whether the sheet was adorned by a black gondola, a weeping willow, or an Ossianic harp, and whether the title of the song was "The Sigh of an Exile" or "The Last Day of Mary Stuart."

An atrocious and infantile thought flashed through my mind: "If I let out a scream, all the patients will rush to their windows and stay there showing me their faces, which are all the same and pocked full of holes like the cork floats dangling from a seine net hung out to dry after the day's fishing."

In the frame of a curtainless window, beyond the glass, flitted something that looked like a pale gesture shooing away a fly or beckoning to me. Surely nothing but a thin sheet of glass separated me from death—and that unknown hand was about to smash it.

I remembered how a cousin of mine at Nice had once had the good fortune of being splendidly loved for an entire afternoon by a canoness from Krakow who then expired that same night.

But my unique and doomed woman's door was closed; and in the small garden a maid servant wearing a bonnet and wooden clogs was washing a chestnut poodle whose color seemed to melt under the lather as if it were made of chocolate, while the dirty water crept down the narrow garden path and into the street towards me, like a crippled hand groping along the ground, growing larger and broader as it searched for something I had lost.

I could not imagine what.

I expected someone behind me to call out eagerly: "Turn around, Sir, look, you've dropped this" whatever it was. But nobody breathed a word; nor did that dripping hand rise from the ground to return to me whatever I had lost; it went on feeling its way until it reached the gutter, breaking up a seminar of caterpillars assembled at a sort of hemp stalk that looked at once like the sloughed-off skin of a snake and the tiny cells of an emptied, dried-out honeycomb.

Meanwhile a small cart shaped like a basket was moving

toward me on its three wheels, pushed by a mustachioed, gray-haired man who performed that office with the dignity peculiar to survivors of the nation's glorious battlefields and to professional rescuers assigned to drownings and conflagrations. Inside the basket lay an old woman who despite her moribund appearance retained some mysterious gleam of fury in a pair of eyes at war with the universe, eyes which bulged at the top of two wizened pouches, recalling the ferocity of the octopus attached to his melancholy sack, and it wasn't quite clear by what accident the eight tentacles stippled with suction cups were missing. At a few paces from me the cart came to a halt so abruptly that I was startled.

A line of grubs was crossing the street, and moved by some obscure impulse of compassion, revulsion or superstition, the worthy trundler was trying to find an ingenious way to avoid the holocaust. When, from behind, he pressed down on the rim of the basket to raise the front wheel, on feeling herself being bounced up and down in that manner the old woman rallied all her energies to spew the venom of her two feelerless polyps at the bumbling fellow. The wheel dropped and cut into the hairy, soft entrail. The two rear wheels and the two shoes followed, completing the resection.

I turned away in disgust and saw a boy laughing behind a fence. He had porcine eyes smothered in a face so huge and lustrous that it seemed to me on the verge of bursting open, as though, through a hole at the nape of the neck, someone were continually stuffing it with lard and ground meat.

Is not the maggot-ridden carcass of a mongrel dog upon a pile of garbage an almost enjoyable sight when compared to certain apparitions of human ugliness dressed up in clothes?

A strong gust of wind swept over my head, one of those sudden breaths that seem to come from the miraculous frontier of another life which can be perceived only at times through certain flashes of remembrance or incandescent flickers of anxiety, when the spirit, perhaps remembering, perhaps presaging, struggles in vain to escape from the habits, manias, lies, grimaces, fears—the innumerable contagions that make up our lives.

Pollen seemed to steam from the shaken branches and gild the lacerated cloud which suddenly allowed me a glimpse of the most angelic countenance among all those faces of the air, framed between two edges that looked like linen bands dusted with that sylvan gold.

And even before I heard the faltering note of a novice nightingale I felt that at the passing of that breath the pine tree, like a wind instrument, swelled with music from foot to crown.

And that gracile note sufficed to change everything.

So I hastened to the town, thinking that music was perhaps about to interpret the enigma of all those images introduced in me by an obscure, cruel sense superadded to my normal vision.

A young musician from the *Schola Cantorum,* trained to emulate the grace and power of the ancient Italian harpsichord players, had written to me with proud courtesy that at his concert that day he would play only for me.

An excellent precaution, I might add, for I realized upon entering the Casino that the greater part of the local swine—*more biblico*—were not attracted by pearls.

The audience was small, scattered through the vast hall which was entirely and lavishly adorned with murals in that Turkesque style which has the uncommon quality of inflaming the imagination of the lower ranks of the soldiery in brothel parlors. The only thing lacking was the scent of those famous aromatic tablets called "pastilles of the seraglio." The local Euterpe, a bony, brusque female, assigned to guide each of the rare auditors to his seat, thrust her hand from time to time into the pocket of her smock, arousing the hope that she might be reaching for one of those lozenges and would burn it in the small polished bowl meant for tips, but each time her gesture was followed by disappointment.

A fresh downpour splashed against the skylight; after which lo and behold, the agile spirit of the water seemed to suffuse the squalid gloom with the mysterious earthly fragrance of joy.

The walls opened up; the huge carcass of iron, wood, stucco and varnish was swept away by a single gust of wind, almost as though it were a little heap of pine needles on a beach washed by the Atlantic.

Clear, swift springs burst forth from all sides, as in the quiet remote corner of a park where, with a mysterious smile, the host leads his unsuspecting guests and, unseen, turns the key hidden inside a cupid's quiver to start the fountain's tricks and deceits.

From the shorn grass, from among the symmetrical shrubs, the trimmed box-hedges, from the Naiads' breasts, the Tritons' shells, the dolphins' backs, the cheeks of the bronze frogs squatting beside the benches or at the grottoes' thresholds, from the mouldings of the balustrades along the terraces and ramps, from the domes of the small rotundas and the arches of the covered walks, from every side the jets spurt, leap, whip out, pursue, smite, formidable as swords, as rapiers, as pikes in an ambush.

Ladies and courtiers shriek, laugh, run, shy away, recoil.

But in every shelter, every hiding-place lurks the cool insidious pursuer; here a diagonal dart finds the nape of a neck, an ear, the hollow between the shoulder blades; there a low spout plays beneath a hobbleskirt like the clapper inside a muted bell; here a rude burst of water snatches at a wig, tousles it, undoes it, turns it into a curlicue of its own foam.

Fleeing Amaryllis trips on a rosebush. Falling full length, she scatters the petals and pricks herself. The mischievous spurts overwhelm her like a swarm of transparent gnomes and ravish her defenseless charms. A plume, a veil, a ribbon, a bow, a silken beauty mark, a tortoise shell comb, a tiny slipper of golden cloth, each airy item dances upon a tip of nimble spray like a punctured, emptied egg shell; and also a green leaf, a white petal, a russet thorn.

"Help! Help!'

The gallant Palamedes does not tarry, or turn around, or hear; he runs off as fast as he can accompanied by a great tinkling of pendants and trinkets, his tassels askew, his stockings glued to his illustrious shanks, clutching the limp sheath of his dirk.

They all flee shrieking, panting, hugging the hornbeam espaliers, heading toward the pink marble stairs, looking like a mixed flock of goslings and swans chased from their lake by sudden fright.

The lovely fugitives now think they're safe and are shaking off the drops when the little marble sphinxes—flesh-colored, well kempt and prim like young ladies in waiting poised on their paws with harmless claws—from their unenigmatic lips begin to spew broad entwining fans of water along the entire length of the stairway.

The delightful rout resumes; and the stairway seems to grow like Jacob's ladder into the mild eastern sky where shuttling swallows weave melancholy's violet veil.

And lo! suddenly the first pearl necklace snaps, the grains come spilling off the string, flow tumbling down along the smooth roseate steps which the water descends in miniscule cascades.

There snaps the second necklace—of seven strands?—then the third—of twenty-one?—and another, and another yet, of strands beyond number.

The pearls multiply, imitate a mild hail, scatter in all directions, resplend, resound, rebound, mingle with the rivulets—now they look like precious bubbles of the water, now like drops scattered by drenched, pouring beauty.

And when the sphinxes cease puffing, the peacocks perched

in the hornbeam rise with a shrill cry, flock upon the path as if attracted by unexpected feed; they pursue the grains, trailing their folded ceremonial fans over the moist slabs of marble.

And suddenly arrives—no one knows from where—a supple pack of Angora cats as white as cream and as gray as smoke, with red eyes, with blue eyes.

And suddenly arrives—no one knows from where—a troop of Barbary Apes as black and sparkling as jet, with tiny, pale, wrinkled hands, a golden bell tied to their tails.

And the cats and the monkeys rush after the resonant pearls, stop them, seize them, fling them back and forth, laughing, gamboling, brawling, vying with turns and twists and gestures of always fresh and effortless grace.

And up there the necklaces keep on breaking, spilling, rippling, almost as though some miracle were transforming the carnal laughter of Youth into those scattering gems, fugitive and irretrievable. (And down there, what of Amaryllis? Has she swooned in the rosebush? Or surrendered her soul?)

He was playing Domenico Scarlatti's sonatas.

The young musician's shaven, angular face was dotted with any number of bristly warts *à la* Franz Liszt. He wore a pair of professorial gold-framed spectacles on his almost Grecian nose, flaunted Jacopo Peri's ancient shaggy fringe of hair and a double-loop cravat over one of those long velvet vests we see on elegant gentlemen in Gavarni's lithographs. But his fingers' prodigious artistry and his intuitions proved him to be a true "maestro of the harpsichord," worthy of the eighteenth century and the divine Neapolitan.

That music's vigor, audacity, elegance, gaiety, directness, and fickleness miraculously renewed and refreshed the sense of life in me. Each sonata with its single theme, developed by a two-part movement, seemed each time to draw the brief line of an ever-varying perfection and to embellish the lively strength of its most limpid elements with unexpected modulations.

During an intermission, while my lids were still lowered over one of my enchanted fantasies, I was reached amid a tenuous rustle by a woman's perfume which was like the scent loosened from a shaken rosebush; so that at first I thought I was being perturbed by my own dream. Was it Amaryllis?

However, on turning, I saw a young woman about to sit down on the chair next to mine; and the first thing I noticed was the quality of her eyes which did not seem to help her find her way. Instantly the world created inside me by that music crumbled and dispersed as if one of those crystal globes that represent the terraqueous globe and are poised on the palm of an English angel of creation had slipped from my hand. The water-spurts stopped their fencing match, the necklaces no longer broke and scattered. My soul, magically delivered from itself, leaped back over the intervening centuries.

Our life is a work of magic which eludes the reflected light of reason and the farther on it moves, the richer it becomes, realizing itself in mystery and often in conflict with the order of perceptible laws. Nor, when we are sleeping and dreaming, are we really asleep but rather the Magician rests and ceases to help our faculties grasp the virtue in things with his unpredictable and unfailing skill. Left for a short while to ourselves, we could perhaps spy on him, find out what he is like as well as detect our secret, if he did not arrest some mechanism in us—like some factory worker who jams a nail or some little wedge into his machine so that it cannot be used. But man is always awake, since the world's beginning; and in truth no Macbeth can murder the sleep that never comes to him.

Human sleep is an error, as are time and space.

Our bed is nothing but the symbol of an incomprehensible or misunderstood rite, like Adonis' ancient catafalque or the bier of Jesus erected in the church's nave before Easter. It is not man but the waxen image of a god that lies down in it.

The woman's eyes were of the kind that leave us perplexed and desperate, as when confronted by a sheer granite wall without an opening or foothold. The edges of her eyelids were hard and clean, holding her eyeballs firmly gripped as bezels hold precious stones, and they made me think of the eyes of a god or athlete cast in bronze, eyes made of bluish silver or a vitreous paste, poured or set into the metal sockets to become immortal and perpetually demand offerings or praise, while giving nothing in return.

But the color of the skin on her naked face was by contrast so delicate that it moved me as hitherto I had only been by the first small single blossom budding from the bare branch of a peach tree. It was a pallor lit up either by some lofty quality of the blood or by the powerful molding of the features, for I had never before seen the planes of a living countenance treated with such a plastic magnificence that, in the narrow confines of a face, it could remind me of the stately sweep of the earth in noble landscapes, the inimitable rhythm of valleys and hills in the frailest, most silent season.

I covered my eyes with my hand and, my head lowered, I listened for several moments to her breathing beyond the music, or perhaps in the depths of that music which no longer seemed to flow over the keyboard but rather to even out and grow quiet like those pools of water left behind on the beach by the tide at sunset, when my Mediterranean-fed imagination finds a cause for their sublime beauty by making believe that some of the statues lost at sea below the Cyclades have been washed ashore.

The sense of the human presence seems to me so prodigious that I wonder by what aberration or what cowardice I have chosen to live for so long among the trees and on deserted shores. But it must be said that even the sturdiest, most alert spirit shies away from uninterrupted strain, and that an extraordinary charge of attention is needed to reach beyond the opaqueness of the blunting screen of habit and to perceive the secret rhythm of a stranger's life.

I was immediately submerged by a wave of sadness, as if that creature had retraced my walk among the homes of the sick, endured the gaze of those ferocious senile eyes bulging over wizened pouches, and were bringing back to me the ashen thoughts pawed by that filthy hand groping along the ground.

With the impact of an hallucinatiion as irrefutable as reality, I was suddenly, pervasively, vaguely overcome by a sense of misery and disaster, not connected with that face and that body but rather diffused—as when you climb a sinister staircase, hesitate along a drab, dingy hallway, and then enter a dimly lit room which still contains the traces of a crime that has been committed there. I think that in the semi-darkness I would have discovered some revealing object—had I not removed the screen from my eyes and turned to look at my neighbor with an involuntary rudeness which seemed to surprise rather than offend her.

Her beauty adhered completely to my senses as if it already had its proper place in them and were simply returning to occupy it, in the way a rare jewel fits smoothly in its case, a bas-relief slips back into its original mold. My mournful insight receded, delivering me completely to my new emotion.

The line of that form obeyed the law governing great plastic works; for wherever I might imagine its inception to be, there, by a sort of fluid necessity, it was brought to completion: departing from the nape of the neck it returned to the nape of the neck; departing from the knee it returned to the knee, with a continuity and fullness uniquely its own, with a movement that was suitable to it alone, like a specific musical form, like the three-quarter time of *andante*, like the six-eight time of that *allegro* by Domenico Scarlatti.

She wore a short chinchilla coat softer than the down of an ash-gray swan, over a narrow skirt of heavy gray cloth which clung to her unchastely. Beneath her hat, made of stiff and lightly woven horsehair, turned up on one side and adorned with two feathers like two knives, skeins of a golden chestnut silk, soft and shining, were held up by neither visible comb nor hairpin but rather by their own vivid thickness.

She was completely sheathed in the exquisite style of the fashion that in those years seemed to deck women out so they could lie comfortably inside the long narrow coffin of some pharaonic princess. On her chair she took up no more space than that provided by one of those Egyptian biers of painted wood. But even through her most up-to-date elegance, from the line that flowed from the curve of her cheek down to her toes, she was, for me, drawn just as artists must imagine the ancient Leda of the Eurotas. From the waist down her beauty seemed inflected toward the mystery of "the divine Olore," as Polyphilo would have put it.

And I thought again of that Leda by Leonardo which Cassiano del Pozzo, Poussin's friend, could still see at Fontainebleau in 1625 and which I always dream of rediscovering in some improbable manner.

"Beethoven?" I asked in a low voice, surprised by the accent of the music I was hearing again after the indefinite interval of my distracted silence.

With spontaneous curiosity, the woman glanced at the programme that lay on her muff and, as if prompted by my expectant pose, she replied: "Ferdinando Turini."

She had proferred the Italian name with a childish, almost affected shyness accompanied by a blush that seemed to wipe out the power of her features like the vermilion juice with which the virgins of Apulia used to tint their sad faces before preparing to embrace Cassandra's funeral statue.

"Would you say," I asked, thankful for the pretext, my heart pounding, "would you say he was acquainted with the early Beethoven manner? I can't really make up my mind. If we could be sure that he did not know it, what original and significant value this sonata in D flat would take on for us!"

I caught the profound, innate indifference of her spirit to this kind of subtlety and problem, just as from a single testing note a singer becomes convinced of a room's faulty acoustics. Between the precise edges of her lids her eyes once more became impenetrable. Instinctively I leaned slightly towards her, over the brink of her secret, but bewildered, no longer possessed of that gift which during the first instants had revealed in her a dark mass of obscure misery.

Her perfume dispersed the force of my scrutiny: and now I gazed at her like someone gazing at some supreme object for whose sake he has made an incredibly long journey. A flood of remote life, similar to the sudden breath I had felt sweep over my head and over the pine trees, was rushing toward me to overwhelm and submerge me. I felt as though a pathetic necessity were hovering over me and that I was already disposed to that sort of contrived folly of which the enchantment which precedes passion is composed.

And indeed I considered every detail in an indefinable light that seemed already enveloped in the past, like someone who studies and then with utmost care wraps objects to be put away, objects on the verge of turning into precious souvenirs from which he will derive a certain sure intoxication when in the future he chances to hold them in his hands. So past and future converged in that complex feeling of mine, and the present was merely a kind of leaven.

Inside myself I spoke to her as if on some future day to come: "Everything is clear in my memory. You were leaning a trifle forward as if to better receive the music. You seemed not to listen with your ears, covered by your hair, but rather with your full, swollen lips, as children sometimes do when entranced by a fairy tale. You kept your right hand inside your muff. Twice you took it out and then thrust it back in with strange haste as if to prevent something from falling out of it. The glove covered your wrist but your hand was bare, slipped through the slit, and the slough of soft leather dangled from the back of your hand, preserving the shape of the living fingers. Along the thumb I noticed an indentation, like the slight bruise produced by contact with some mysterious harshness . . ."

I don't believe she was really listening to the Italian sonata. I had the impression that her musical sensibility was very slight.

Music infuses an aerial quality in the bodies of women who respond to the innocence of the melody, like the air that fills the hollow bones in the wings of flying birds. Once, I don't know why, seeing my mistress bowed by illness and quivering with the sovereign lamentation of a famous violin, I thought of those air bubbles which the hunter sees rise through the warm blood of the wounded wing where the shot has broken the shoulder. A beautiful and profound image, which returned to my mind as I considered by contrast the density of that woman's life, the cohesion of her very substance, the sort of complete animality dissimulated by the volumes of so noble an architecture.

And yet within her dwelt an anguish that at that very moment must be pounding against the hull of her rib-cage as if to shatter it. And the sorrow that rose from time to time to swell her lower lip was so evident to me that I was almost surprised not to see its wave ripple over the delicate fur like certain shudders of agony that, shaped like a fishbone, furrow the pelts of sick animals.

"Are you suffering?" I dared ask her, in a changed voice that undoubtedly touched her.

She turned to me the enigma of that face of hers, with its broad planes strongly joined as in the head of some shepherd king carved from basalt.

"Not at all," she replied; and she laughed a dry, sharp

laugh without resonance, as whores will sometimes laugh at someone standing behind them, while the mirror reflects that fixed, curt expression with which they stick a long hatpin in their hats.

Then all my fantasies again disintegrated. She began to chatter like a little Parisian prostitute, with a soft, rubbery mouth that exaggerated the shape of the words and syllables to the point of grimacing. She poked fun at that Turkesque hall, at the shaggy pianist, the insipid audience; she aired her contempt for the petty, boring life in that awful town that had grown up around the shacks and sheds of a settlement of resin gatherers; she complained bitterly at being forced to vegetate there almost the entire year round.

"But why?" I asked timidly. "Because of your health?"

She laughed again, acrimoniously.

Here and there a throat coughed in the dim light, which seemed to grow gradually colder while a new downpour crepitated on the gray glass ceiling.

"No, of course not."

She sat up in her chair, straightened her torso with an abrupt, almost involuntary movement, like the harsh spasm sometimes sent through us by an inexplicable shudder. I noticed the breadth of her shoulders and her breasts, a solid structure that corresponded to the style of her head. Through the opening of her muff I caught sight of something shiny, ivory and steel, which looked like the butt of a revolver about to slip out.

"It's for my car," she said, smiling, almost in answer to my probable surprise at seeing her armed. "After the concert, I have to drive all the way to Bordeaux."

Truly now it seemed that those lips belonged to another woman, living another life in the middle of that face, those lips with their frivolous mobility which was in such conflict with the hewn firmness of the other features and the formidable mystery of her naked glance. I thought again of certain

Sardinian dances danced with a closed and darkly ominous expression, of certain Arabian dances in which only the belly moves, moves incessantly upon a body fettered by some unknown snake-like fascination. The artificial red of her lip-rouge was fresh, applied perhaps just before entering the hall, and with a hasty hand, for it was uneven, slightly smudged at the edges and corners. Her teeth were strong, the lower ones set a trifle irregularly, resplendant like chips of some precious substance, made of an enamel so dense and pure that you thought of the carats that measure perfection, as though they were gems to examine on a jeweler's tray.

"Listen," I said, stirred by some notes in a passage in the second movement of a sonata by Domenico Paradisi, the last on the program.

I watched her from under my lowered lids.

The force of dissimulation suddenly left those lips over which an emotion of unknown gravity seemed to draw a real band of gauze, woven as tightly as the one worn by Berber women in our white and crescent-shaped Ghadames.

And yet, the cadenza having almost come to its resolution and my heart dreading its end like a farewell, I looked at her again as one looks at a supreme thing for which one has journeyed the very greatest distance.

She was so smooth that it seemed she must not be marked by a single furrow in the palm of her hand. She was truly polished by the waters of the Eurotas, since in my memory brilliantly shone the flat stones of that swanless, laconic river, amid the narrow blue shadows of oleanders and reeds. "What are you, who are you?—you who certainly harbor a cunning serpent behind your low forehead, even though your heart is heavy with tears."

As many other times before, my whole being clung to the unknown which is at the root of life, because of the shadows the body contains, the darkness that fills the secret recesses of the flesh, the mystery of viscera and precordia.

I felt sorrow and death trickle toward me like drops oozing from the walls of a deep and gloomy cave.

Desperate poetry became my very flesh.

She stood between chair and chair while the audience left the hall like some fluent pulp swept toward the door by Euterpe's broom. Every human shape seemed to be bowed, deprived of backbone, faded and limply dragging along—save for the one standing in front of me, whole, silent, throbbing with a unique sickness similar to a truth or the profoundest lie, which in her took the place of life.

The most solitary places are not in deserts or mountains, not among sterile sands or rocks, but where the soul confronts its destiny, breathing for a few seconds an air that no one even nearby can breathe.

Now, looking at me, she slightly narrowed those lids which I had been so certain were immobile, like the raised ridges of bronze surrounding the eye-socket cavity in archaic statues. A horse-trader examining a beast put up for sale never had a colder and shrewder look in his eyes. But it seemed to me that in the depth of her pupils that scrutiny had the sheen of a deadly weapon by which I would soon be wounded. She kept only one hand hidden inside her pearl-gray muff, her ungloved hand; and in it she certainly clutched the small weapon to make sure it did not fall. But the darting light in her eyes was a much greater danger. I don't know why, but I felt more fragile, more mortal, tormented by an apprehension not unlike the one we experience when a doctor palps our body to discover our weak spot. And (I report this with absolute truthfulness even though later on it may appear unusual) a spontaneous image flashed through my mind, arising perhaps from a forgotten episode in my past: the bizarre and lugubrious image of an insurance company physician, intent on palping and probing a customer's stomach, liver, lungs, heart in order to estimate his approximate life expectancy. I realized that my spirit's craft could not prevail over this creature whom the divine, as in the myth, must approach in the guise of an animal.

Under her appraising glance I was only a miserable body, worn out by excesses, torn by restlessness, continually threatened by the collapse that inevitably follows extreme tension. "Yes, no doubt," my irony urged me to reply to that scrutiny, "it would be easy to finish me off. All my vigor is concentrated at the base of my skull. A sharp little blow would be enough, or a tiny puncture no bigger than that made by the weasel in a chicken's head . . ."

Now, from which feature of her face did that murderous aura come? Why was she herself revealing to me at that moment the evil and destructiveness of her secret depths?

And yet she was not simply lying in wait for prey, there was also an indistinct cry coming from her which did not yet reach my ear but already touched my soul.

"We must go," she said, moving with sudden haste toward the squalid maze of chairs.

Now, as when she had first arrived, her eyes did not seem to help her find her way. Brushing against a chair with her legs she tipped it over, then overturned another. She kept on like a blind person, running into an uninterrupted series of obstacles. To get through meant tearing them down. It resembled certain obsessive and ridiculous dreams.

I don't really remember whether the hall had gone dark, but to me it resembled an ugly church, reverberating with echoes in the service of Darkness. And the skeletal custodian came rushing up to us with the zeal of a sexton infuriated by desecrators. The offering of a coin placated her and roused in her an inexhaustible hilarity: the lady I was accompanying having laughed her false laugh out of flattery, the custodian echoed her without restraint, picking up chairs and convincing herself and us as well that this was the most amusing prank in the world.

Outside, the rain had stopped. A cool wind, thick with resin, like the rain water that fills the crocks hanging from the pines, cleansed my face. The crest of clouds in the West was like incandescent foam.

Something silvery, almost a shimmer of mother-of-pearl flickered in the unknown woman's eyes. The first quarter moon hung in the greenish sky as if Morgan le Fay had set it there to mirror the pallor of the barrens.

"Do you have a car to drive home?" she asked with a hesitation on which my shyness failed to seize.

Did this mean that she knew my way home and me?

"I'm walking home," I replied.

She looked at me, debating within herself something I couldn't see and which nevertheless seemed to affect the horizon and charge it with an energy akin to the lightning that flashes through the sky on certain summer evenings when our entire soul is ready to spurt in sparks from the apex of our heart, like a flame assailed by the wind. Her face was distorted by a muscular tremor that, becoming unendurable for me to watch, almost transferred to the joints of my jaws like the spasm that doctors call trismus.

My awareness was the axle of a wheel spinning at tremendous speed.

"Goodbye," she then said, walking over to her automobile with the short, jerky steps imposed by the hobble skirt.

What pathetic irony there was in the contrast of that dark will impeded by those stylish fetters!

"Shall we meet again?"

The hand holding the weapon still remained hidden inside the soft fur.

"Who knows?"

Amid the roar of the engine, beyond the glass in the door I glimpsed a gesture of the other, gloved hand, a white gesture similar to the one I had seen behind the curtainless window in the town of the sick and dying. A second later, on the road, between the two grooves cut by the tires, remained only the reflection of the dazzling cloud caught in the liquid slush.

The unknown woman had disappeared. Forever.

Certainly, for me, a hearse could not have taken her into a deeper mystery, a gloomier annihilation. Did not her absence and the night have the same countenance? I had to summon up her face from a darkness as impenetrable as that of a grave.

I walked back the same way, passing again through the Ville d'Hiver; but more than of my own direction I was aware of the distance traveled by that destiny made of flesh along the rectilinear road which the young moon was beginning to mark with shadows of a tenderness excruciating to a desperate heart.

It was already the hour when household lamps appear. And each time another lit up, my melancholy overflowed as if to feed them.

I could detect no expression in any of those houses: they no longer seemed to contain any life other than that concentrated within the luminous circle where the shadows flocked to imbibe light as at the quiet edge of a fountain. Beyond that circle everything was shrouded in a human mist as if, out there, the slight, obstinate fever that begins to smolder in the diseased colony after the setting of the sun were sending off its fumes.

The twilight was still bright enough for me to distinguish a starry cobweb spun between the bars of a garden gate or, among some blades of grass, one of those small downy spheres whose name I've never known, lighter than the first fluff of a cocoon, destined to fly away and vanish, driven beyond the borders of the world by the breath of a puff-cheeked arrogant boy.

A poplar quivered, solitary, clothed in iridescent silver, at the corner of a garden; and through the rippling rustle I heard: "Look, look—there she is."

Suddenly the one he had announced with such trepidation

appeared. But much whiter, and fresh, all nuptial jubilation, a modest bride, arrayed in her own virginity: the blossoming of an apple tree.

Every appearance was an apparition to the fervor of my senses; but each one was accompanied by a stabbing, blinding pain which seemed to me almost physical, similar to the one I experienced in the past from avidly inhaling marine air with a chest where three broken ribs were not yet healed.

I suffered the urgency of a force over which I had no control; and of which I did not really know whether I contained it or was contained by it.

That cinereous taste in my mouth as I descended to the unexpected encounter now returned to me commingled with a peculiar blood-like sweetness, against which a revulsion rose in me as bitter as nausea, and my thoughts had a hideous resemblance to those leeches that as a child I had seen placed in a dish full of ashes to make them vomit the blood they'd sucked.

When at last, having left behind the domain of illness and agony, I found myself in the wild wood and felt the invisible threads woven from branch to branch brush softly against my face, my neck, I understood that these were the caresses of spring and that perhaps until now I had been obscurely suffering the pangs of the new season.

A drop fell on my hand, another on my lashes; a brittle pine cone crackled under my heel; something flaccid hopped across the path, a toad perhaps; the scops owl played its oboe with a single note; the nightingale in the shadow picked up that note of dark brown velvet and transmuted it into limpid, voluble, crystal warbling. The entire wood was suddenly filled with lament and song, it dripped with rain, was drenched in resin, pungent as a dish of mixed herbs, ineffable as the sentiment of puberty.

But within that vast breath my anxiousness searched only for the memory of that perfume "similar to the scent that wafts from a shaken bush," which had come to me from the fettered woman. The eternal anxiety for adventure seized me again and agitated me again with mad violence. What further novelty of possession could I hope for? What other communion could I expect? What other disillusionment could I reap? Enraged regret bit and clawed me for not having been able or wanted, with an audacious initiative, to prevail over the unknown woman's momentary perplexity, when double sharpness of dilemma had shone in her fixed eyes. I was filled with contempt for myself as if I had let a magnificent prey slip away out of slackness or foolishness. I forgot how, amid that maze of chairs, her scrutinizing gaze had filled me with apprehension.

The ferment of the wood communicated to me an illusory energy, from which were born senseless resolutions. I tried to orient myself towards the place of the distant race, towards the highway. Would I have the time to get there, so as to be there waiting when she passed upon her return in the evening or night? It seemed to me that across the barrens a remote folly was calling out to the folly in me. I quickened my pace. Twice I lost the path and found it again, hastening through the thicket, broom and prickly bushes, my heart pounding like a bandit lying in ambush.

In my house too the lamps were lit. Having occupied the sky again, low-lying clouds now grazed the roof, in flight towards the Orient. When I entered, the ground-floor rooms were full of that indistinct fright which seems to fill deserted rooms until a familiar presence dispells it, for when man gets up and leaves it seems that a ghost takes his place and sits down where he was sitting just before. The tide was rising; and something like a female multitude clamored threatfully against the moon, resounding with a hollow sound out on the balcony.

"Did anyone come?" I asked the servant.

"The signora," he answered.

Although I could have no doubt to whom he was referring, in my heart I felt a thud as the other woman's image presented itself there.

"She looked very upset," he went on. "She waited here until six o'clock. She begs you to go to her immediately after supper."

There are hours of the solitary life in which the body's sensitivity seems to dilate all the way to the walls of the house, just as, at times, when lifting an arm we feel our heart throb all the way to our finger tips, and beyond.

The entire house seemed to be getting ready to receive something unknown. A silent event might enter through any door. The attention of the walls was turned wholly towards the night. No room retained its feeling of privacy, but harkened to what was about to happen outside and ceased to keep the warmth and to conciliate the thoughts of the objects gathered and arranged in it.

I looked among my prints for some of the known Ledas. The first I came upon was Ammannati's, which is at the Bargello. A very remote Florentine remembrance arose in me; I found it in the secret book of my memory, under the date of the twenty-second of September 1899.

I read, with a confused emotion which I did not dare examine for fear of dissolving it: "Yesterday, incredible to say, some attendants at the Bargello, wanting to move the Leda, dropped it; and the marble statue broke into seven pieces. Today the fragments have been taken to the stone workshop to be restored. I went today to see that dismembered voluptuousness. The parts that expressed pleasure most intensely are intact. The head is cracked, like mine . . . From the workshop I then went on to the Museum, to see the void left by the shattered group. My imagination has filled it with a more arduous beauty. Now, as I was standing absorbed in this fantasy, suddenly all those silent and abandoned bells that clutter the loggia—gagged mouths—began to toll in my head . . ."

The next page seemed to have been written in a slight delirium, nor did I know any longer because of what love, what absence: "It seems to me that, lifting my head, I could seize something of you in the space and pull you in through the distance, as a child pulls the string of a kite which the wind threatens to carry away beyond the clouds. The space lights up, and you open your mouth to drink in the coolness of the speed. You laugh. I hear your laugh; I touch it as one touches a necklace, grain by grain. One could weep . . ."

Never before had the magical sense of life become so profound in me. Just as the music of a forgotten score relives intact and again exerts its vigor, as if it were created that very moment when the musician touches the strings, so that rhythm of the past goes in time with the breath in my mouth. Some of the words appeared to me like those scrawled on a mirror by the little finger of a baby sister, in a distant past, which became visible only when the glass was misted over by a breath. At last I read: "There is an old burial stone in England that shows Lady Beauchamp's head resting not on a pillow or on her faithful greyhound, according to tradition, but on the back of a swan which seemed to be floating around Arthur's island. I am sure that if I could secretly return to the workshop tonight, this is how I would see the dead Leda . . ."

I closed my eyes; and on the face of the fettered woman, along the edge of her upper lip I searched for the tiny spot which, free from rouge, had looked slightly bruised during her nervous tremor, while the delicacy of her nose had seemed to grow thin and take on, around the nostrils, the smoke gray hue that usually accompanies a fainting spell.

My man came to tell me that the lantern was ready. I carried it to find my way between the puddles along the sandy path leading to the garden of my mistress.

The barrens were dark beneath the cloudy sky; but the air was mild, as in our nocturnal Maremma when the wind blows from the east or the south and amid long pauses you hear a quacking of mallards in the tamarisks, a chittering of foxes along the swamps tender with young green reeds, a crumbling of stones under the feet of boars making their way over the low stone walls, the lamentation that rises from the depths of the centuries.

Here I heard the faint cries of the sea birds beyond the dunes, similar sometimes to a sad whimpering, and the voice of the regretful, plaintive ocean, and the note of the owl which each time touched the most aching part of my heart as if it knew it better than I.

A sudden homesickness saddened me, engendering in my senses phantoms so ready that a torn part of myself seemed to rise from one of those grassy marshes and then plunge again into some pond, or issue from a low swamp, follow a track, and browse beneath a cork oak. Then the animal hallucinations broke off; and the lyrical feeling for my homeland was like the murmur of spirits who dream in the shadow of distant gods.

"I cannot see her, speak to her, hear her," I thought, coming to a halt and setting the lantern down on the sand inside the imprint of a man's foot.

I felt I could no longer endure the presence of the tortured mistress who was waiting for me, nor the contact or proximity of any other petty, troubled being that would remind me of myself, force me to return to my senses, force back again into the usual tracks that extraordinary life that flowed impetuously from my breast and embraced thc entire horizon, lusting for remoteness, new things, creation.

The lantern stood on the ground before me; and from the footprint it occupied began other footprints that led in all directions and disappeared beyond the limits of the light. The furrow made by a wagon shone white as though strewn with flour that had fallen from a torn sack, and it was the pollen fallen from the cloudy sky; in another parallel furrow a chain of caterpillars crawled towards eternity with the light and frightful contraction of its myriads of rings; a broken, leafless branch lay aslant, forked at the end like those branches used to discover buried treasure. There was little light on the ground; but it seemed to me that, had I wanted to, I could have ignited at the summit of my spirit one of those all-seeing beacons that from the turrets of a battleship explore all the hostile space and shed light on the cautious advance of death. I could have scrutinized the depths of the night had I raised another lid that was deeper inside than the physical one on which I liked to feel the marine coolness, by closing it as though under a fleeting kiss. But the anxiety to create arrested at every moment the expansion of my spirit, my aspiration towards the infinite, my inclination towards the abysses, as though I had in me a kind of mysterious rennet that curdled the ideality of the world in specific figures.

A great silence had come over the Landes; which was nothing but the silent growth of night. Just as birds dive into the glass of the lighthouse, just as insects fly around a lamp, the life of solitude pressed to the brink of the dim luminescence, breathed towards me, spied on me without being seen.

I strained my ear for a singular sound, not without fright; for it seemed now close, now distant, now in the air, now under the ground, like the rhythmical beat of two sticks striking against each other with the tinkle that needles make as they clash when one knits. Was it the shepherd?

It was certainly the immortal shepherd of the Landes, on his stilts, there in the shadows, leaning against a scaly pine tree, at his feet his wild dog with its eyes that throbbed like the flickering lights of a glow-worm. Was he clothed in leaves? Was his beard a swarm of bees hanging from his chin? Did there issue from the assiduous activity of his fingers panicles of corymbs?

The shape and its metamorphosis were so alive in my imagination that, had I doused the lantern, I would certainly have thought I saw the man and the demi-god with the pupils in my head.

Again I strained my ears, anxious; because the strange beat continued without interval. Following the sound, I entered the shadows with an inexpressible emotion; as if leaving the circle of brightness I issued from myself to assume I know not what nocturnal nature, and perceived the throb of my own pulse in the substance that was about to engulf me. It was nothing but the wind playing with the hard, tapered leaves of a certain liliaceous plant that grows densely along the beaches.

And inside me there was nothing but the dark monster of love, not yet subdued, not yet bound, which still changed and changed again, taking on a thousand shapes, tempting me and deceiving me through a thousand images, tormenting and renewing me with a thousand wiles.

Just as inside me, so outside me everything was travail and change, anguish and frenzy.

I walked forward at random, holding the lantern low, dangling and swinging to cast light on the edges of a world prodigious as the world a diver sees through the glass opening in his helmet. As on the bottom of the sea, plant life and animal life had the same appearance. The bushes were bristling with horror, an alert voracity strained through the branches. And I was urged on by the fate of the man who, having glimpsed the shadow of a mermaid at the threshold of the cave, could no longer find his way back to the surface.

Where was the woman of the myth at that moment? Were the headlights, preceding her speeding wheels, lighting up the deserted road down there, the muddy ruts, the heaps of pebbles, the rim of the ditches? Had she been totally shattered by her secret pain, like that marble statue which was restored to its former shape?

Suddenly there fell like lead upon my heart the severe sadness which had overcome me when, having covered my eyes with my hand, I had listened tensely to catch her breath through the music. In an instant that sylvan delirium of mine faded away. I felt exhausted, as when a fever falls. To walk on the sand became painful. Nothing was left in me that was not human, sickly, miserable.

I found my way back to the path of habit.

A dismal sultriness slackened the vividness of the air. From the dense overcast a few almost lukewarm drops began to fall. You could hear the crackling in the bushes grow little by little. A scops owl complained in the thicket: and it seemed to recall to me the words written in the secret book of my memory: "One could weep . . ."

At first through a windowpane I saw a pink lamp burning in the house. For some reason my heart was pounding, almost with fear. Near the gate, as I stooped over to put out the lantern, I was called by name by an anxious and hoarse voice, a voice of disaster which chilled the blood in my veins. I approached, I too called out her name. I saw my mistress's shadow inside the gate, agitated, all white, who, both her arms bare, was shaking the slats of the gate, trying to open it.

"What's wrong? What happened?"

Her hands passed through and touched me, trembling, already wet with rain, as if to feel me alive.

"Push!" she said in distress. "Push hard! I can't get it open."

I pressed with my shoulder, but the gate would not budge. The new wood had swollen in the dampness and fresh paint had welded the edges together. My repeated attempts to push it open were in vain. Crushed bubbles of resin made my fingers sticky.

"We'd better call the servants," I suggested, trying to laugh, as seemed appropriate.

"No, no," she cried, vexed and greatly upset, her voice already stifled by tears, clutching the slats again. "Try, try some more!"

I tried. Her hands reached through again, touched my face, dismayed.

"What did you do? What did you do?"

The rain fell harder, crashing down. The scops owl continued to complain. The entire barrens seemed oppressed by an inexplicable despair.

And love sobbed as if I had nailed it against the dying wood and flogged it.

The figures of that afternoon and that night were soon stripped of all reality, even by the time I awoke the very next day. The remembrance floated like the shadow of a dream over the uneasiness of spring. All desire to obtain information and to investigate was immediately stymied by the habitual discipline of my withdrawn life, by the rule of monastic seclusion devoted to study, by the wise resolve not to give way to temptation again. Chance favored neither another meeting nor the discovery of any sort of useful information. To these causes for renunciation were added the suspicions, the vigilance and the constancy of my tenacious mistress. Then followed the torments of our break, an illness of a nostalgic order, a long convalescence in a country of hills and meadows, a diligent renewal of meditation and contemplation.

Nevertheless I had a frequently recurring image of Leda without swan, a living breath issuing from lips that the game of dissimulation could no longer distort, lips never perfectly closed but always slightly parted, like lips that must allow more than one soul to breathe.

It visited me sometimes at the hour of the lighting of the lamps, when the servant prepares and lights them in the room below and they seem present already owing to a divine something which seems to precede them on the already darkening stairs, that interval becoming the occasion for those divine thoughts which accompany the departure of the other light from each of our friendly objects as it returns to the West.

Then, since for the solitary man the whole long day is nothing but a construction of the will, he likes towards evening to leave a small door open through which may enter beggar or witch, herbalist or poisoner, in short an emissary of the Unknown; and he likes to tremble again in expectation of the unexpected. Most times nothing enters but some harmless ghost.

That guest of mine was tied to life by a great number of knots and enchantments, fettered by more than just her hobble skirt; and each time she leaned towards me she seemed to be pulling at a chain, to have to snap a thong, break a rope. To encourage her I would say: "Don't be afraid. Come forth. I am ripe for your coming. I understand everything, I sense everything."

It seemed that my consciousness strained toward the glorious moment when it could accept and render everything safe and immune, like those cities of asylum where the accused without guilt or beyond guilt sought shelter, those sacred places that in ancient times welcomed "the dregs and knavery of the world." But its acts were not without ambiguity and contradiction. At bottom, it toiled in the hope of creating a new emotion, one capable of guiding the most turbid energies of instinct and rising higher than voluptuousness. In this art, justice and compassion are worthless. Other guises, other rules, other rites are required.

Meanwhile, with the new spring, the anniversary of the strange day approached, almost brought back by the long procession of caterpillars upon the road again yellow with pollen. And, almost on the same date, the young maestro of the *Schola Cantorum* returned with the nightingales to give his Italian concert. This time he had brought along his companion: a small Spanish woman from Cuba, golden as an exquisite leaf of tobacco, and who, in promising to sing arias and ariettas by Carissimi, Caldara, Antonio Lotti for me alone, made me think not without regret of that breed of dogs that do not bark which the Conquistadores discovered on her miraculous island where today the breed no longer exists, even its memory being lost.

However, the harpsichord's honors were for Domenico Scarlatti. Like a magic formula his sonata in A Major conjured up from the past the mysterious hour whole and alive, as if the unknown woman had come again to sit beside me and I with all my acuteness were again leaning over the brink of her secret.

Although the audience was more numerous, the chair next to mine remained empty.

I saw a shadow approaching along the row.

From second to second my disquietude increased so fervently that I turned, with my soul in my eyes and my heart leaping in my throat, as if to receive all at once that beauty which already had its place in all my senses. Two thin, bony hands with spatulate fingers were held out towards me, and my name was pronounced by an unforgotten voice.

I immediately recognized a friend of mine from whom I had not heard for some time: a musician of great talent and high reputation, who more than once had been a guest of the sad Ville d'Hiver, hovering between getting worse or better.

"I didn't know you were here. Since when?"

"I spent the whole winter here with my mother—not too well."

"But you look wonderful."

To sink his teeth into his pain he still had a lean jaw from which the razor seemed to have scraped away layers of dead skin replaced by the greasy sheen of glycerine.

"No, I got burned."

His cheeks were red and veined like the leaves of a wild vine hanging from a wall in autumn, not without some greenish remnant and a few traces of snail-slime. For his wretched condition I had—alas—the same implacable eyes that would have noticed the slightest wave in the opulent silk of a certain woman's hair or the gap left by a single fallen lash at the edge of certain eyelids.

"Burned by what?"

He made an almost brutal gesture of indifference, but fixed on me the kind of stare that from man to man delves deeply and seems to search in your heart for a point of support, the place of masculine sympathy.

His eyes now also seemed to me deprived of their outer skin, as if they had been brought into direct contact with external ruthlessness, as if they were the exposed apexes of his sensitivity and there was no medicament that could soothe them. The look in them pained me.

"Are you staying any longer?" I asked. "Would you like to get together?"

"I'm leaving in two or three days, Saturday perhaps. My mother is tearing me away."

He had the smell of port wine on his breath, but his white teeth still gave his mouth a youthful quality.

I felt his humanity with unusual force as if I had for some time been his nurse and had endured the smell of his sweat and knew all his petty troubles and manias.

And from him too I was already expecting the unexpected.

"Come and have lunch with me tomorrow. I'll send the car for you."

"Very well. I'd like to."

And he grabbed my hand and squeezed it with his convulsed fingers. The Sonata in F Minor was beginning, and we fell silent. It seemed to me that the music did not bring us closer but separated us, for I thought that as a craftsman he must hear it in a very different way. He sat there unable to restrain his restlessness, and he communicated it to me.

"What's troubling you? Whom are you looking for?"

Since he had twisted around, I turned too. In the back, standing to the right, leaning against the wall, was the unknown woman, facing our way, nodding. My inward commotion made her features waver and then wiped them out, like a pastel dipped in water.

"Do you know her?" he asked me, with one of those exclamations that seem to hiss in a breast suddenly emptied of everything.

"No. I just saw her once. Who is she?"

He said the name, that did not adhere to the person but remained suspended in the air, an extraneous, meaningless sound, like that imposed upon the beauty of a distant hill which for a long time has been living nameless and ideal in our feelings.

"Till tomorrow," he added, getting up as the cadenza was ending.

Just as the flame bursts from the ember veiled with ashes, so the fever lit up his ruined face. I saw him go towards the woman, his shoulders faintly hunched but with an anxious solicitude that permeated even his clothes and the prematurely gray hair over the collar of his coat. I saw him stop in front of her, exchange a few words of greeting, and then leave with her. Behind me I heard the vicious comment of two people in the audience. I restrained the tumult inside me, shook off the impurities of my solitary fantasies, regained the sharpness of my vision, braced myself to plunge my hands again into the living substance. I forgot the play of the water, the broken, rippling necklaces, Amaryllis' tiny shoe dancing at the tip of the jet, the merry chases over the pink marble stairs, and heard again sorrow and death trickle towards me like drops oozing from the wall of a deep, dusky cave.

My friend came, as agreed. I still pitied him; but I realized that I now looked at him rather as an instrument I must tend to, a tool for dealing with this episode with a delicate or rough hand. And my kindness, as is often the case with me, was only an aspect of my energy.

Lucidity sometimes accompanies an almost animal hideousness which seems the punishment inflicted on those who break the spell of illusions, flout convention.

When eating he had the bad habits of an ill-mannered

invalid; he chewed noisily, drank with his mouth full, smacked his lips, displaying a voraciousness and a thirst unchecked by the least civility. And this gross behavior in that monastic room furnished with books and prints, where I was in the habit of taking my brief meals while reading or following my thoughts—this behavior that I found unbearable was worsened by my insidious emotions; for I kept loading his plate, refilling his glass, intent on stuffing him, making him drunk as you do with a chum when you want to have him at your mercy.

It really seemed he had to fill huge vaults or to appease the appetite of the one inside him who threatened not to leave him either cartilage or bones. Next to that shriveled face, flushed by a touch of intoxication, framed by long hair and a fluttering bow tie, still with a certain resemblance to Henri Mürger, I set the enigma of that other face with its broad planes strongly welded together as in the head of a shepherd king carved in basalt.

And I asked almost silently: "So, she is your mistress? Do you know the shape of her knees? Do you touch her with your spatulate fingers? Eat, drink up."

A breath of monstrous creation stirred within the walls thickly lined with books, where my soul was vibrant as the air imprisoned by the dry wood of a well-constructed violin. That which from immortal books mingles with the fluidity of life in the silence, the eternity which is fixed in the pathetic fragments of masterpieces, the myth which burdens an invisible temple with the wine-colored flower of the hyacinth, the transparent splendor of the wine similar to the corporeal presence of the god it dissolves, bread, fruit, a knife, a strip of meat transformed by fire, the rim of a glass touched by the grace of a ray of light, everything before me and around me expressed myself to myself. Full of meanings, I played with love and with death. With the figure of my guest, with the figure of the absent woman and with my sober intoxication I composed one after the other the scenes of a new *Danse macabre.*

"Who is that?" he asked, looking toward the fireplace.

It was a complete cast of one of the eight hooded men who carry the burial stone of the Great Seneschal of Burgundy. He stood near an andiron, stooped, but his shoulders unburdened, his face hidden inside the hood, only one long-thumbed hand exposed.

"Really," he said, "this isn't a very cheerful place you've made for yourself."

And, fixing a murky stare on something only he could see, sadness overtook him, as the soul does when it curls up on a stuffed bag.

"Come, come," I said, suddenly standing up and taking him familiarly by the arm, with a bold cheerfulness. "Tell me about your new love affair."

"What love affair?"

"I'm dying of envy. She's a magnificent beast."

I made him sit down in a comfortable armchair, while the servant brought liqueurs and cigarettes. I went and stood in the shadow of a bookshelf, away from the light, as if lying in wait.

From a small wooden box he took out his tobacco mixed with opium and rolled it in the paper between thumb and index stained yellow as if with iodine. He was affecting that vain, effete smile of his which I knew so well, that disgusted smile of a womanizer who sees no difference between one affair and the next. As he sat there with his weak legs outstretched, one of them trembling while he stared at the tip of his shoe, there arose again in my memory the image of a peasant I had seen in a field looking calmly at his bare foot, to which the head of a viper seemed stuck forever like a sixth toenail.

"Why do you call her a beast?" he said. "Do you know her story?"

"I know nothing. Who is she?"

He smeared her with a filthy word; and then turned his tongue in his mouth as though it had suddenly dried out.

"So you are in love with her?"

He began to talk—rancorously, dismayed, talked about revenge and spells; there was something unbearable about it, like the sight of an agony; something false, like a clown's routine, alternately pitiable and odious, tragic and ridiculous.

Now Leda without swan was there, so smooth that it seemed she could not even have the mark of a furrow in the hollow of her hand, truly polished by the waters of the Eurotas. And her life was something else.

She came from one of those mixed races whose tragic quality is the product of an obscure confluence of blood and destinies, like the potency of those stimulating concoctions in which mandrake root is boiled in the urine of a mare. Her father, a great lover of horses, had kept a famous racing stable; then he had lost all his money, had lived by expedients, as a swindler, sinking lower and lower, stumbling more than once into the arms of the law. After living in daily contact with grooms, jockeys, trainers, giving rein to her innate, hereditary recklessness and to her exhibitionistic tendencies by riding three-year-old colts on the public bridle paths, at the age of eighteen she had married a French gentleman. She had divorced him at twenty and had found herself first with a lover who was a cold calculating scoundrel and then alone, in straitened circumstances, at loose ends, harassed by her father who would have liked to turn her into the source of a good income that not she but he would pocket. Unable to cope with poverty, ready for anything, at a spa she had run into some sort of procurer in search of accomplices and victims, who, through a sequence of lucky moves, managed to get her engaged to a foolish young man just barely come of age, an orphan, already very rich and about to inherit an even more lavish fortune. She, the fiancé and the matchmaker had lived together for two years "hitting the high spots," roaming from hotel to hotel, from pleasure to pleasure, from boredom to boredom, from one sleepless night to the next, from one gambling table to another, in unconfessable promiscuity; for the bride-to-be enforced the rule of fasting and abstinence until the ascent of the nuptial couch, and the best man had managed to maintain complete domination over the dupe, something akin to a perverse spell, with the help of that philtre which is offered in a golden syringe. The morphine, administered by his skilled hand, had generated such a rosy feeling of benignity that with no trouble at all and no suspicions an insurance policy for one and a half million was obtained for the austere bride-to-be, as a nuptial guarantee. After the first payment was made as prescribed, foresight advised getting rid of the benefactor. One day, on a twisting, dangerous road in the Pyrenees, a stronger dose of the drug was followed by an accident prepared with exquisite caution. After a casual halt, the car was started and then plunged headlong into the ravine, with the murderer left behind unharmed on the road.

Was I not listening to things I had heard many times before? Undoubtedly, similar cases abound in the judicial annals and the scarlet thrillers consumed by janitors, washerwomen, housemaids. But underneath that vulgar hodgepodge meandered I know not what dark track along which my soul had traveled before and was traveling once again, confusedly recognizing the signs of its first passage. And those depths filled me with eagerness to delve even deeper into myself, to reach in myself a more real me that would not fail when confronted by what was about to take on substance and manifest itself.

"How do you know about all this?"

From time to time, enlivening his tale, he injected here and there personal confidences which can be entrusted to another person only by someone recklessly confessing in order to incriminate himself.

"I know it from her."

"She accuses herself?"

"She does not accuse herself; she talks. She has no idea of right or wrong. First she tells you something dreadful, without looking at you, with a kind of timid smile, like someone testing the strength of a plank laid across a stream before venturing over it. Then she bends you under a weight, piles on a guilt that crashes down on you and you've got to support with main force."

"Are you sure that with all these things she wasn't and isn't putting together some sort of imaginary life?"

"She wears the shackle of reality well fastened to her foot."

"What do you mean?"

"She lives with the murderer."

"Where?"

"In this town."

"How long has that been going on?"

"For two years."

"Was she already his mistress before the accident?"

"She was, yes; but in payment for his mediation, and afterwards because of their complicity. She loathes him."

"Then why does she put up with him?"

"The circumstances surrounding the prospective bridegroom's death aroused some suspicion. And the insurance company seized on this to challenge the validity of the policy. There was no evidence or it was too vague. Nevertheless the case was taken to court and is still dragging on. Consequently the man holds the threat over her head of a wild denunciation that would destroy them both. I believe that after the trial, whose favorable outcome is by now assured, the two of them will divide the money according to some kind of agreement they have already made."

"Just what sort of dregs from old detective stories are cluttering your imagination?"

"It's all true, and it is only a particle of their everyday

reality. Just picture it: they live together on the Basin over there in one of those rackety little villas with thin walls and ceilings where you can hear a heart beat or a lung dilate in the next room, where it is impossible to escape the smell of the person you hate or the splash of his wash water."

"And what kind of a man is he?"

"Think of a head the shape of a truncated pyramid, a real python head, exact like a geometrical creation, rigid as a problem or a condemnation, with two colorless eyes behind a pair of lenses as thick as the glass in a dark lantern . . ."

"And who pays the bills?"

"His background is just petty bourgeois, his father owned a china factory near Limoges. She still has something left from her dowry. But that little would not be enough to pay for her elegant, expensive habits, at least externally. Belief in the trial's favorable outcome makes available to her a ruinous credit with the money-lending wine-dealers of the Gironde. And for those extortions too the cold python willingly acts as go-between."

"And what does he think of you?"

"I'm the chosen victim for the usual swindle. Two or three times, while I was at the piano there, in the villa over by the Basin, I saw him appear in the doorway, snicker silently, then leave hurriedly like someone rushing off somewhere to enjoy his mirth to the full. And every time he appeared he had for me the look of one of those phantoms produced by certain dissociations of a mind on the brink of madness, which terrify the patient with their intermittent presence. A colleague of mine, poor man, before entering a clinic, was assiduously visited by such a caller; and he never dared turn his head for fear of discovering him at his side. Now something of this sort is happening to me too . . ."

"But it is quite obvious that you are dealing with a tolerant, even obliging ghost, my dear friend."

"He does not interfere with the workings of chance and of

fantasy, the caprices of boredom and cruelty, he merely watches them from nearby or from a distance. Only one thing interests him: to keep his accomplice tied to him, on a long leash he can slacken at will, if convenient. His one fear is of flight, of her escaping, her "giving him the slip,' let's say. Now, the arms he uses against her and the threats you can imagine leave her no earthly way out. But there is a possibility of escape toward darkness, there is the possibility of escape to the nether world. And this is the only threat she can oppose to the threats that oppress her."

"Do you believe she would be able to kill herself?"

"At any moment."

Again I saw the steel and ivory weapon gleaming through the opening of her pearl-colored muff. Again I saw the woman with the concealed hand, standing before me, intact, silent, her evil sickness filling her like a truth or like the profoundest lie, which in her took the place of life.

"At any moment, just like that—as you might open a door, cross a threshold, go down a step."

Until that point the things he had told me were no less alien to her ideal figure than, for example, to the cast of the Piombino Apollo resting over there on a square revolving bookcase beside the piano. I was unable to understand or even feel that such could be the true substance of her life. Her mystery remained as untouched as the obscure divinity of the statue which, glowing like gold in the afternoon light, attracted my gaze. Such definite acts were as unlike the unhappy creature I'd met as an Homeric hymn or a chapter of mythology differed from that intent form inhabited by a spirit no less unknowable than the vigor of a tree which provides its fruit.

Where was the hand that had shaped above the god's brief brow that symmetrical, double row of curls? No less forceful seemed to me the power of a past in whose unyielding mould her soul must be imprisoned. My spirit found nothing coherent in that mass of cheap, distasteful facts, but was possessed by a poetic emotion that contained, mysteriously combined with it, what comes into existence under the protection of man's silence. That is why instinct so often guided my eyes toward the Apollo that, finished in every detail like the work of a goldsmith, expressed through every line an infinitude of poetry. Once again form became for me a clairvoyant faith; and listening to so many degrading details, I believed only in that which the beauty polished by the waters of the Eurotas signified for me.

But then suddenly that beauty appeared to me to cling to death like one of those cameos engraved in the white vein running through a dark agate. The contrast was so fierce that everything else vanished. I could hear my heart pound so violently that I was surprised my friend did not hear it. But he was certainly deafened by his own agitation, on which every so often he poured a fiery gulp.

"Why?" I asked him. "Is it because she alludes to it cunningly; because, like so many other women, she uses it as a charming bit of bravado . . ."

"Two years ago, during a period of particular exasperation and rage, she defied death almost every day. She used to have one of those light speedboats you see at the races in Monaco, equipped with a sixteen-cylinder engine, the gift of an Argentine admirer. A daredevil mechanic was always with her, at all hours of the day or night, when that damned North wind would whip up a storm in the Basin and the ocean channel became murderous, and nobody dared venture out past the cape. Through monstrously clever ruses she eluded the closest surveillance and every impediment. She almost always returned just when all hope of seeing her reappear seemed lost. For hours on end the foaming waves would have lashed at her as at a figurehead. Whoever kissed her then must have got a good long taste of the salt on her dried lips."

I could see her so well . . . as if the mooring-place were within me—I could see her wrapped in her waterproof slicker, her face hidden inside the oil-cloth hood, diaphanous as the light of the floating Portuguese man-of-war. And I had waited for her only in order to set off with her again in the dusk.

"At a fasionable Normandy seaside resort, shortly after her divorce, she was assiduously courted by a young polo player who let her ride his delightful horses. Without ever granting him anything, she was able to arouse such an insane passion in him that he asked her to marry him. She laughed him off and tortured him with such subtle perversity that one day he summoned the courage to leave and perhaps went off to play his game on some good English polo grounds in India. She was not in love with him and she had grown accustomed to him only as to a slave she could use for inventing and experimenting with different tortures; but she dearly loved one of the polo horses, a young bay roan that had been given the Shakespearian name of Petrucchio. When she found out they had gone she poisoned herself the same evening, swallowing a number of pellets of corrosive sublimate, and hovered for days on end between life and death. From the bed where she lay in terrible agony she kept holding out the palm of her hand, repeating the gesture she made when she offered lumps of sugar to her Petrucchio."

Now, before my half-closed eyes, I could see that naked hand, freed from the glove; that long strong hand with its lean polished knuckles, grazing the thin delicate lip of one of those small Phidian horses that gallop on the plaster reproductions of the Frieze hanging along my wall. The slender, elegant Athenian riders lacked only the wooden ball and the mallets with the long flexible handles, the hooves of their neatly poised animals lacked only the shorn, springy meadow grass. I could see the slanting sun strike the lush green meadows of Normandy; and a sheaf of light like a golden blade sever with a clean stroke two nervous feet digging into the ground in a sudden, abrupt halt. But my rival's heart leaped with wild joy to the words: "She was not in love with him."

"A year ago, actually around this date at the beginning of April, one evening . . ."

My heart stopped. Inside me I could again hear the overturned chairs banging noisily to the floor, down there, in the dim hall filled with echoes, like a church during the Tenebrae office.

"One evening?" I said, encouraging the voice that had broken off as though intimidated by my anxiety. I could again see the uncontrollable tremor affecting the unknown woman's features, and in her eyes the reflected shimmer of mother-of-pearl.

"One evening, at Bordeaux, for a similar reason, while she was sitting in the car arguing with the uncle of some poor boy that the relatives wanted to prevent her from seeing anymore, she suddenly shot herself in the breast with the revolver she was carrying in her muff. The bullet grazed the lung and lodged under the shoulder blade. Once again her life was in danger for weeks and weeks, again the horror of a hospital confinement, the disconsolate python at her bedside . . ."

All the appearances and all the premonitions of that distant spring evening streamed through me with increased vehemence, giving birth to a kind of immense sorrow with which I would become thoroughly acquainted only at a later time. There was no doubt in my mind; nevertheless I asked:

"What day was it? Do you know?"

"Yes, it was the fifth of April."

"Because of some hopeless love affair?"

An obscure jealousy tormented me.

"Because of some imagined love. And out of weariness with life's stupidity. That Paolo, the youngster she had corrupted, was the nephew of a wine merchant with whom the python had made some usurious deals, borrowing at exorbitant rates against the hoped for bundle—against the devil's own harvest, so to speak. Just see how strangely everything worked out! Almost by way of retaliation against the crook who had fleeced her, she took possession of the boy who was quite charming physically and had rather delicate feelings. In no time she transformed him, made him into her belonging, which she held on her fist like a young hooded falcon. Become aware of the danger, the boy's family decided to put a stop to it, taking at once the most effective measure. They sequestered Paolo, dragged him away, hid him who knows where. This was enough to turn her thwarted whim into frenzy. She asked to see him once more, to talk to him one last time. Their answer was no. Almost every evening she drove to the street where his relatives lived and sent a message; but nothing came of it. That night, having received an imperious and threatening note, the uncle ran out to speak to her, to try and persuade her to give it up. She was sitting in the car; he talked to her standing on the running board. Obstinately she kept repeating: 'I want to see him.' Obstinately he refused. From beneath the fur the gun suddenly went off, almost as if by accident. The usurer took her wounded body to the hospital. When she regained consciousness and could whisper a few words, she begged them to let her see Paolo just for an instant. In vain. The law those merchants laid down was implacable. Only the python remained beside the white bed, with spring clinging to the windowpanes. The bullet was extracted. The scars . . ."

"Ah. Please, describe those scars to me."

I could no longer control my agitation. At those words he had broken off to gulp down yet another drink, to pour yet another dose of liquid fire into the cavern where his tired heart was gasping. His spatulate fingers enveloped the glass completely, so that index and thumb surrounded the rim which he touched with his lips to inhale the aroma of the lukewarm liquor. His nostrils twitched, limned against that worn mask of vice. Everything about him now repelled and irritated me. Between his deformed fingers and the almost crushed glass, I could see the glint of some strangely loathsome smile. I thought of the demonic pigs that often inhabit that particular kind of artist, waiting to be expelled by the exorcism of inspiration.

"So tell me, tell me. How did she finally come to you?"

He laughed brutally into the circle of glass.

"She smelled the carrion, perhaps."

"It would be more graceful, funereally, to say to hear the song of the swan. Doesn't she remind you of a Leda? Look at this group by Ammannati."

He heard the hostility in my voice.

"My dear friend," he said, violently agitated, staring at me. "Tell me the truth. You weren't putting on an act yesterday, when you asked me who she was? Didn't you know her before me? Didn't you too go through it all?"

"No."

"Then why are you jealous?"

"I am not jealous, but perhaps a little annoyed. You know it: I do not conceive of life save in the guise of expression. Now, with your opaque stories, you have denied, line by line, her expression in me. I must rediscover it and recompose it at the cost of love and pain."

"She'll come to you, and you will love her, and you will suffer because of it."

"Are you bequeathing her to me?"

"I assure you, I would like to die at her hands. But I'm being wrested away, like Paolo, I'm being snatched away from that enviable destiny. And this is her peculiar fate: at the crucial moment, each one of her chosen victims escapes her. Even she escapes from herself."

"To a lung already injured by a bullet, weren't you afraid to communicate your disease?"

The air in the room seemed to have become harsh, like that which fills places without laws and without lies. I was no longer capable of forbearance or kindliness. On one side I saw that stupendous figure moulded with a magnanimity as severe as that revealed by the examples of ancient art through whose presence my sense of the world continues and is confirmed; and on the other side I considered that human hotbed of infection, that species of ignominious sensuality which I could not separate from an image of filth and fraud. Their commingling seemed incredible. Deep down my question contained a malevolent curiosity, for I knew he was a braggart and quite incapable of admitting that he'd been jilted, like Petrucchio's rider.

"Did you really hold her in your arms? Did your breathe your breath into her?"

My eyes bored into him. An involuntary contraction of his lips seemed to me the clue I was waiting for; but he canceled it with a strident burst of laughter, rising to his feet with a slight stagger.

"Careful of you to collect information beforehand. And impudent too. But the contagion that attends succession would be my revenge. What time is it? She'll be here at five o'clock, to pick me up and take me back home. You'll see her. She wants you to show her your dogs. I am leaving with my mother tomorrow morning, that's definite. One might say I'm handing you the torch on the run."

I opened the glass doors to the verandah, with the haste of someone on the point of being stifled by some evil emanation.

The tide, which is female, was mounting toward the dune bristling with reeds. The entire surface of the sea trembled and glittered, submerging the sand banks, pale and languid like the bodies of shipwrecked sailors sucked dry by sirens. There was a murmur deep as must be that which announces the spring breaking through in countries that winter covers with ice. The declining sun left behind it a resplendent path upon which it seemed its great white horses, unyoked, must descend. The myths of my race were rushing to invade the deserted places without history. My spirit was fervid, fecund, irresistible as at the beginning of love. The fulfillment of a prophecy was near, and the blood's oracular utterance had been rightly interpreted.

I no longer had the strength to turn and see again that ravaged face, the horrible skull, the harsh, bony mask covered by worn skin. Something stronger than I and that miserable presence was being born right now; and would soon resemble me. A spirit voice said: "Only that is that does not yet exist, and you are living in the future, you have no memory but of the future." My heart said: "I take all upon myself. She is guiltless. I absolve her. Look, there she stands."

It repeated the words of that evening's lone poplar, clothed in irridescent silver, at the corner of that garden. Returning, my twilight and nocturnal visions flowed through me and vanished.

I heard the sharp sound made by the raised piano lid; and I did not turn but waited, shivering as if his hand were touching my shoulder and not the keyboard.

The soul of the instrument vibrated as if shattered by sorrow. The doomed man spoke his true language. His despair seemed at times to reproduce the cry of a terrible happiness and seize his fate by the throat with a claw as powerful as Beethoven's. All that had been or thought before, all became small, empty, and distant. The light of the sun became a kind of blindness.

I turned my face to the jamb, I laid my hand high against it and against my hand I laid my brow, my eyes closed. I created night inside me, to see the dazzling light which the music intermittently poured into the vacuous bottom of life. A pause suspended me over my own annihilation. It was as if that silence would last eternally. The lament resumed; then fell silent again. Resumed a third time, as if halting before the threshold of a door that might remain closed; then it ended. We did not move.

Suddenly we heard the roar of an engine at the garden's gate.

And he rose, and I turned; and I saw myself discolored in him, deadly pale and with bloodless lips, breathless like someone returning to the surface from the bottom.

There are emotions of some curious plastic quality which almost seem to knead human nature and remold it into a momentary appearance.

As we were walking down toward the gate, still under the influence of the musical power, it seemed to me that we were a single being, greater than either of us, inhabited fully by a primitive soul, and that that fantastic, unearthly creature was staggering along, limping in the same direction. It was only an instant, inexpressible, which faded into the immensity of spring, and fled beyond the boundaries of the world. Had the woman's eyes possessed a magical power, she would have seen coming to meet her that lopsided embodiment of Love, like an evanescent chimera. But with each step we separated more and more distinctly. I felt my companion's emotion rise confusedly through his hazy intoxication, through the toxins in his blood, the impediments of his diseases. I felt mine flow like vigorous lymph through the lightness of my body almost completely empty of food, grow with each step as if my heel's contact with the ground enriched me with the fervor of the earth.

She had remained in the car, in front of the gate. When she saw us draw near, she jumped out, with a movement that provoked innumerable waves in me, as in the waters of the Basin the leap of a certain fish, golden and arched like the young moon, sometimes does.

She no longer wore her fetters. That inflection of her beauty from the waist down, which I had noticed earlier, and made me think of Leda in the act of embracing the swan, seemed enhanced by her skirt draped and somehow rolled up toward the front over her legs in a manner that suggested the tightly curled petals of those large gloomy irises called lilies of Susa.

Every fold and the shadow within every pleat and the light on the flounce and the yielding cloth and the recurrent pattern were expressions of her fresh life, which moved me like the outline of her chin stretched taut by divine youth. I took her in, simple, single and manifold in the way that the mass of the air presses against us and simultaneously penetrates each of our pores. Everything in her was known and unknown to me, for that fleeting moment and forever. And she certainly read this wondrous discovery in my eyes.

Inside me a spirit repeated "More! More!"—the word of those who are never satiated and know that after something beautiful there is something more beautiful still.

Visible and invisible things passed through the light, as if carried along by a current, with that precipitous onrush we see near a cataract.

The large garden was transformed into a cradle of warmth by one of those sudden flashes of heat that on the barrens seem the deception of the Western Morgana intent on simulating the breath of summer. The gold of the sun and the pollen of the trees mixed the same dust with the pulsating wind. At their tips the pine trees each bore a drop of vivid blue.

We talked. Each of us three had the air of listening to the other and of answering him. But it was as when in a dream we see the lips of the dead or the living move and do not hear any sound. A silent vortex formed from the fluid substance of two lives; and the third life was like one of those pieces of flotsam that a vortex attracts, spins round, then rejects. Everything was hidden and everything was manifest, everything took place at the deepest root of the soul and at the ends of the nerves, it resembled initiation and final perdition. And assuredly one of us was lost and perhaps two were lost and perhaps three, as in the Greek song of Charon.

"What are you doing!"

Seeing his instinctive gesture, I could not hold back the

exclamation but I was able to muffle it: he had seized the woman's arm and was clinging to it, almost beside himself, imploring and frightened. And nothing could be sadder than the manner in which by managing to control his feelings, he tried to give his involuntary gesture the appearance of an innocent familiarity.

She flushed, then she moved away, and began to run toward the kennel where the young dogs were already in a turmoil. We entered together, as if into the foam of a breaking wave. He did not dare, wary of the onslaught he remained outside, against the bars of the iron fence.

"Leda! Leda and the swans!"

She seemed recaptured and re-fashioned in juvenescent nature, inhabited by a spring welling up behind the crystal of her eyes. She was the source, the river, the banks, the plane-tree's shadow, the quiver of the reed, the velvet of the moss. Huge wingless birds assailed her; and certainly, when she stretched out her arm toward one of them and held it by its plumed neck, she repeated exactly the gesture of Testio's daughter.

"Leda and the swans."

She was leaning against a tree to resist the assault; and, when I tried to chase the frenzied animals with my stick or voice, she cried: "Oh, don't! Don't!"

It was a litter of borzois born in August from my pure white Thamar; but the divine image of sea-foam was linked to their birth as it is with the Hellenic name for Venus. They came racing to my call as the waves rush to the shoal; and I must say that each time I was astonished not to hear water crashing at my feet. Certainly they were made of the most precious substances; and no sea-shell was so delicate as their muzzles in the transition from the roseate hue of the gums to the white of the teeth. Some in their variegated, clear eyes had all the ramifications of marine flora as though concentrated in an incorruptible gem.

"Don't!"

Rearing on their hind legs, they were trying to lick her face and neck, seeking the touch of her hand; but one more than the others, dazzling, though touched here and there by a mark as light as the shadow of smoke—one dog more than the rest pursued and pressed her.

"Oh! This one!" she said with a loving voice, electing him.

I managed to lead the others away and leave her only that one.

Oh imagination, omnipotence of all-powerful desire, insight of poetry!

My heart brimmed with an unknown voluptuousness. Leaning against the tree, she was covered by the quivering beast; and she spoke to him with those words tenderness dissolves into empty sounds. The long, slender muzzle lay against her cheek; and both the feral and the human mouth had the same youthful freshness. Her naked fingers burrowed into the beautiful coat as into the downy feathers under a wing.

There are looks which as they meet celebrate a mystery with each flutter of the lashes. There are others, or even the same ones, that exchange such gifts that the value of all the rest is impaired.

The straw of dry pine needles made a dry, crackling sound under our feet as the three of us walked back to the gate in silence. The trunks to one side shone resplendently like copper armor, on the other they looked dark as if smeared with pitch. The edges of the path were yellow with wild floury dust. Seminars of caterpillars were assembled under what seemed a ragged bit of canvas that bore a resemblance both to the slough of a snake and to an emptied and dried-out honeycomb. I shivered on suddenly hearing close to my ear the sinister tinkle which in that distant night had evoked the figure of the silent shepherd intent on knitting his interminable garment. It was the vespertime breeze among long leaves shaped like iron spears.

"Goodbye then," said my friend, when we got to the car. "Are you really leaving tomorrow?"

"I am."

"Perhaps I'll be at the station when the train leaves, to say goodbye to your mother."

He twisted his mouth as if it had suddenly filled with gall. He climbed into the car with an effort, sat down next to the woman of the myth.

It was as though she no longer recognized either of us. Now, between the hard, sharp edges of her eyelids, she had those eyes that leave you perplexed and desperate, like a smooth granite wall without an opening or a foothold. The same slanting glow, which transformed the scales of the tree trunks into red armor, set fire on her temple to the metal of her hair.

"Goodbye," my friend repeated, waving the hand that had drawn the nocturnal lament from the keyboard.

"She does not love you, she does not love you."

Amid the roar, the wheels spun, cutting deep into the sandy road, leaving between the two furrows some of that fascination which my lantern resting on the ground had illuminated in the distant night.

The roar died down, faded away. Yet I stood there still listening. Now I only heard the beat of my heart drumming at the nape of my neck. An anxiety like a melting blast of fire dissolved every thought in me, and vehemently brought back to my mouth the taste of ashes and blood that had been under my teeth during the walk interrupted by that filthy hand trickling and groping as it searched for the thing it had lost.

I returned to the kennel, as you would return to the place where a miracle of life or art was accomplished, to ask again the questions that remain unanswered.

The long, slender, moist muzzles strained towards me through the bars, and the eyes darkened by the oncoming night stared at me like those of swans when one walks along the water in a garden already invaded by shadows and sleep.

I went inside; I spoke, with those guttural sounds dogs understand. They were all around me, imitating on their four paws the crest of the wave when it forms a volute, or rearing up like dancing goats to commemorate the satyrs. One, however, apart, was in the throes of a wild happiness, as puppies are when they find a bone, tossing it into the air and then seizing it again between their teeth, although what he had hold of I was unable to see clearly. He was in fact the one Leda had liked best.

I called him several times. He stopped playing, looked at me with wily distrust, hesitated for a few seconds, more sinuous than a wave in a Japanese drawing; then went off again, leaping and cavorting on the pine needles. A sterner order made him obey. He came over, stealthily, almost crawling, with pleading grace; he took the last few steps bending to one side, then rolled over and lay on his back at my feet, as if he were about to faint or breathe his last. But between his teeth he still held the object with a careful strength which gripped it without breaking it.

"What have you got there? What is it? Let me see."

He pawed the air in supplication. To force him to release it I pressed my fingers on the articulation of his jaws. Thus I managed to take away his find; it was a comb of light tortoise shell, a small comb that had slipped out of Leda's hair!

I felt it moist and sticky with slaver. As I held it upon the palm of my hand I felt it live with a secret life. It weighed no more than a starfish. The dog was still there, stretched out, as if waiting to be forgiven for a transgression; and between his half-closed, fringed lips his fangs shone vividly, evoking in me the phrase "carats, measure of perfection."

I had a single, tormenting thought, generated by an obscure anguish: to try to see her again before night. The lost comb was a plausible excuse. Perhaps she had returned home, after having accompanied her lover. I thought, trembling: "If I could only find her alone; if I could talk to her!" Every delay seemed to me to favor some hostile power and lessen my chances. Anxiety cannot breathe unless things move swiftly.

I jumped on a bicycle and went down the road at top speed. The first steep slope cost me no effort at all. A strange vigor ran through every muscle in my body, and the evening breeze played in my chest as through young foliage. I crossed the Ville d'Hiver, the town of the diseased. Here and there I glimpsed a lamp lit behind a glass pane. I thought I could see, to the right, before a bend in the road, the silvery raiment of the apple tree once again covered with blossoms. The bell tolled above the chapel. At the end of a tree-lined avenue, past a tall crucifix, the Basin glittered.

I knew that the house was close to the pier: the fourth on the left. To find it I dismounted and walked slowly, my courage ebbing. There was darkness in all the windows. I followed the garden wall, where the glossy leaves of shrubbery were still glistening. French doors into the entrance hall stood open: at the far end I also saw a balcony open onto the pale sky; and the breeze swelled the curtains, scampered along the arched, vaulted ceiling. The house seemed deserted. The waves' backwash resounded through it, as underneath a wharf. "Perhaps she is over there, sitting quietly in the dark. Now she'll recognize me, she'll jump to her feet, she'll cry out."

I waited immobile in the current of air which carried my life away with it in sparks. Now she was no longer before me; she was behind me, like a block of ice.

At the sound of a footstep I turned around. Someone was coming into the garden. Some unfathomable, instinctive revulsion and then the glitter of the thick spectacles warned me that the man with the head shaped like a truncated pyramid was approaching.

"Who's there?" he asked, in a sharp, penetrating voice that cut through the murmur of the tide.

I told him my name; I briefly explained my presence; I

handed him the small package containing the comb, asking him to return it to the person who had lost it.

"She has not come back yet," he said.

And, with a clipped, cold courtesy, he invited me to wait for her.

My eyes now accustomed to the darkness saw the unmoving head of the python as if I were in the midst of an incoherent dream where, unsuspectingly entering a room, in a corner one suddenly discovers an enormous snake, escaped from its cage, erect on the heap of its coils and staring fixedly from eyes at a man's level.

"Thank you," I said, unable to dominate my strange feeling of terror. "I must go now."

I left; I resumed my race; I reached the end of the promenade bordering the sea, hoping to meet her. I turned off over the dunes. I returned home; among my books and casts I was met again by the odor of tobacco blended with opium; I saw again the open keyboard and the shadow of the Immortal on the mute ivory.

I lived part of that night like someone who knows he no longer possesses his entire self. I stayed there listening to catch the cry which did not yet reach my ear but already touched my soul.

The lethargy due to my exhaustion had lasted for I cannot say how long when my spirits revived with the vehemence of a suddenly alarmed multitude. I found myself propped up on my elbows, shaken by a clamant pounding of the blood, my eyes staring into the dark, with no sense of time, place or what was to happen, like the man who wakes up to die in a house that is crashing down upon him. As always, my window was open; and I sensed the approach of dawn from the color of the starry sky. The cool air soothed me. I lay down again on my back, and stayed awake.

No shore is so lapped by the melancholy of the world as

this westernmost shore at the beginning of each new day. The cock on the barrens crows hoarsely, as though remembering his descent from a cock consecrated to a divinity begot of Night and unaided by any other god. Man, whom that crow awakens, knows he is a shadow before resuming the burden of his body to drag it again to its pain.

Again exhaustion overcame me.

When the full morning light roused me, I at once remembered my promise to pay my respects to my friend's mother. I hurried so as to be on time, and I took a bunch of violets with me.

The North wind had sprung up in an intrepid sky, laden with fecundity, with migrations and returns.

"Perhaps he won't leave," I thought, seeing before me his bitter mouth, hearing again his strident laugh. "No, he won't leave."

But another spirit, mindful of the burst of shattering pain that had torn the fibers of the instrument, told me: "He is leaving. He won't stay. He is vanquished."

And I had drawn a veil over the enigma of that ancient and new face with its broad planes strongly welded together as in the head of a shepherd king carved from basalt. I was expecting some occult message from some horizon, to expose it and to contemplate it without fear.

I walked onto the squalid covered platform. The train stood motionless on its tracks, black, stupid and massive. On a long counter were stacked certain cages made of cane full of dazed chickens. The face of every human creature seemed to be branded by servitude and infamy. The cock of the barrens had already crowed for them.

I was walking past the cars in search of my friend and of myself, when I saw him leaning broken against his mother's shoulder, waxen, as if stupified by a drug, with his legs sagging limply, a bit of the whites of his eyes showing through his partly lowered lids. A gesture of the old lady forestalled the inopportuneness of any word, any act on my part. She leaned with the greatest cautiousness towards me, making sure not to disturb her son, and whispered:

"Last night she killed herself."

This is what Desiderio Moriar told me.

Since his story seemed to have reached its end and he remained silent, staring at the arched sand bank in the middle (pale slope without asphodels and without relics, belonging to the world of the depths), I asked:

"Did you see her on her deathbed?"

"I saw her," he answered.

"Was her face intact?"

He nodded affirmatively, lowering his head, and his hands trembled slightly on his knees.

I added timidly, in a low murmur:

"And how was her face then?"

He made night inside himself, covering his eyes with his open hands, and remained silent.

The ebb-tide had left the immense beach bare; and the low water no longer breathed but immobile mirrored the immobile sky. The canals, the sand banks, the dunes, the long thin spits, the thrusting promontories, the low undergrowth, all the internal lines went in accord with the line of the ocean's horizon, obeying a rhythm of sublime perfection granted to man only during the hour that follows his passing.

In a silence the same as perfect nudity, the beauty of the Occident lay there supine.

In the Landes, June, 1913.

NOCTURNE

Nocturne

Aegri somnia.

I HAVE bandaged eyes.

I lie in bed on my back, my torso immobile, my head thrown back, a little lower than my feet.

I raise my knees slightly to tilt the tablet resting against them.

I write on a strip of paper wide enough for only one line. Between my fingers I hold a soft lead pencil. Thumb and middle finger of the right hand set on the edges of the strip make it glide as the words are written.

With the last phalanx of the little finger I can feel the lower edge and I use it as a guide to keep a straight line.

My elbows are motionless against my sides. I try to impart great lightness to the movement of my hands, so that their play will not go beyond the articulation of the wrist, so that no tremor is transmitted to my bandaged head. In my whole attitude I sense the rigidity of an Egyptian scribe carved in basalt.

The room is utterly emptied of light. I write in darkness. I scratch my signs in the night which presses solid against either thigh like a nailed board.

I am learning a new art.

When the doctor's harsh decree plunged me into darkness

and in the darkness assigned me the narrow space my body will occupy in the grave, when the wind of action grew cold on my face, almost cancelling it, and the ghosts of battle were suddenly excluded by this black threshold, when silence reigned in me and around me, when I had relinquished my flesh and recovered my spirit, from my first confused anxiety arose once more the need to express, to signify. And almost immediately I began to search for some ingenious way to elude the rigors of the treatment and to trick the stern doctor without transgressing his orders.

I was forbidden to speak and in particular to sculpt my sentences; nor could I overcome my old aversion to dictating, and maintain the secret modesty of art that rejects intermediaries and witnesses which stand between the subject and him who works with it. Experience advised me against approaching the page with closed eyes. The difficulty lies not in the first line but in the second and those that follow.

Then there rose in my memory the way of the Sybils, who wrote their brief sentences on leaves scattered to the winds by fate.

I smiled a smile that no one saw in the shadow as I heard the snicking sound of the paper which Sirenetta,* stretched out on the rug in the next room in the light of the low lamp, was cutting into strips for me.

Her chin must be lit up as it was by the reflection from the burning sand when in the time of joy we lay next to each other on the beach at Pisa.

The paper makes a regular, rustling sound which in my imagination evokes that noise of the waves' backwash at the foot of the tamarisks and junipers scorched by the southwest wind.

Beneath the bandage the depths of my wounded eye flare like a high noon in summer at Bocca d'Arno. I see the sand

---

* D'Annunzio's pet name for his daughter, Renata.

corrugated by the wind, streaked by the waves. I can count the grains, bury my hand in them, fill my palm with them, let them stream through my fingers.

The flame grows, the great dog days rave. The sand glitters in my vision like mica and quartz. It bedazzles me, fills me with vertigo and terror, like the Libyan desert on that morning when I rode all alone to the tombs of Memphis.

I have the protection neither of eyelids nor of any other screen. The dreadful fire is inside my forehead, inescapable.

The yellow turns to red, the plain convulses. Everything becomes bristling and sharp. Then, as a creating hand molds figures from the yielding clay, a mysterious breath lifts from the glaring expanse the reliefs of human and bestial shapes.

Now the solid fire is carved like chiseled stone.

I have before me a steep wall of red-hot rock sculpted with men and monsters. From time to time it flutters like an immense sail and the apparitions writhe. Then everything vanishes, borne away by the red maelstrom, like a huddle of tents in the desert.

The rim of the torn retina burns and curls up like the Dantesque papyrus, and darkness effaces the words on it one by one.

I read: "Why have you twice deceived me?"

Salty sweat runs down into my mouth mixed with tears from my compressed lids. I am thirsty. I ask for a sip of water. The nurse refuses to give it to me, for I am not allowed to drink.

"Thou shalt quench thy thirst in the sweat of thy face and in thy tears."

The sheet clings to my body like the sheet that envelops a drowned man dripping with salt, pulled ashore and laid out on the sand until someone will come to give him a name, close his foaming lids and howl over his silence.

It is no longer an apparition; it is a continued presence that repulses whoever draws near. But the first apparition comes back to me with an aura of terror.

It is the evening of the burial.

My sorrow is nevertheless still entangled in his decayed flesh.

It is the night of St. Stephen. His fire is lit. I sit where he always sat. Again and again he annihilates me. I lose myself in him.

I can no longer hear what the living at my side are saying.

Cinerina is there, with that strange inspired face of hers which reminds me of the young Beethoven, with her extraordinarily large eyes whose gaze is enriched by melancholy and irony mixed together like a mysterious cosmetic. Manfredi Gravina is there too, to comfort me, to convince me that there are still friends in the world, that there are still comrades sworn to war.

"How is the weather outside?"

Cinerina says that when she arrived at seven o'clock the sky was clear and full of stars. Manfredi says that now there is a thick fog.

It is ten o'clock. It is time to go. Renata is tired.

I put my large gray cape on over my thick aviator's sweater. We make all the gestures in the entrance hall that we did when he was there. But his small black cape is not hanging on the gilded hook, nor do we hear his gracious, ironic voice.

We go outside. We chew the fog.

The town is seething with ghosts.

Men walk noiselessly, shrouded by the mist.

The canals steam.

From the bridges one sees only the white stone edge of each step.

The singing of a drunk here and there, a shout, a sound of shrieks and uncouth laughter. Blue steel lights in the haze.

The cry of the air raid look-outs hoarsened by the fog.

A city of dream, a city of another world, a city washed by Lethe or Avernus.

Ghosts pass by, graze us, vanish.

Renata walks in front of me as she did *then*, and Manfredi walks at her side. They speak as Renata and my comrade spoke. From time to time the fog separates me from them.

We cross the bridges. The lights shine like will-o'-the-wisps in a graveyard.

The piazza is full of fog, like a basin filled with opalescent water.

The ancient Procuratil Palaces are almost invisible. The top of the belltower dissolves in the haze.

The Basilica is like a rock in a misty sea.

The two columns in the Piazzetta are like two columns of smoke risen from two identical heaps of ashes.

On the Riva degli Schiavoni, the lights of the boats at their moorings.

The gay music in the Café Orientale, behind the frosted doors; a dance rhythm.

The song of the drunks.

The wandering ghosts.

Tonight the dead are abroad; roaming the streets, as on the night between All Saints and the second day of November.

We say goodbye in the lobby of the Hotel Danieli. I hope Renata will be able to sleep tonight.

I start back to the Red House, alone. My friend is with me, in spirit. A profound regret trickles from my heart.

I look at the edge of land where his small boat used to lay to, where every night we shook hands and said, "See you tomorrow."

In the Piazzetta a man turns around at the sound of my steps. He turns again, walks away, becomes a vaporous shadow, is engulfed.

I enter the arcade of the Procurator's Palace lit by blue lamps. I am astonished when I hear a large family talking about the usual things with the sluggish stupidity of people returning from a night of guzzling. Are they alive? Are they dead? I pass ahead of them. They become shadows.

Beyond the Ponte San Moisé, while I am thinking with a shiver that I will have to pass in front of the alley of Corte Michiel, I catch sight of someone walking at my side, noiselessly, as if he were barefoot.

It is someone of the same height as my comrade, with his identical figure, his way of walking.

He wears a sweater, an indefinable suit of a grayish color, and a cap, also grayish.

He is silent, his is a singular silence, as if no voice at all or breath ever lived inside him.

He walks without heels, without shoes, without sandals.

I have an instinctive sensation of terror. I slow down. I see him ahead of me.

He walks like my comrade. Shortly afterward he is again at my side, there, in front of the passage which leads into Corte Michiel. The street is deserted.

I switch on my flashlight at the corner and slow down. I manage to keep a distance of two or three yards between us. He never turns his head.

His step is so soundless and so strange that the rare passersby look at him, stopping for a moment. We have reached the church of Santa Maria del Giglio. The fog is in my mouth, fills my lungs. Toward Canalaccio it fluctuates and accumulates.

The stranger becomes grayer, evanescent; a shadow.

Now I walk faster, so as not to lose him.

In front of the house where every evening one hears the sound of a piano, in front of the house where the antique dealer is, he disappears, suddenly.

He did not fall into the canal, he did not cross the bridge, he did not go through a door. Doors and shops are closed. I examine them with my light. I retrace my steps to make sure.

Then I run up the bridge and all the way down the *calla* to make sure I am not mistaken and that he is not still in front of me.

The *calla* is deserted. Campo San Maurizio is deserted.

Perhaps I shall find him again in the narrow *calla* that leads to the Red House? My heart falters. A tatter of fog brushes against my cheek. A swarm of drunks brawl down there at the end of the ferry.

We hear somebody come up the wooden stairs and knock at the door, calling my name.

It is Renata's voice. I open the door.

Renata is pale, beside herself.

"Come, there's been an accident."

"What accident? Miraglia?"

I think of him immediately.

"Come, Genua is downstairs. He will tell you."

I go, my heart in turmoil. I find Memmo Genua at the door, very disturbed. He tells me that he has found out from telephone calls from the air defense look-outs that the plane piloted by Miraglia has crashed into the sea and that the pilot's condition is serious. The mechanic, Giorgio Fracassini, our Fracassini, cannot be found! Perhaps he went to the bottom.

I rush back upstairs, I say goodbye to Cinerina, who is dismayed. I run back down.

Genua, Renata and I start running along the Zattere, looking for a gondola, any sort of boat.

Miraglia has been taken to the Naval Hospital. I keep questioning Genua to find out the real truth.

My knees shake. My tongue is mired. I leave Renata at Campo San Maurizio. I continue down Via Venti-Due Marzo. I pass Miraglia's house, at the entrance to Corte Michiel. People stare at me. I am unable to master my horrible fear.

We run into a sailor who is walking quickly. Genua stops him. I cannot hear what he says to him, I come closer. The sailor was on his way to my house. I learn that the body has been taken to St. Anna's Hospital.

The body! He is dead.

Genua steadies me.

I begin to run, looking for a way, any way, to get to our destination and escape the curiosity of the passers-by. The sailor catches up with us and offers to take us in a launch waiting near Santa Maria del Giglio. We go.

The small bay in front of Saint Mark's—bright blue.

The sky everywhere.

Bewilderment, despair.

The immobile veil of tears.

Silence.

The throb of the engine.

The Giardini.

We turn into the canal.

On the right, the bank with its naked trees; it looks funereal and remote.

Ahead of us, in the low sky, close to its shelter, the foolish and obscene shape of the anchored blimp, the color of silver.

It is about three o'clock in the afternoon.

We arrive. I jump onto the dock, I go inside.

I ask the officer on duty for Giuseppe Miraglia. He points to a door. I enter.

The corpse lies on a trundle bed.

Bandaged head. The lips tightly closed. The right eye injured, livid. The right jaw broken: beginning to swell. The skin dirty olive in color: an expression of unusual serenity. The upper lip slightly protruding, slightly swollen. Cotton plugs in his nostrils.

The look of an Indian prince wearing a white turban.

Hands yellowish, crossed over his chest. Both feet swathed in white gauze bandages.

The right foot is broken. The thumb of one hand is broken. One leg broken. Several ribs broken.

He wears a blue jacket with gold buttons. The jacket he had on yesterday.

They try to drag me away. I refuse. I remain on my knees. Beg them to leave me here alone.

When I am alone, I bend over the dead man, call him several times. My tears rain down on his face. He does not answer, does not move.

I fall on my knees again.

The sounds of the day.

The throbbing of engines on the canal.

The thud of steps on the boardwalk.

A sailor enters with a sheaf of candles; sets four candles at the four corners of the bed.

Luigi Bologna comes in, Carlo della Rocca comes in. I cannot move, cannot get up.

Somebody places a bunch of flowers at the feet of the corpse. I think I recognize Silvio Montanarello, the youngest aviator.

Two sailors come in with fixed bayonets and take up positions at the head of the bed, standing there immobile. Another sailor attaches a ship's flag to the rear wall, facing the window. A flag is placed at the head of the cot.

After a period of time that I cannot reckon a sailor arrives with another bundle of candles and opens the door in the wall opposite me.

The door has been closed.

I hear shuffling feet. On a stretcher two sailors are carrying in the body of Giorgio Fracassini, found after two hours amidst the torn canvas and twisted wires, when they were taking the plane's wreckage back to Sant'Andrea.

They cross the threshold, put him down in the other room.

I get up to go and look at him. I bend over him.

Memories of the flight over Trieste, his advice about the gasoline pump, his cleverness in stowing away all twenty-one of the small green-white-and-red sacks . . .

He looks as though he were sleeping. His face is composed, severe. He is wearing his leather suit.

He looks like a monk to whom the crossing has brought beatitude. His manly face, almost always shiny and dripping sweat, with its pale, daring eyes, its broad open forehead, its hooked nose, has become peaceful, ennobled. He is truly at rest.

I return to the adjacent room and find my comrade's body covered by the black cloth with the golden cross.

His face, too, is covered with gauze.

A sailor is about to remove the flag from the head of the cot and replace it with a small Red Cross flag. I stop him. He was taking it to put up on the wall in the other room.

I arrange the red and the green, right and left, over the black cloth.

The magnetic life of the Navy's battle colors.

The white roping as on the border of a sail, the slip-knot . . .

They go to find another flag for Giorgio.

Admiral Umberto Cagni arrives, accompanied by other officers. I see him dimly through burning eyes. He approaches, uncovers the dead man's face, murmurs a word, what word I do not know. He also goes to look at the mechanic. Then he comes over to me as I lean against the wall and make an effort to control my horror. He takes my hand, clasps it, saying in a rough, soldierly, almost violent tone: "Goodbye!" He leaves.

The boat's crepitating sound. The launch moving away.

Here is Manfredi Gravina, then Alberto Blanc. I do not move. A sailor puts a black cushion under my knees, the cushion from the *prie-dieu*.

Night has fallen. I hear the first call from the look-outs: "Over the air keep watch!" I think about Renata, I think about the flowers she has put in our vases for him.

I get up, go outside on the pontoon dock.

Low, opposite me, the golden moon shines in the sky.

I step into the boat, go back down the canal.

The walls of the Gardini, the shore with the bare, stark trees, the blimp's black bulk.

Genua accompanies me, to pick up the parcels I had prepared and give them to Alberto Blanc who was supposed to take them to Rome.

With me I carry death, the smell of death. Renata is waiting for me: she knows everything. We embrace, weeping. She wants to come and see him.

I go into the dining room to get the flowers. There are three settings! I gather all the flowers from all the vases. I take them with me in a sheaf.

Again I enter the mortuary chamber.

The candles burn. The small flames waver, reflected by the blades of the bayonets. The two sailors are at attention, on guard, rigid.

I arrange the flowers on either side of the corpse: I feel the shape of his thighs, his legs.

I put the white jonquils on the red and green of the flag.

I uncover the pitiful face. The right cheek is swelling out and turning black. The mouth seems closed.

Again and again reality escapes me. I reflect. I close my eyes. I imagine him alive as he was yesterday. Then I look at him and see him inert, bloodless. Is it true?

The vigil begins.

Opposite me is the door to the other death chamber where Giorgio Fracassini lies, illuminated, filled with wavering shadows.

The two stock-still sailors; the stiff gleam of the naked bayonets.

The plash of the canal below the window.

The shout from the sentinels on guard outside.

A singular atmosphere, like a block of impenetrable crystal, surrounds the corpse.

Around ten o'clock the Commander-in-Chief arrives. He

enters with a firm, energetic step. Dominates his emotions. Kneels, prays. Rises, goes into the room where Giorgio Fracassini lies. Shakes my hand in silence, leaves.

I hear the throb of the launch. Then everything returns to silence.

Faces faces faces, all the passions of all the faces flow through my wounded eye, innumerably, like hot sand through the fist. No one stops. But I recognize them.

Is it not the enormous Roman crowd in May, in the evening at the Campidoglio? Enormous, fluctuating, howling.

I feel my pallor burn like a white flame. There is no longer anything of me in me. It is as if I were the demon of that turmoil, the genius of the free nation.

My perseverance over thirty years, my love and my worship for Italy the Beautiful, the courage of my solitude, the song in the desert, my contempt for obscurity and vituperation, the patience of my waiting, the restlessness of my exile, are transformed for me into a single mass of incandescent force. The whole past flows together toward the whole future. I live my *Credo* at last, in spirit and blood. I am no longer intoxicated with myself, but with all of my race.

Faces faces faces, shaped in the smoldering flesh, printed in the blood-red fire.

The turmoil has the breath of a furnace. The gasp of a voracious crater, the crash of a savage conflagration.

I lead and am led. I ascend to crown and I ascend to crown myself.

An epic spring uplifts and carries me off as if this ancient triumphal stone were melted by scarlet lymph.

Riots of swallows graze Marcus Aurelius' green horse, which at each shrill cry seems about to unseat the emperor and rear up towards the ultimate fate.

The confused delirium of the multitude becomes a clear voice within me.

I speak. Each of my words echoes under my skull as if cast back by domed metal. Each breath strains the circle of my breast. I suffer and am proud that my joy is mixed with pain.

It is like the suffering of creation, like the anguish of a birth. The crowd howls in labor. The crowd howls and writhes to engender its destiny.

Beyond the lead-covered ledge I see thousands and thousands of faces, and only a single face. A face of passion and expectation, of determination and redemption, which burns in the center of my breast like a generous wound.

Like a sudden *chanson de geste*, my words separate into ample loops which the clamor completes and lofts on high.

Overwhelmed by a cry higher than any other, I lose my voice in the pause. The imperious cry seems to demand more than speech.

Before me on the leaden ledge an unknown hand sets down a large sabre, curved like a scimitar.

I grasp it and draw it from its sheath. That cry demanded that gesture. A flash of lightning seems to pass over the turmoil.

It is Nino Bixio's sabre, the weapon of the slashing hero, with the names of victorious battles etched on the honed blade.

I press my lips against the unsheathed sabre. It does not feel cold because my lips are bloodless. All the blood flames in my heart.

The silence of the crowd is like a maelstrom that attracts me, surrounds me—like a vortex that drains and destroys my life.

I fling away my life, abandon my soul to delirium. The last words are like those blows of the founder's mallet struck to open the tap out of which the molten metal flows into the mold.

The crowd is like an incandescent pouring of metal. All the mouths of the mold are gaping. A gigantic statue is cast.

I turn. I descend. I sway, prey to a slight dizziness. Thirst devours me. I beg for water. The women of the people crushed in the crowd surround me with compassion while I wait. A rough hand gives me a glass of lustral water. I quench my thirst and purify myself. I drink and spill the libation that precedes the sacrifice.

I descend. I am carried down, I do not know by whom. All is ardor and clamor, creation and inebriation, thirst and victory, beneath a sultry battle-like sky through which shrieks a flashing of swallows.

We suffer because we are defenseless. We suffer because we are not fighting, because we are not transformed into a thrust of swift legions crossing the unjust frontier.

Dishevelled youths with wild faces, dripping sweat as if after the struggle, throw themselves at the wheels as if to shatter themselves.

Workers darkened by the dross of labor, bent by concentration, gnarled by effort, workers of all works, who it seems to me have all wielded the hammer, pounded the boiling iron on the anvil, reach toward me with their strong hands as if to seize and crush me in their sudden love,

Women, powerfully carved like the mother of the two tribunes, with the same gesture throw me a flower and give a son to the war.

The fold of a flag blindfolds me. It is the red flag of Trieste. It is continually over my head. At times it waves, drops and covers me. I pour my yearning into its folds.

In the red shadow of its folds I hear the first chime of the Capitoline bell. My heart cracks. I rise. The wheels stop. The crowd falls silent. It is nothing but the chain of vertebrae traversed by an identical shiver.

The bell tolls. The roar of the bronze penetrates every marrow. An immense shout drowns it, rises above it. To war! To war!

Does it ring from the depths of the dead centuries? Does it ring from the depths of centuries to come?

We are carried by the twentieth wave of the centuries—ten and ten—by the second decennial tide.

The bell of the people proclaims war. It no longer is a call of bronze. It is a call of red fire at the summit of the Latin sky. The entire Fatherland hears it and leaps!

To war! To war! The splendor of the evening is defeated by these thousands of flaming eyes, by this stirring of flags and threats, by this sublimation of the free populace once more possessed by its true god.

Faces faces faces, all the passions of all the faces, flow through my wounded eye, innumerably, like hot sand flows through a clenched fist.

It rains wildly on the evening of Ash Wednesday. A cloudburst in March. I listen intently to the crash of the water.

My ear now—it seems to me—is more sensitive than when it composed the music of the poem "Rain in a Pine Grove."

I distinguish all the strings on the great harp of the meteor, and I almost test them.

If only I could open two holes in the wall facing the garden, and push my dessicated hands outside!

Won't the downpour be too violent for the fuzz of the small, delicate, new leaves?

Nerissa sends her little maid through the rain to bring me an armful of flowers she had found in Padua this afternoon.

The moist air comes into my room, cool freshness spills onto my sheets.

Speaking about the maid, the nurse says to me proudly: "She has come without an umbrella! She is dripping like an eave. The flowers are all drenched. We must wait until they dry."

My relentless thirst sniffs out the moist smell that immediately impregnates my darkness. My heart throbs. I beg the compassionate one to come close, to let me touch the flowers.

I beseech her. I threaten to rip off my bandages, to throw myself from the bed to the floor. I get my way.

The flowers are placed on the counterpane. I have them under my seeing fingers. I palp them, separate them, recognize them.

There is the hyacinth. In small bundles tied with thread. The stems are uneven. Together they form a thick cluster. As I inhale, their perfume grows like the pain of a small cut.

There is the zagara. It is the Arabic name which Saracen Sicily gives to orange blossom. I learned it as an adolescent on my native beach, from a cabin boy off a schooner. It pleases me so much that if I utter the name, I can smell the perfume.

There is the hot-house zagara: a bunch of leaves which vibrate under my touch and, at the center, the hard buds. I feel them one by one. Some are closed, some are split, some are half open. Some are delicate and sensitive like nipples, fearful of a caress. The scent is candid, unripe, infant-like. But one must seek it out among the ice-cold, dripping leaves which wet my chin and enter my mouth.

There is the rosemary. It is the most rain-swollen, completely saturated with water from the clouds. It smells most strongly at the apex, like the last phalanx of a finger putting on eye-shadow and rouge. There is at the bottom of its scent something of the milky fig, the small, green fig. There is also, if I persist, something of the ripe greengage plum. More the smell of grass than flower, more of fruit than flower.

Most of all I like the zagara, both name and thing. It is more tenuous, rarer; not nuptial but virginal. I search for it again, inside the leaves. It pales the fire in my eye. It is hard and white like the sclera.

I remember the large orange groves at Villacidro on the island of the Sardinians. I was a lissome animal. My ankles were slender. I used to take off my shoes and walk with my young feet on the snowy flower which wove over the ground.

I remember a walled-in orange grove at Massa, in the direction of the Amalfi coast, if my memory does not deceive me. I had not quite recovered from an evil potion. I was bewildered, as though I had entered an unimaginable labyrinth. The trunks of the trees seemed carved from the stone of secret grottoes. The flowers were like the foam of which immortal flesh is born. The shade was almost aquatic, modulated by the dying song of some mysterious Siren banished from the sea.

The rain does not cease. I hear it splatter in the garden, on the embankment, the small piazzas, the alleyways. My generous friend will not dare to venture, as her maid did, through the deluge which has submerged gloomy Venice. I had thought the flowers were to announce her.

The tedium of immobility oppresses me. Dull anger tautens me from the nape of my neck to my heels. I am getting up, I will throw off the bandages and walk under the eaves.

My melancholy pleasure is already exhausted. The nape of my neck throbs. From the stems of the hyacinths oozes a disagreeable fluid which glues my fingers.

And where does this scent of violets come from? Are there violets in the room? Who has hidden them from me?

I reach out with cautious hands, groping around. I find a bunch that had slipped from the counterpane to the top of the bed. My heart flutters. For nothing at all, my heart is startled!

It is a bunch of violets. Wet, they had no perfume. The warmth of the bed gives life to them again. It is an exquisite surprise. I am delighted by them as if I myself had gathered them at the edge of a strange meadow. They are no longer violets from Padua—for me they are wild violets from golden Pisa.

I remember a March cloudburst in Pisa. We were on Piazza del Duomo. We took shelter under the architrave of the main portal, shaking off the drops. There we lingered, waiting for the rain to stop. *Imbres effugio*, said the speaking emblem on the door.

The rain fell on the short grass with an even crepitation which to us seemed as intimate as the sound of a shell held against one's ear. Leaning back against the bronze of the doorjamb, we began to possess it, merge with it.

The dampness seemed to augment the preciousness of the material. Like curious children, we stuck our fingers in the metal foliage, fondled the tiny wreathed head which gazed out from among the olives and branches. Above us spoke the symbols: *Fons signatus*, *Hortus conclusus.** Astonished, amid the leaves we kept discovering lizards, snails, frogs, birds, fruit—endlessly. In our fingers we felt the pleasure of the artist who had shaped those forms, his wisdom and his whims. The more we looked at the bronze, the richer, more powerful and deeper became its patina. It was enhanced by our loving eyes and returned love for love. Above us spoke the symbols: *Onustior humilior, Tantumodo fulcimentum.*** The crashing downpour slowly diminished. The sound seemed to reach us and be stilled within us like the harmony produced by the interior echo of the Baptistry; the empty meadow had a sense of derelict gentleness along the walls in the direction of the old town. Archbishop Ubaldo's graveyard was closed and meditative, withdrawn around its fifty-three shiploads of soil from Calvary.

Then we descended from the smooth threshold. We left the bronze and marble for the grass. Dusk was falling. We were alone. And life led us by the hand, indulgently.

It was said that from channels and canals beyond the Camposanto a silent fever would rise toward evening and come to roam the holy meadow. Yet we felt nothing but the shiver of the soggy, softish spring.

We walked between the Camposanto's wall and the side of the Duomo, where there was a mystic space for our music. In our fantasy the interior frescoes shone through to the outside.

---

* Sealed fountain; closed garden.

** More burdened are the humiliated; Only a support.

And our music had the face of that robed woman whose cheek rests upon her psalter.

I was vigilant and attentive to my desire.

I was what I am when my nature and my culture, my sensuality and my intelligence cease to struggle and are wholly renconciled. I was a musical mystery, with the taste of the world in my mouth.

When I halted, my companion, who for me bore the name of Ghisola, would ask: "What are you seeking?"

Dusk was falling. The marble's shadow was cerulean. It is a marble that at sunset exudes blueness like lapis lazuli. It blued the grass almost like a brush-stroke of ultramarine.

The silence opened up before us, divided to right and left, flowing along our sides as the river polishes the swimmer. Our feeling was simple and ineffable. We were poor and unburdened, we were rich and unburdened. We were like two beggars without wallets and like two sovereigns without diadems.

"What are you seeking?" beautiful Ghisola asked me at intervals, as if in cadence.

Was I a magic seeker for treasures or wells of water? All my wells and all my treasures were within me.

I sought for my desire. And suddenly I had found it.

I stopped, closing my eyes to keep my happiness beneath my lids. I was no longer anything but a single sense. My entire brain throbbed in unison with my knowing nostrils.

I stooped in the watery shade, deftly probed the moist grass with my fingers. My lowered face also felt suffused with ultramarine; even my hands turned a faint blue.

"But what are you trying to find? What?"

I had discovered a clump of violets.

Sirenetta has a voice that soothes, that lulls. When she speaks my heart is assuaged, my pulse slows. It reminds me of the young voice of my mother who every evening made me fall asleep in a small boy's bed with a fairy tale.

Sirenetta reads the poets, and the stream of dreams carries me into the shadow of the laurel groves.

She stops reading, and immediately pain bites into me again.

Her speech is Tuscan, with a Siennese purity. This is how St. Catherine spoke as a young girl when she tended her garden.

A bee has left sacrificial honey in her mouth.

Through her mouth the sonnets of *Vita Nuova* touch me deep inside as when, at sixteen, I read them on Affrico's grassy banks, around the time of the Resurrections.

And as I dwelt with bitterest sorrow "like those who cannot stir," I too saw faces of dishevelled women who said to me: "Your youth is dead!"

And also, after those women, I saw faces different and dreadful to behold, which said: "You are dead."

Having a beautiful voice, the dear child is sensitive to beautiful voices. She tells me which one she loves most among the people in our family. She speaks about them as about the taste of water from different fountains.

Then she tells me about a night of full moon when she was a pupil at Poggio Reale and was taken with several other girls to the observatory at Arcetri. In her memory she sees large terraces whitened by the moon, large terraces piled one above the other, leading to the stars as to the abode of an astrologer invented for a poem of chivalry.

And there she heard the world's most beautiful voice.

It was that of a modest assistant, who while at the telescope spoke of the lunar mountains and valleys, of Saturn's rings and Mars' reddish glow. All the young girls hung from his lips, entranced by the spell of the full moon.

The pure voice was like a note of the celestial harmony. And the crown of virgins pulsed like a humanized constellation, encircling the student of the stars.

My daughter has dark Oriental eyes, those Saracen eyes which blossomed in Sicily at the time of Frederick II.

Sometimes, when she suddenly bends over me, they seem set in her temples like those of palfreys which gaze out of ancient miniatures.

A head, white in color or rather the color of peach blossoms, with a dark tightly curled mane difficult to divide into braids.

Sometimes, when she sits on a low cushion and cuts for me the strips of paper which rustle slightly like dry palm leaves, the poem "The Flower of Soria" written by Frederick, comes to mind.

She had gathered small olive branches in the Garden of Gethsemane; and was braiding them with the skill that adorns Palm Sunday and she had learned in our region.

With them she made a mat the length of my body, for me to lie on.

Entering the shadow, "The swallows have arrived," Sirenetta says, in a restrained tone which seems the shadow of a cry.

I recall, I don't know why, the sound of my voice of long ago, when as a boy I lifted the ironbound cover of the well and, leaning over the stony rim furrowed by the rope, flung a shout to its bottom where I glimpsed my face in the shimmering water.

In my eyes I see that muffled, silvery sound in which the levity of maidenhair fern shivered.

I would lower the cover cautiously, so that the clang of the iron latch would not drown my secret cry.

And it seemed to me that I had imprisoned in the cool dark well something living, like a bird that continued to fly and sing, fluttering its wings against the damp bricks.

Sirenetta speaks, remembering that one evening I took her to see the staircase of the Bovolo* and, to prepare her for the delight, blindfolded her lovely eyes with my hands in the

---

* A winding staircase in Palace Contarini del Bovolo in Venice.

narrow alley there, before coming out in Corte Contarini. Sirenetta says: "Don't you think there must be nests hanging in the Bovolo stairs? I want to go and look at it again to find out if the swallows go to live there, as I would if I were one of them!"

O child, unnail me from here and then take me with you.

I am immobilized by two nails in my armpits and two in my feet.

I remain silent. But a leaping instinct of my tired flesh imitates the flashing swallow.

Her tiny wild eyes open beneath my bandage.

She enters Corte Contarini. A cry, two cries.

She comes from Riva degli Schiavoni.

She passed over Chioggia.

She flew to San Francesco del Deserto.

She circled around the Oriental belltower on Isola degli Armeni.

Alighting for an instant in the mouth of the Lion on the column of the Piazzetta, she was tempted to build her new nest there.

She enters Corte Contarini. A sharp cry, a white flash.

She descends toward the dry wells, set apart by iron fences.

Then she brushes against the loggias spiralling one above the other, with the musical rapidity of a hand executing an arpeggio on the strings of a sculptured harp.

She shimmers and flutters around the last balustrade.

Then I see her disappear, hear her shriek under the low ceiling.

Then I see her dart like an arrow, cross the roofs, pierce the azure.

I hear her cry of pain, cry to the sun of my suffering.

While my body is being washed and perfumed part by part by compassionate hands, like the body of someone dead, a faint drowsiness comes over me. All the apparitions of my sleepless night have dissolved in the light of morning.

My left eye is allowed to see a little light.

The shutter is almost closed so that the sun cannot enter, but down over there the old rose-colored silk of the wall turns golden. The glimmer touches my naked lid together with a mild warmth which is nothing but its own sweeetness. I feel my wasted knees rub against each other, I feel them as polished as the knees of graveyard statues.

The sleep which the spring equinox brings me is like the sleep of Ilaria in her tomb at Lucca. This glow resembles the glow of the stained glass window which there in the Tuscan duomo illuminates the reclining statue.

This musical tone of fatigue brings back to my joined feet my love for the most beautiful of my young borzois.

I surrender to sleep with reluctant slowness, and know that I may never wake again.

Compassionate hands cover me with a fresh sheet which gives my blind eye a vision of whiteness.

I have escaped from the night.

The sad soul seems "purged in the fire of suffering," as the mystic says.*

My sleep is no longer a flaming of formidable phantoms, but rather a quiet, even lightness.

The nurse said: "The front of the house is already dressed in green *like Ornella*."**

The wall dissolves without dust and the small new leaves tremble against my face. My breath stirs them.

How long did I sleep? I immediately feel my sick eye lacrimate under the bandage. A tear has reached down to the joining line of my lips.

The tears expressed by the soul and those shed by the irritated lid—are they bitter with the same salt?

---

* A quotation from *Le Poesi Spirituali* of B. Jacopone di Todi. (Tr.)

** She is quoting from D'Annunzio's play *La Figlia di Iorio*, act 1, scene 1, verses 6-7. (Tr.)

I sense the afternoon. There lingers in my puny body almost a golden hue from the diurnal sleep slept in the light.

I call. It is three o'clock in the afternoon. I have slept for a long time. The nurse smiles and says that the musicians have come to play music.

From the small adjacent room I hear the tuning up of the cello and violin.

Sirenetta appears on the threshold. She wears a striped dress and her beautiful dark head rises from a white collar moving on her bare neck with that grace which is peculiar only to birds and therefore seems dictated by the singing instinct.

She is an angel in a tunic stepping out of a Florentine singers' gallery. She precedes the music and announces it.

The first notes of the Fifth Trio by the Flemish Beethoven truly touch my heart, physically, as drumsticks strike the kettledrums in the living marble of Lucca.

It is the trio also called "The Ghost Trio."

I listen to it as if after death.

The musicians are hidden, they are in the other room. The small, enclosed room acts like a soundbox. Harpsichord, violin, and cello are three voices which speak as though in a religious drama, a sacred mystery.

I have pulled the bandage down over my living eye too.

When, after a long pause, the instruments begin the *largo*, I see a yellow stripe blend into a purple stripe. Then I see a purple cloth with a yellow border over a shape which is that of the crucifixion. The ravaged knees protrude, lifting the cloth in the center; and when the violin resumes the theme, at the center the cloth turns scarlet.

And then each time I feel a deep, piercing agony.

From vein to vein all the way to my heart each note drives the dregs from the cup of life, what I have not as yet tasted, what I have prayed should be kept far from my lips. Each note drives them closer to my heart, and the heart will not open to receive them but twists and rejects.

They have suddenly reached the rim, it is near. The heart falters, and is suddenly possessed, filled, replete.

I discern the shadow of my childhood bending over my face. Her light fingers touch my cheek beneath the bandages, become wet with my tears. Over chilled, sticky tears, warm weeping gushes from my lost eye.

The soul's life drenches the bandage.

I do not deceive myself. I am certain that the tide has poured first from the blind eye socket, then from the other.

Now both eyes are alive with the same sublime life. They are two living founts.

I no longer know where my misfortune is. My misfortune is a blessing that is unknown.

The tears overflow. My child has immersed her fingers in them but does not dare to dry them.

I feel her head close to the pillow.

And my daughter, the daughter of my flesh, says a material word to me on the threshold of old age, the tender word that mothers say to children!

I feel that with that word she takes me upon her lap like the ancient Pietà and assuages my wounds.

Once more the demon has kindled all the fires deep in the depths of my eye; and he blows on the sinister pyre with all of his madness, as during the most desperate hours of this remorseless martyrdom. The burning in my eye reduces my whole wretched body to a bundle of brushwood just at the edge of the flame.

The fern leaf I have inside my eye multiplies, rises, thickens. And now I am like that clump of ferns, the color of copper and gold, which I saw in the burning forest of the Landes, untouched at the borders of the fire.

The flame had grazed it without burning it. And I was filled with wonder and superstition at seeing that fragile, so burnable thing on the rim of the fire, intact. It was ready to flare up in an instant, turn to ashes in an instant, and the voracity of the fire had spared it for a miracle.

Who is swathing me in searing ashes? The heart's apex sparkles and traverses the ashes.

I am my ashes and I am my phoenix. I am opaque and I am refulgent.

I survive the pyre, intoxicated with immortality.

Who has lifted me onto my horse with such an imperious hand?

The spirit of attention invades me like a god armed with a thousand eyes.

Attention creates that which it contemplates.

I create ardor.

My intimate fate is this.

Oh woods of the westernmost shore! Oh forest of fecund wounds! Oh exile of my power drained in tears like resin.

I ride through the already burnt stands of pine.

I ride through the already parched pine woods. I roam through the young pine plantings without a future, sacrificed like prime adolescents on the idols' searing bronze.

The ground is hot and smoky and here and there blackened, streaked with whitish ash.

The pine trees are dark, scorched to the crown, without needles and only naked branches; but all standing straight like unvanquished martyrs. Some are charred; the fire still smoldering in the mutilated trunks seeks out the roots, gnaws away underground.

Some carry their blackness covered by impalpable flakes of ashes all along the craggy trunk.

The hoof of my horse could sink into an empty trunk as into a smoldering sheath. I never relax my vigilance. I am all eyes and all acumen. The black twigs threaten to pierce the sole, strewn like those iron tridents which once lamed the enemy's chargers.

The smoldering ashes are burning hot. I perceive the smell of the burnt nail, as though I were at the door of a blacksmith's shop. I breathe in the flame, I hear it interspersed with gasping, crackling, scraping. I am drenched and I pant.

Who is that man who, the skin of his face burnt, his clothes in flames, rolls in the sand of the fireguard and shrieks?

I continue across the ashen barrens. I ride over ash and sand through the dark wood.

Now and then a silent gust lifts the ashes to great heights.

In the silent sky I see the slender twirl of a waterspout that wavers.

It casts a spell.

I turn my horse toward it to observe it from closer by.

As I approach, it disappears.

And another rises farther away.

And casts its spell.

And I approach. And it fades away.

And another rises still farther off; and then another; and then another.

Silently they vacillate in the burning air; beckon; dissolve and disperse.

They are like the ghosts of holocausts.

I cross the ditches; pass beyond the wide, sandy roads, which in the Landes are called fireguards, which did not suffice to preserve the adjoining woods. The sand on them is mixed with a dust of ash and ground charcoal.

Beneath a landslide a knot of roots burns and smokes, hissing, squeaking, crackling.

Here and there amid the carbonization and incineration I see a dry blade of grass intact, an untouched leaf of fern. I discover here and there along the edge of the ditches where the fire has reached, a tuft of grass, a stem laden with small rosy or purple flowers.

The astonished soul alludes to itself.

No longer ghosts of ashes, but gloomy columns of smoke.

And a sinister roar, which seems to rise from the heart of the earth.

Among the burnt pine trees I urge my horse toward the expiatory abyss.

The serpentine fascination of danger encircles my breast.

The ground smokes and splutters under the hooves.

The fat cloud of smoke swallows the flames farther away.

The acridness of the resin bites into my throat.

The world grows larger, pounds at me, deafens me.

From deep inside me a song bursts forth against this when suddenly between the tree trunks living flames appear.

Beauty of the fire, you are newer to me each time than the time of spring.

The multitude of flames is deployed on the field before me like an impenetrable enemy.

Higher than the splutter of the turf, above the sizzle of the resin, above the crashes and bursts, they sing.

They are deployed in a single line which advances, voraciously.

They eat away at my eyes, devour my face.

They have an orange color, which receives again and again an admixture of blue and green and gray. They darken at times like embers; dazzle at times like lightning. Their very diversity perturbs me, like the looks of an enchanter.

They have left behind the carbonized, smoking forest. They advance in a long, endless chain. Deploy a battle front which disappears into the distance, diving into the cloud of black smoke.

Their violence is such that it does not seem to spring from

the surface of the ground where the stubble is rooted, but erupts from the depths, surges from the abyss, like the vomiting of open craters.

They have violence and tenacity, impetus and perseverance.

They teach us how to fight.

Here are the modes of the flames' artfulness.

They assail the trunks, first testing the evident roots, the exterior outcrops. Then they glide upward over the scales.

They seem to fondle, they seem to search for the place into which they can sink their fangs most effectively.

They stroke where a branch was pruned, where there is a resinous wound, an aromatic sore, and then they dig in there.

In a lull of the wind they fall lower.

But the one that has bitten into the trunk at the vital spot, that flame does not let go. She remains alone, suspended, intent on biting, intent on devouring, detached from the others, alone with her hunger and her fury, obstinate.

I think—I don't know why—of those naval battles, those boardings and assaults when fists and jaws seize the ship's rails and enemy axes chop through wrists, sever necks; and the dreadful hands still remain clinging to the wood, the teeth remain sunk into the wood, while the bodies plunge down and sink below the water. Thus the red claws of the flame, thus the red maw of the flame cleaves to the trunk severed from the body, which subsides.

Oh inert combatant, remember the brother of Acschylus.

Certain tree trunks burn only on one side, bursting out from inside through the vertical incision made by the resin spike.

The fire is like a tattered flag hoisted on the tree.

Now the wind grows stronger.

All the victorious flags snap and unfurl and tear into shreds which dissolve in flight.

A great salty squall comes from the open sea.

With the roar of a tempest, the fire bounces up again and

again, drives past the tree tops, envelopes whole trees, reddens them from root to crown.

Flaming scales of bark and blazing pine cones spurt far out like crystals of solidified lava from a volcano.

The innumerable nests spun by caterpillars' larvae catch fire and fly even farther and propagate the fire even down there in the safe wood.

The resin sizzles, bubbles, splutters. The clay resin jars, boiling, searing, brimming over, leap, fall down again, explode like hand grenades. Every explosion hurls myriads of red needles.

Within the clamor a mysterious melody takes shape, stretches, uncoils, flows.

Are the salamanders singing?

The flames flee with the smoke into the sky. A vortex of dark, sinister smoke fills the air, attacks the sun. Through it I see the sun like a reddish disk about to turn cold.

I no longer see it. It is swallowed.

The wind makes a truce. The smoke thins out.

I see the disk again. Little by little it turns from red to russet orange, from russet orange to blond. But in the shadows the fire surpasses the splendor of the sun.

Then suddenly all around their edges the smoky clouds turn blond, resplendent.

Is the sun triumphing?

For an instant it blazes in the blue, while the huge flame collapses and crawls.

But up there, in those high knots of the trunks, the small flame survives and gnaws. But up there, in the eaten-out trunks, already abandoned to death, the small obstinate flame searches for the last morsel.

And, during a respite in the attack, the mysterious melody becomes more distinct. It is light like a soprano voice. It enraptures me in a way that is beyond all ardor.

Are the salamanders singing?

* * *

The Ocean once again hurls its powerful volleys between the bold dunes. The thunder and crash cover the magical voice which releases the burning victim from his suffering. The thunder and crash change into the lowing of buffaloes; the roar of lionesses. Infuriated again, the flames advance taller and thicker, in battle order.

"The fire is mine!" shouts the implacable leader who has my warlike mask. "The entire forest and all of its aroma!"

He leads the charge; and is the first to seize the bristling mane with his red hand.

"Men with me! With me, people of the forest!" shouts the audacious adversary who has my warlike countenance.

Fire will overwhelm fire, flame will kill flame, so that from the two hostile ashes the earth may be made fertile.

Who is this man with the scorched face, the burning vestments, who flings himself on the sand and burrows into it as if to bury himself?

And he is not extinguished.

Against the chain of flames is set the human chain. Against the front of flames is set an opposing front.

The counterfire flares up.

With long branches of fresh pine, the young, the old, women and children strike the savage red beast to force it to advance against the other advancing savage beast.

Help! Help!

The beaten flame writhes, the gusts of wind drive smoke over the fire-fighters. The increasing heat from the flame singes lashes—eyebrows—beards—clothes. Throats become dry, eyes begin to tear.

Help, help!

The counterfire advances. The enemy approaches. In turn yellows, reddens. Shatters into myriads; recomposes; dissolves; disintegrates. Roils, shrieks, croaks, squeaks, hisses, crashes.

Help, help!

From what bowels rise this howl of pain and terror which splits my soul open?

It is no longer the voice of the element; it is the voice of the creature.

Caught between fire and counterfire the crazed beasts try to find a way out.

The fire drives them from behind, the counterfire is upon them.

Blinded by the glare, they ram into trunks that crackle in the growing blaze.

Down the long torrid corridor of the labyrinth without exit they plunge on, howling; and the lugubrious howl shatters the sooty suffocation into a turbulence of blazing scales, chips and burning pine cones.

Help, help!

We trample on embers, pound the smoldering bits of wood, swallow sparks.

Are these tenacious fire-fighters a phalanx of martyrs compelled to fight the fire of Our Lord? Each has looming before him a flaming angel and a thousand swords. The children weep; the old fall to their knees; the women howl as if in the throes of a bad childbirth.

And who is the Lord of this scintillating battle?

And which of the far centuries does this battle redden?

I see the ancient Sybil without her turreted crown and without her lions.

I see her robes variegated by water, earth and fire.

I see her pine bearers, hirsute teams of her *dendrophori* that resemble the sacred tree.

Who howls? Who roars? Who calls from the abyss and from sleep?

The sun is obscured.

Is this the thunder of the Last Judgment which dominates the collision of the two roaring adversaries?

Where they clash, everything is already devoured. Everything is black char, embers and hot ashes. There is no more fuel for it. There is nothing more to catch fire.

The fire dies.

The fire is dead!

Sorrow is dazed, and terror falls silent.

But, suddenly, a quiet vortex seizes the ashes which still throw off sparks and lifts them to the sullen clouds which are thinning out.

I see the tall, frail vortices rise, sway, go off.

It is the ghost of the holocaust.

To be a beautiful Italian pine tree
on a Roman hill
when the moon is full
and hear the wind of night
move the tender pinnacles
which are reborn among the old needles
at the summit of the ancient branches
rosy as children's fingers.

To be the tallest, darkest cypress tree in Villa d'Este
after the twilight
when the fountain
removes the veil of maidenhair
from its dripping ear
to spy on the remote drone
of the Tiburtine waterfall;
and fondle the grace of evening
with the light, sensitive green
that edges the funerary leaves.

To be in the Forum
the spirit of a blind herb
and toil patiently
to discover the fissure of aged stone

over which the Triumphs clattered
and at last find it
and strain up with the slender head
and burst forth, and bloom, and delight in the sun
which saw nothing greater than Rome.

Horses, horses without number, as at Versailles during the first dog days of the French war.

They are tied to a line strung between tree trunks, under trees which still display the adeptness of the pruning shears; and hay, straw and dung befoul the polished surface of the noble avenues.

But a large bunch of roses rests on the shoulder of that wounded man; and that other man, whose ravaged legs were black with blood and flies, is covered by a shawl of Flemish lace.

The regal city is transformed into an equine city.

I see the horses around the abandoned basins greenish with floating putridity. The palace is a dead thing, inexpressibly dead. The sweep of the broad canal, like a Styx compelled not to twist, thrusts into the melancholy of an infinite Hades.

I see other horses around an even sadder pond. They neigh towards the doleful, grim water which reminds me of Lake Nemi's face beneath a cloudy sky. Their makeshift troughs, shaped like black boats, stand in the shadow of the elms. A heartbreaking odor of stable has invaded the King's delights.

Now they are dead; they are all killed, slaughtered en masse.

The Battle of the Marne leaves them behind, reclining in the grass strewn with empty bottles and unexploded shells. They all hold the same pose, all the way to the horizon they all make the same lugubrious gesture, with a swollen belly and a hind leg rigid in the air.

In the sweet meadows of erba medica, swollen bellies, lifted legs, yellowed gums, whitish eyes, flocks of ravens, swarms of flies; and in the valleys and the fields and the streets, everywhere—slain horses; and the horror of that always identical gesture; and the glint of iron in that petrified underbrush beneath a jet of lacerating sunlight.

In a field of sugar-beets, behind a pile of wrecked gun-carriages and large ammunition caissons, I come upon a surviving horse. He is alone. He cannot walk. One of his fetlocks is smashed, there is a deep wound in one of his haunches and another in his withers.

But he is quiet. His eye is tranquil. The clamor has ceased. The inferno is ended. All is silence. The birds do not sing. A man walks down the path in the distance beneath the drizzle, a folded burlap bag on his head. Close to a ruined house a threshing machine sprawls, toppled over, belly up, like the carcasses. The grassy knoll curves so gently that it seems to express some arcane tenderness of the earth. The weather-vane on the bell tower rules over the silence, which the fine rain soothes. At rare intervals the wind raises a damp gust. The smell of death chokes his breath off.

Stretching his neck, the survivor tries to eat the grass near his mouth. He is alone. Soon night will fall. A lost, voiceless swallow grazes his flank.

> Oh sadness sadness
> why bring back to me
> from so far away
> what you already found
> so heavy to bear?

And now you are also leading me back to him who was the favorite of my childhood in the comfort of my home when my mother was the pensive flower of my healthiest youth in Pescara, my native city.

He comes to me, moving through the dense crowd of my memories, as when he parted the tall, not yet scythed grass with his chest.

He opens a furrow through my life which bends from side to side, touching the good soil with its pliant, grassy tips.

He was a small Sardinian horse. A tawny bay, with a white fringe above his hoofs and a white muzzle. His mane and tail were long and rich. His name was Aquilino.

In the stable, between his stall and that of the pair, there was an empty stall where I would have liked to put my small wrought-iron cot. Whenever I was able to slip away, I went downstairs, my heart beating with excitement, and went inside from the courtyard. Aquilino, recognizing my light step, neighed softly as if to prevent anyone from hearing and finding out. Each time my joy was so great that the corners of my smock in which I carried the booty slipped out of my hands.

Then his neighing trembled with impatience; and while I gathered up the bread, apples, everything I had been given for my afternoon snack, and whatever I had been able to filch from the pantry for my sweet-toothed friend, I stilled my hunger with a smile which had a nourishing quality I have never tasted again.

One of the stable doors opened on the coach room. This room was almost always empty, lit by a chapel-like light that shone down from the colored panes of the fan-window. There stood the large, covered wedding coach, lined with blue cloth, silk curtains behind the glass, and silver handles on the doors. There was a gig with its collapsible hood, and a wicker basket on two wheels. And hanging against the wall there were the harnesses which I never grew tired of contemplating: collars, pectorals, cruppers, straps, traces, bridles, buckles, loops, rings, always sparkling, and the long whips for which I yearned.

That child stooping over the floor to gather the bread and fruit he had denied himself for the sake of his love, that child already avid for a singular life and mysterious communions, entranced by that neighing as by a magical voice, illumined by his own smile as by a subterranean lamp, leave that child within my reach. Let me recognize in that act of his, in that pleasure of his, an image of fleeting happiness which is peculiar to me and which from time to time flashes through me even on this bed of sorrow.

Was I already then possessed by the lyrical daimon that exalts and transforms my whole being? Was the magical sense of life already awakened in me?

And just as Aquilino neighed to me softly, so I spoke to him in a whisper. Just as he understood me, so I understood him, happy to stand with my two feet on the straw on a level with his four hooves.

He took the pieces of bread from the palm of my hand, the slices of apple, the squares of sugar, with a careful grace which tickled and sometimes made me burst into convulsed and smothered laughter or yelp unrestrainedly. But I was intimidated by the two large coach horses that continually rattled the wooden balls attached to the ropes of their halters; and I tried not to be seen by them.

And little by little that trepidation and cautiousness and understanding created in the closed stable a mysteriously fantastic sense of remoteness. And that black gaze which Aquilino kept fixed on my face as he chewed and that face of his marked by his lips' white and rosy spot, mobile as the muzzle of a hare, and that way of demanding with a greedy quiver of his nostrils when he had finished, and his teasing way of nibbling at my shoulder when, to goad him, I hid what was left behind my back, and all his ways of pretty duplicity gradually merged in me both his species and mine and bewitched me.

"I'll give you the rest if you'll let me take a hair, if you'll let me take two hairs, three."

I remember that when I ripped them out I had to overcome a slight feeling of shame, of remorse. Did it hurt him? Did he know that I wanted them to make snares for the swallows that lived in the eaves?

My sister Ernesta was the one who had put me up to pulling them from his mane and suddenly I felt sick at heart, perhaps for having given on condition, bartered, perhaps for having thought of bringing death and mourning to the small mud nest.

When I pulled, many more than three were left in my fist.

The stable boy who was an accomplice of my secret forays came in. And he lifted me up and set me astride "the Sardinian."

I liked to ride in a dream without moving. But I did not like to be watched.

I would say to the stable boy: "Go away and come back later."

I closed my eyes. I was bewitched. The door opened onto the edge of the woods. Night was falling. It was impossible to see the end of the path.

But that day the manger remained fixed against the wall, and the wall did not open up; and the horse did not move, even though I talked to him in whispers.

I still had those hairs in my fist and that shadowy regret in my heart.

A sudden sharp cry, a white flash.

Had a swallow entered through the broken pane, the crack? Was there a nest attached to the ceiling of the stable? How long had it been there?

I shivered with astonishment.

A light feather descended through the enchanted air, wavering: the one feather I needed to put in the mane as a lure.

I did not wait for the boy to come back and take me off. I lifted one leg over his back and let myself slip down onto the straw.

"I'll be back, Aquilino. Before evening, I'll be back."

And I went straight for the hearth with a brow on which the vertical furrow of willfulness was already being scored.

And I threw that fistful of hairs into the magical fire.

Oh sadness sadness
why bring back to me
from so far away
what you already found
so heavy to bear?

I, my brother, and my three sisters, had gone downstairs into the coach room, we had climbed into the old wedding coach where the blue cloth lining smelled of dried rain and a cushion was still warm from the cat who had slept on it.

The door to the stable was open. Aquilino lay on the straw in the agony of death. My father knelt at the side of the dying horse between the coachman and the whimpering stable hand who held the cup full of medicine and the wooden spoon.

Through the window of the coach, huddling together in dismay we watched without crying, with hearts so pinched that neither a drop of blood nor a tear of grief could flow. We watched death for the first time, we who had never thought about it except on the eve of All Souls, waiting for the gifts it would bring us.

I could see the convulsed movements of the hoofs, and the one leg marked by the white fringe hurt me most; and the tremor of the poor white muzzle hurt me even more.

But I could not cry; and, alone, I kept back the grief of all five of us.

The stable boy burst into sobs. I pushed mine back into my throat with a feeling of indignation that I cannot describe. I saw that the poor legs had stiffened.

We huddled even closer together and together turned to ice beneath that dark sky formed by the carriage, in that feeble light from the fan-window. And for the first time with ten fixed eyes we looked at death. But I received its mark for all of us.

Then my father rose, crossed the threshold, halted, turning toward us in our dismay; and, over the icy silence in my breast, said in a tone that now rings vivid and precise in my ear and soul: "Gabriele."

Oh sadness sadness
why bring back to me
from so far away
what you already found
so heavy to bear?

I ask one of the musicians to show me his cello. He brings it to me with a modest smile.

This Alberghini is a very clever hunter of instruments, scouring the mountains and valleys in search of them. Whenever he hears about a violin hiding away somewhere, as others when they hear about a boar or hare, he sets off and will not abandon his search until he has found it.

This cello of his was made by Andrea Guarneri. He came upon it in Egypt, in Cairo. I smile, thinking that under my hand I have a thoroughbred like El-Mar, and that even its coat resembles that of my sorrel.

The varnish is intact and rich, of a beautiful reddish-brown color which allows the gold beneath to shine through. The golden sheen comes through more frequently on the back in streaks, in patches, and here and there on the sound-holes which smell of amber. The back of the neck is pale, polished by the sliding hand. But the true miracle of gracefulness is at the back's center: there a bird of paradise has once mirrored the brief treasure of its throat and the reflection is still there, captured in the everlasting varnish.

The musician tells me that, in Cairo, he traded instruments

with a colleague whose hand was short, giving him a small Gagliano.

The cello had been bought near Cremona. A rustic had been playing it in the choir of a country church. One day, during a solemn service, the chancel had collapsed, along with organ, cello, musicians and singers. The cellist broke a leg. The back of the instrument was damaged but not its sound-post. A few days later it was rescued from restoration by an inexperienced mender.

"Don't you think that with its delicate bridge and its sound-holes ending in large open tear-drops, it looks like a beautiful face with a beautiful voice? It is alive. There is no need for a bow. It plays by itself, sings by itself. In Mexico City the women used to draw near, fascinated by its angelic timbre, and wanted to touch this skin, more precious and sensitive than their own."

So says the artilleryman from Emilia, dressed in his gray uniform.

"A woman's skin eats into the varnish. At Nice I saw a Stradivarius almost completely stripped by the violinist's bare arm and shoulder.

"But then in Ferrara I saw another Stradivarius under a glass bell. It is one of the earliest, when he was still an apprentice to Amati. The wood has turned almost all to dust but the strength of the varnish alone holds it together. And I remember that I was afraid to breathe in the presence of that relic.

"Who can say anything absolutely certain about varnishes? Red varnish? Yellow varnish? To be so impregnable it must contain the dust of diamonds."

My hands rest on the shoulder of the cello while the soldier, seated, holds it by the fingerboard. And before they reach my ear, the things he says seem to travel through the sensitivity of the strings and the wood.

"There exists a strange similarity between man's structure and that of the instrument. There is a definite relationship between the player's physical condition and the quality of the sound. Earlier they played without a ferrule, resting the cello on their joined ankles. Movement of the legs stopped any vibration that might reach the sound-level too forcefully. Bones are musical, you would say that a good musician's bones ought to contain air rather than marrow. Both tibia and femur exert a continued influence on the sound. Each note can be corrected by expert pressure.

"The bow is also very important. Depending on the kind of bow the sound is more or less full. Between the wood of the bow and that of the instrument there must be a vital correspondence. The fiber of the wood, not bent by firing, immediately transmits the intention of the hand.

"This is a Tourte, it is nervous, the rod is octagonal, the heel ebony, the eye is mother-of-pearl. Here is another, its round rod covered with black leather tooled with the design of small hoofs, the heel is dark tortoise-shell, the eye is gold.

"Here is a Dodd, it's English, it has an entirely different gracefulness or perhaps it has none, with its whale-bone sheath, its ivory heel, its octagonal pommel made of ivory and silver.

"And here is another one, nameless and unadorned, indeed, poor thing, a truly Franciscan bow that would suit *Il Cantico delle Creature*, and there is nothing to recommend it but for the reddish-brown color of its wood, attuned to my Guarneri.

"And only this bow, who knows why, suits my cello; and only this bow, who knows why, can extract from its soul all of its voice.

"They understand each other. From what you see by examining the two woods closely, you might even believe that this bow was extracted from the cello's rib just as Eve was from Adam's."

The soldier laughs openly like a child and plucks the first string.

I say to him: "It could be. Instruments have a demonic nature. Sometimes, at the end of the neck, instead of the scroll, the old masters carved the image of the splendid Enemy. I saw a tenor viola with a neck ending in a horned head. In my hometown in Abruzzi, I saw a viola d'amore with a kind of screech-owl, its very long neck bending toward the player to tempt him and instill its perfidious fascination in his heart."

The soldier no longer speaks in jest: "There is no doubt," he adds. "The great violin-maker is a magician. Only magic can illuminate him in the choice of woods. Why does a Testore go and pick the soft wood which immediately becomes saturated with sound, and so that the sound circulates through it uninterruptedly like a dry lymph? And why, on the other hand, does a Guarneri del Gesu not attach too much importance to the choice, feeling able to transform any wood by his mysterious influence? There you have the true occult poet. He does not work unless inspired. He cuts two imperious sound-holes into the violin's face; and the face lives, expresses, speaks, is anxious to sing.

"So then, what is the sound-holes' influence on the harmonic plane? Guarneri's sound-holes resemble neither Amati's, nor those of Stradivarius, nor any others. How did he find them?

"And is he not a magician, that Gennaro Gagliano the Translucent, who hurls his small striated tigers at the throat of Music?"

I admire the animation of this exquisite cellist attached to a heavy artillery unit, who feels and expresses with such lyrical intensity the life of living things.

He says: "There was no such thing as a muted cello for practicing. So I decided to build one, with a very narrow sound-box to fit the extended strings. And by chance a new instrument was born, which has a delightful English horn sound, perfect for dance melodies."

I say to him: "Let's call it an *Alberghina.*"

He goes to get his Alberghina. He returns, and plays a jig, a courante, a galliard.

Halfway through the galliard we hear the lugubrious howl of the siren followed by the roar of canon.

Beauty of the night, how many times have I lost you?

To see, to look, to know: I was avid, always. Insatiable, always. And yet, my restless eyes, you have not seen enough, you have not looked enough, you have not been able to take in all the faces of the manifest deity.

And one of you is already extinguished, and the other grows turbid and tired and is perhaps fated to be obscured.

"Look! Look!"

Under the full moon echoes that voice which knew how to match every tone of misery and every note of happiness: the voice of Giusola.

"Look! Look!"

She was rousing me from sleep. I had drowned in sleep as in a black river. It felt as if, her hands under my armpits, she was trying with all her strength to lift me up from that torpid whirlpool.

"Look! Look!"

Thus she pulled me to the window. And I lifted my heavy eyelids; and saw the tall sapphire peaks, the supernatural summits of a planet without men.

"Look!"

I saw the transfiguration of the Tuscan Alps in a lunar night arisen from the depths of some ecstatic god's millennial memory.

I closed my lids again, pressed down by inert sleep.

"Look!"

I opened them again and closed them again. The divine spectacle was erased by the wave of the forgetful stream.

I descend the stairs with infinite caution, carrying my eye inside the reliquary of my lifted head.

Sirenetta is there, ready to support me.

Here is the last tread.

Here the downstairs room.

Here the green dazzle beyond the panes covered with lace.

Here the living air which like an unaccustomed potion fills my greedy mouth with its new taste.

Here the garden, here the leaves, the flowers.

My hand rises to the blindfold. It is a sterner bandage than usual. It is not white but dark. It is not of linen but of silk. My eye is dressed in mourning, clad in weeds.

With her childlike grace Sirenetta seizes the mad hand, draws me toward a rosebush trained to a tall, slender trunk, and says to me: "Look at this little rose."

Mystery of an intonation which can make of a young girl and a rosebush a single creation.

As she holds the stem between her middle and ring fingers, the little rose seems to have sprouted in the hollow of her hand, almost the beginning of a vernal metamorphosis.

She wears a striped dress, white and green, which seems patterned after one of those silvery poplars that shiver with all their tender branches in the wind from the river bank.

The little rose is grafted into her, it is the flower of her tenderness.

It is so pure, so fragile, so delicately constructed that no corporeal thing can be compared to it but perhaps only a chaste, ineffable thought.

There is no form of infancy equal to it.

One must kneel and worship it.

Its perfection is so shortlived.

I think I see its petals open with each instant.

By early evening it will already be open, and in vain.

The inertia of so many days had imprisoned me in the feeling of solitary transiency amid inanimate things. Now once more I regain the ear of the poet, resting on the bank of time's stream; I hear again the melody of the perpetual flux.

Sirenetta minutely knows the garden's brief fairy tale. She

knows where to find the caterpillar, the bee, the spider, the scarab, and what they are doing. She knows the sick branches, the number of buds; what is late, what is about to open. She complains about the gardener's laziness and fetches a small bellows to blow a healing dust on a rosebush that crawls with greenish insects. With hesitant compassion she leads me to a large white rose whose deepest heart is being devoured by a scarab.

"Why don't you shake it off, why don't you get rid of it?" I ask her.

"The rose is done for by now," she answers. "And if the scarab does not get enough of this, it will go looking for another."

I sense that her compassion is divided between the insect and the flower, just as the heart of St. Francis included the famished bird and the pecked worm, the burning fire and the burnt garment, the ailing flesh and the herbs crushed to heal it.

I halt before this spectacle of devastating passion.

The insect is nailed into the flower's sweetness with a craving which resembles both perdition and rapture. It is dazzling, like a gold lamella shining through a polished emerald. It is a stupendous jewel and a savage force.

It is forgetful of everything, oblivious of all risk, all surprise, all threat, submerged in its delight as in a crime that fears no punishment.

I sense again, as in my early youth, what there is of the divine in thirst and hunger.

The entire heart of the rose is spoiled and, surrounded by a crown of still intact petals, appears yellowish like a trace of honey.

The sore oozes nectar, the murder is sweet.

Unsatiated love does not know guilt.

Who feeds on beauty grows in beauty.

I would like to linger and catch the instant when the scarab will extend its wings outside its carapace and fly away along a ray of sunlight.

The afternoon wanes. Even the slightest breeze is gone. The new leaves breathe and hope, the old meditate and remember.

A vast flowering of wisteria, which covers the entire wall up to the roof, issuing from a trunk similar to a tangle of ropes, calls forth the image of a net that I saw pulled up on the Atlantic shore filled with futile, almost violet jellyfish.

The swallows riot and screech furiously, and I suffer ancient wounds as if they were stabbing me through and through like lightning bolts.

In a corner I see two overturned watering-cans and, I do not know why, they give me a sense of silence, create a pause amid the lacerating shrieks.

"Here is your speaking laurel," says Sirenetta.

It is a rounded laurel on a slim, bare trunk, as tall as a man. It has a certain allegorical air: it seems transplanted from a grove in the dream of Polyphilus. It lacks nothing but the flutter of a scroll wrapped around the middle of its trunk. Its foliage is somber, harsh, thick, so that the Muse cannot reach into it without the cutting edges injuring her hand. And from the perennial foliage, at rhythmic intervals sway the small new leaves, so lively that they seem to chatter like small impatient tongues filled with "the will to speak."

Sirenetta's fresh young soul has immediately heard the soundless rhythm.

The laurel speaks. It says: "So as not to sleep?" or does it say "So as not to die?"

Never was sleep more alien to me, nor was I ever so deep in death, filled with so much eagerness for immortality.

I still have a deep song in my tempered heart.

The sun sets beyond the bend of the canal which now is as green as the speaking laurel. The bells are silent, but the air seems to quiver with the expectancy of their angelic sound. My bandaged eye brims with luminous wisteria; yet the other eye, disaccustomed, is lost in reverie.

Outside of time a slow harmony unfolds.

Core's house is nothing but a vast garland supported by the heads of lions bent over the water. From Palazzo Doria to the church of Santa Maria della Salute, brick and stone, under the rose-colored light, become almost carnal. The two façades support each other, like women leaning one toward the other so as not to fall, overcome by the sudden languor of April.

A huge black boat loaded with resplendent sulphur, propelled by long oars, glides by like an apparition from beyond the millennia and memory.

Along with the broad ram it has the ancient rudder with its long tiller, held by a man who resembles a Phoenician helmsman.

As it enters the shadow, the sulphur takes on a color for which there are no words. That yellow has the power of an unexpected theme which suddenly raises a waning symphony to sublimity.

A strange silence falls within me.

I no longer hear the swallows.

And my heart trembles for fear that a knell interrupt this tacit music.

QUARTET ENCOUNTERS

Aharon Appelfeld · *The Age of Wonders*

Aharon Appelfeld · *The Healer*

Aharon Appelfeld · *The Retreat*

Alain · *The Gods*

Lou Andreas-Salomé · *The Freud Journal*

Gabriele D'Annunzio · *The Flame*

Ramón Pérez de Ayala · *Belarmino and Apolonio*

Ramón Pérez de Ayala · *Honeymoon, Bittermoon*

Gaston Bachelard · *The Psychoanalysis of Fire*

Giorgio Bassani · *Behind the Door*

Giorgio Bassani · *The Garden of the Finzi-Continis*

Giorgio Bassani· *The Heron*

Thomas Bernhard · *Concrete*

Robert Bresson · *Notes on the Cinematographer*

Hermann Broch · *The Guiltless*

Hermann Broch · *The Sleepwalkers*

Mikhail Bulgakov *et al* · *The Fatal Eggs & Other Soviet Satire*

E.M. Cioran · *Anathemas and Admirations*

E.M. Cioran · *A Short History of Decay*

E.M. Cioran · *The Temptation to Exist*

E.M. Cioran · *The Trouble With Being Born*

Paul Claudel · *A Hundred Movements for a Fan*

Louis Couperus · *The Hidden Force*

René Crevel · *Babylon*

Stig Dagerman · *A Burnt Child*

Stig Dagerman · *The Games of Night*

Stig Dagerman · *German Autumn*

Grazia Deledda · *After the Divorce*

Grazia Deledda · *Cosima*

Grazia Deledda · *Elias Portolu*

Heimito von Doderer · *The Demons*

Marcellus Emants · *A Posthumous Confession*

Per Olov Enquist · *The March of the Musicians*

Péter Esterházy · *Helping Verbs of the Heart*

Ennio Flaiano · *A Time to Kill*

Peter Paul Fuchs (ed.) · *The Music Theatre of Walter Felsenstein*

Carlo Emilio Gadda · *That Awful Mess on Via Merulana*

Andrea Giovene · *Sansevero*

Remy de Gourmont · *The Natural Philosophy of Love*

Julien Green · *Avarice House*

Julien Green · *Each Man in His Darkness*

Julien Green · *Midnight*

Julien Green · *Moira*

Martin A. Hansen · *The Liar*

Eugene Ionesco · *Fragments of a Journal*

Gustav Janouch · *Conversations with Kafka*

Ernst Jünger – *Aladdin's Problem*

Ismaïl Kadaré · *The General of the Dead Army*

Pierre Klossowski · *Sade My Neighbour*

Dezső Kosztolányi · *Anna Édes*

Miroslav Krleža · *On the Edge of Reason*

Miroslav Krleža · *The Return of Philip Latinowicz*

Pär Lagerkvist · *The Dwarf*

Pär Lagerkvist · *Guest of Reality*

Valery Larbaud · *A.O. Barnabooth: His Diary*

Valery Larbaud · *Fermina Marquez*

Arnošt Lustig · *Darkness Casts No Shadow*

Arnošt Lustig · *Diamonds of the Night*

Arnošt Lustig · *Night and Hope*

Osip Mandelstam · *The Noise of Time*

Norman Manea · *October Eight O'Clock*

Ana María Matute · *School of the Sun*

Henry de Montherlant · *The Bachelors*

Stratis Myrivilis · *Life in the Tomb*

Romola Nijinsky (ed.) · *The Diary of Vaslav Nijinsky*

Pier Paolo Pasolini · *A Dream of Something*

Pier Paolo Pasolini · *Theorem*

Fernando Pessoa · *The Book of Disquiet*

Luigi Pirandello · *Short Stories*

D.R. Popescu · *The Royal Hunt*

Vasco Pratolini · *Family Chronicle*

Eça de Queiroz · *The Illustrious House of Ramires*

Rainer Maria Rilke · *Rodin and Other Prose Pieces*

Rainer Maria Rilke · *Selected Letters*

Victor Segalen · *Paintings*

Victor Segalen · *René Leys*

Fyodor Sologub · *The Petty Demon*

Abram Tertz (Andrei Sinyavsky) · *Little Jinx*

Yury Tynyanov · *Lieutenant Kijé & Young Vitushishnikov*

Simon Vestdijk · *The Garden Where the Brass Band Played*

Boris Vian · *Froth on the Daydream*

Boris Vian · *Heartsnatcher*

Elio Vittorini · *Conversation in Sicily*

Robert Walser · *Masquerade and Other Stories*

Bruno Walter · *Gustav Mahler*

Stanislaw Ignacy Witkiewicz · *Insatiability*

Yevgeny Zamyatin · *A Soviet Heretic*